STRICTL

It took me a long time   ... me is

fundamentally about loneliness.

I know, you're reading this thinking I'm daft, aren't

you? What, with seven billion people on the planet, how can

you be lonely? But, truth be told, I am lonely, I was born

alone, I will die alone, I spend my time searching for places

where I won't be lonely, clubs, pubs, sports arenas,

supermarkets, bars, and I see the faces of men doing the

same thing, all ages, all races, all sizes.   For it is

predominantly men, the loner species, not out of choice. Save

for the widows, widowers and the pensioners.

You just have to understand the rules that this is how it

is.   Once you come to terms with loneliness it's okay, just

about passable, because that is the way that it is.

My mum is a two-time widower in her eighties and all

her pals are dying. She's been on her own more or less since

1992 and even though she's used to it, just about passable,

she'd love to have people nearby, people who she can share life and its experiences with, people to validate her existence. The loss of her friends just creates a vacuum, a soul destroying emptiness.

As a boy, the runt of the litter, I had three siblings, yet I felt isolated, on my own, craving affection, love and approval. My dad got done in an RTA. My step-dad died of wear and tear. God took my mentor. Where on earth would I find unconditional love from now?

Close friends were there when the time chose to make it right; at college, in a job, in a team. But once that cycle was over they too disappeared into the ether, cocooning themselves in family, happily not alone until that inevitable change of circumstance. I never got that. You work with people for twenty years, spending more time with them than with your family, and then you never speak again.

Of course, we all try and garner friendships, enabling security, the comfort of people, disabling solitude. Altruism works. Some try and buy it. We all hope for love. It is not a given.

Even when marriage arrives over the horizon like the cavalry, along with children, two cars and a mortgage, you are never safe. 40% of marriages go tits up and kids soon disappear into their world once they have no need for the comfort and security of the nest, though the bank of dad is always handy. Offspring, like siblings, go their own way, hiding, hidden and safe in their own world until tragedy strikes. And how often is that?

Loneliness is very much a given.

So this story?

Girls.

I was never good with chicks. I'm sure they liked me for my daftness, my sincerity, my total naivety, my literal hint of Asperger's but no one really explained what life was about as far as girls were concerned. Life was about me, my priorities, my schedule, this just a veneer of protection against ignorance. It took years, half a lifetime, to find some confidence. Little did I know that 99% of the people my age were going through exactly the same thing.

So, this story? It is true. I have changed the identities of some people to protect their names, to hide their blushes and so that possibly they don't even know that it's them that I'm talking about. I am the narrator, so if there's anything in the first person then it's me.

After a long relationship, courting and marriage, that ended with no shortage of acrimony, it made Kramer vs. Kramer look like a party in the park, I was left alone, teetering towards middle age, alone, in need of company, craving female company, desperate to be wanted, sated, satisfied, acknowledged.

I wanted sex and I wanted companionship but after the maelstrom of separation I was terrified of commitment, of getting hurt and of being used and abused, physically, mentally and financially. And I was angry, boy, was I angry, and I guess my potential lovers sensed this. Most backed off.

This story is what happened next, how I rebuilt my self-esteem by learning how to pull women, not just for the sex, some good and some bad, but also for the ultimate result of finding someone to spend the rest of my life with, the ultimate solution to loneliness. I have some male friends but to be honest you can't beat girls can you? I love their empathy, their hearts, their eyes, their curves, their brains and the fact that most regale in the bedroom and are keen to satisfy.

Let me set the record straight. This isn't a book about how to be a pick up artist, someone looking for notches on his belt. It's not about chat up lines – saying 'Hi, can I get you a drink?' is normally as good as anything. Of course you may see some similarities and there will be techniques that you might want to try out – men and women – but this book is about the quest to find a lover not a one night stand, it is about how tricky and difficult it can be when you get to a certain age to actually meet the right person, or anyone. It is a quest to overcome loneliness and to add validation to life. To my life.

The targets of my affection have all been single women though one or two married ones or girls in relationships have slipped through the filter. This was a shame and never intentional; I am not a home breaker – just put yourself in his shoes even if he is a tit – but sometimes married women want a piece of what they're not getting at home. Others are in shit relationships and want to get out so if I am an option then so be it but I never targeted married women knowingly.

I should point out something else too. I'm not Brad Pitt but am good looking. I haven't got a six-pack, more of a twelve-pack fuelled by my Watney Party Seven. But I'm a nice bloke, educated, middle class, articulate, I am funny, sensitive and brave; I'm not scared of talking about subjects that many, mostly men, veer away from – love, death, sex, personal health, sexual preferences – more of those as the story unfolds. Although I was born shy I have confidence flowing in my blood even though I fear rejection as much as the next person but I have a couple of key qualities lacking in both sexes. My intrigue levels are genuinely high and as such I am sincerely interested in people.

And I have learnt how to be charming.

<u>ONE</u>

I hauled my large frame off the floor just before Corrie started and got ready to go out. The usual, shave, shower, (I can't understand men who shower before they shave, doesn't seem to make sense), nice clothes, cleaned, ironed, shoes made for the walk, a full ten minutes, a few quid in my pocket, hair gelled, a smile and a song. The Bee Gees CD provided a back drop with falsetto.

Another mile away Billy was doing the same, old enough to be my dad, slighter of build, his a genuine walk, his wife comfortable in front of the telly, him clean shaven, pin stripe trousers, crew cut top and a brown leather jacket that made him look like an extra from The Professionals. He'd shaved twice. Meticulous.

Dan was already in the pub waiting. He'd sent me a text to 'get a fucken rift on, fatty.' Cheeky sod. Who does he thinks he's calling fat? I'm not even big boned. We'd agreed the time but he had nothing else to do so he was on his fourth pint already. When he was off it, he was off it, but when he was on it, he liked his ale. And his lager. And his wine. And . . . you get the picture.

One last check in the mirror, no missed shaving cream in me lugholes or food between my teeth, a descent of 36 steps, and then, the steady stroll, trying to focus on reality not hope. Going out as a single bloke is like doing the lottery. You get your ticket and you cross your fingers. Maybe a couple of numbers will come up, maybe three. Fourteen million to one against winning the big one. With girls, you hoped that the pub would contain some willing to audition, if not the one.

Billy skipped down the stairs of his house, revitalised, buzzing with expectation and anticipation, he lived for the moment, in time, loving every experience, learning from it, bagging the good bits, rejecting the bad. He put his house key under the wheelie-bin like millions of others and started his walk checking out his mobile phone.

The pub, Annie's Arms, was built in the thirties, a tribute to an eighteenth century queen, a refuge for those not rich and fed through devotion to tobacco and the slave trade. The red brick was at ease with its sandstone neighbours, the garden at basement level built into the side of the hill, this city a veritable yo-yo of highs and lows. In the last couple of decades the clientele came from those close by, the Bible Belt, the professional, the lawyers, the doctors, the scientists, those confined to a life in a PLC, the self-made, the frame makers, the interior designers, those who tailored floors not suits. The dark wood and stained paintwork hid the dirt and the nicotine, even though smokers had been exiled for some time now.

Billy took his shandy, 95/5 mix, I glugged my tortoise (Stella Artois – Not The Nine O'clock News, 1979), and Dan sipped his mainstream lager, whoever sponsored the footy. That first mouthful was all I needed really, just that combination of anticipation and quenched thirst, the froth teasing my lips, the nectar beginning its journey of adventure, but I knew we'd have four or five or six or seven depending on how the mood caught us. Add Dan's four already down to his tally. And he'd have had wine first back home to get a little loaded.

For the first hour the bar bustled, we clung to a corner, to stools, caressing our nuts and crisps, stylishly priced. We laughed, giggled, reminisced, repeated old stories, trying to work out if any of us had Alzheimer's, and we watched, observant, body language telling a thousand tales.

The numbers thinned as the night moved on. This was it; there would be no more takers.

'So, Dan, Dan, What's Thy Plan, where are all the birds?' I asked. It was nigh on ten o'clock now, we'd been sitting there hoping and praying, thinking that maybe some skirt would come into the bar but at the moment it was ninety percent blokes, a few young student girls and two chicks behind the bar.

'I thought you said the place'd be heaving?' I continued.

'What on a Monday? Don't be so fuckin' daft,' said Dan without a thought to defending himself. We are a peerless group. 'Nah, this place buzzes from Wednesday to Sunday but Monday and Tuesday it's pretty dead. So is everywhere. Monday must be the night they're all in watching telly or washing their hair or practising self-love.'

'Fat lot of use to us then,' I interjected.

I scanned the room in search of a mirage but none was forthcoming. It would be another lonely desert of a night.

'So,' I continued after another sip, 'what we need is a plan. Focus on the outcome and develop a proper strategy. Come on fellas, we're all smart, we've all run successful businesses, why don't we approach this in a formal way? We want girls, so how? Where? When?'

The others looked at me through thoughtful eyes, each churning the story in their head, Dan picturing the movie of the first night with a new girl, Billy sensing that Mrs Bill wouldn't approve. He was thinking about his businesses not girls.

I continued. 'Where are we going to get some skirt...I know, not tonight...but Dan Dan, we're both single, not you Billy, so where do we go? Hit the city on a Friday and Saturday? Hit the clubs? Fucked if I know.'

'Or not as the case may be,' chirped Billy. Smart arse. None taken.

'You can't pull in the city and in clubs,' said Dan with assumed authority. 'Too much noise, everyone's too pissed, they're all too young, they're all fucking chavs, tattoos, piercings, thick as shit, full of alcofuckingpops. No smart girls hang around in town. Who wants to have a night out in Dodge fucking City anyway? Fights, knives, police vans, police horses, people pissing and puking everywhere...not exactly Shangrifuckingla is it? The smart birds keep well away.'

'Yeah, so where do they go?' I asked.

'I bet they have exactly the same conversation about blokes,' said Billy, wisdom that becomes his years.

'I used to try and hit in supermarkets,' said Dan. 'Loads of mums from 3:30pm to 5:00pm, sometimes with the kids, the executive chicks normally file in after half five except on a Friday when some bunk off early, but I'm not sure they enjoy getting hit on in Tesco's or Asda.'

'So where then?' I continued. 'Or do we just trawl pubs hoping for a group of birds doing exactly the same?'

We all drank together, a simultaneous tasting, another moment to think.

TWO

We'd all gone our separate ways that night, Dan to his flat, me to the house and Billy to his missus and true domesticity having spent the last hour topping up our alcohol intake and trying to figure out where single blokes could actually pick up decent women, where they hung out and how we could track them down. It was unbelievably difficult because we were blokes, we hung out with blokes and we lived in bloke domains. We all worked, some women, yes, but there's always that rule in the back of your head that niggles: don't pork the payroll. But we were used to male societies, things like sports clubs and spectator sport. Sure some women like soccer, rugby and cricket, hey I even found one who loved golf, of all things – they go to watch the arses and the muscles, nature's magnet – but not many. Get me a bird who's into rugby and cricket and I'd marry her tomorrow as long as she didn't look like the back end of a double-decker.

Let's put this into perspective, we're all clever blokes but you'd have thought we'd have had a more cerebral approach to the solution. When I mentioned singles' bars and singles' events both Dan and Billy winced and you could feel the shiver run through their bodies.

'Am I really that desperate?' Dan asked with mock indignation.

'Yes,' I said.

'It's all right,' said Billy, putting a playful arm onto Dan's shoulder, 'I'll come with you and hold your hand.'

'Fuck off,' Dan said, mate to mate, no animosity intended. 'Those events are a nightmare of pure desperation, I mean, who would be so fucking desperate...it really does say, "I'll shag anyone".'

'Yeah, but,' added Billy, 'you might get lucky and find a nice, decent girl amongst the weirdoes and the hapless. You'd be okay. I'll look after you. You can have my dregs.'

'What about the lonely hearts ads in the paper?' I offered ignoring the banter.

'People just up for a shag,' said Dan. 'They are blatant adverts for sex only...might as well ring an agency or go down the red light area for a hand job.'

'Red lights? Hand job? Where is this place?' asked Billy.

We giggled.

'I read a study on newspaper ads,' added Billy, forever trying to extend his knowledge. 'These people are normally into extremes of sex...all the fetishes you can think of...they're all fantasists who just use the columns as a way of getting a contact...then they talk dirty on the phone...they're very honest about their intentions and then it's decision time, if their fetish matches yours, if they're desperate, don't give a fuck, too pissed or coked up to even care...and it's all done without seeing who you're going to meet...could end up with some bloater from chav city with a nose ring and a portable dose of the clap...'

'I knew a bloke once,' said Dan, 'who put an ad in one of these and the first thing that he said to the girl was that he wanted a fuck, no messing about. He said it sieved out the rubbish.'

I didn't believe anyone could be so blatant but then it takes all sorts, doesn't it?

'What about speed-dating then?' I offered having seen it once in a bar in town. Dan answered this one.

'Like the tower of fucking Babel...twenty blokes and twenty birds, all talking at the same time, can't hear yourself think and not exactly a lot of time to make a first impression. Should take place in sound proofed booths like on Mr and Mrs.'

'Yeah, but,' I said, 'you can check out the talent pretty quickly and you can see if she's physically up there...and if you dress smartly and turn up showered and shaved, she might just like you too.'

'But you can't get to know somebody in three minutes,' Billy joined in. 'What do you ask? Who's your favourite pop group and do you take it up the arse?'

'I suppose that would break the ice...' I said. 'You could talk about Glenn Miller and The Beatles you old cunt...'

'Fuck off.'

'None taken.'

'Clears the wheat from the chaff,' added Dan. 'No, it's bollocks really, speed dating...what about Internet dating?'

'Swipe left, swipe right, old photos, women with confidence thinking that they hold the cards . . . men as disposable as internet music and movies . . .and when you meet them they're shitting it . . . '

They looked at me inquisitively wondering where my empirical data came from.

'Do you think people tell the truth?' I asked. 'I mean, they could put what they like on their profile and who would check it? And people aren't going to be that honest are they? FUD looking for someone to finance her middle age? Lonely, boring widow seeks help? Alki seeks similar? On some of the profiles they say, "drinker". What do you put against that? Capable?'

We all giggled a little; we knew this was really close to the truth.

'Fucked up divorcee,' I explained to the quizzical faces just so that there was no doubt.

'Photos always lie too,' said Billy. 'You need to be able to thin slice...'

The term hung in the air for a few moments.

'It's the instant recognition that you do when you see someone face to face,' Billy continued. 'All it takes is just one look...'

'The Searchers?' I suggested.

'Shut up you silly twat,' said Dan. 'Let Billy finish...anyway, it was The Hollies.'

'Well,' he said, 'we all do it. We instantaneously check out someone's size, face, colour, shape, their body language, the clothes they wear...everything in a split second. We thin slice people. We give them an immediate yes or no...and you can't do that from looking at a photo, a photo that might be years old, or that hides the fact that she's got an arse the size of a large country...'

'The Divine Comedy?'

'Shut up you silly twat,' said Dan again. 'Correct...let Billy finish...'

'Let me put it this way,' said Billy. 'Take a look at the mothers in the school playground coming to collect Jessica and Georgiana or whateverherfuckingnameis. Most of them are frumpy, arses like a bag of spuds, dressed in casuals looking like they've never scrubbed up well in their lives yet they must have once, hence the kids. But to thin slice them, take a close look, look at their posture, shit clothes, lank hair, see how ugly most are, see how many don't give a shit about what they wear...and then try and wonder if you would date them, let alone shag them. They feel safe, married, taken, they don't feel the need to smarten up, not many have pride.'

'You could compare them with what they look like on a night out,' said Dan.

'Still plug ugly,' I said.

'Mutton dressed as lamb,' said Dan.

'Never to be shagged again.'

I can be succinct when I want to.

THREE

They're funny these women in the playground doing the school run. Why do most of them not give a shit about how they look when they are out in public? Let's face it, whenever you're out, you're out, you are on show whether you're going to school, the supermarket, the Post Office, the rugby or the pub, so why dress like you've just got up, like you're blind and you've just put on the first clothes you come across? It is no fun, as a bloke, seeing so much rough, women with no cares, little make-up, no fashion sense. I mean, leggings, trainers and a lumpy sweater don't do it for me, especially when you're three stone overweight and in need of botox, a new hair-do and a serious makeover. Nor those who turn up in a nightie and slippers . . . hidden by an overcoat.

I have to add a caveat here to defend some of the women. Some dress okay, some try, but it really is a minority. I know a French girl who lives the other side of town. Okay, she's pretty, tall and slim. That helps. But she has pride in how she looks. Not too much slap – some birds really do overdo the make-up stakes. There is a popular misconception amongst the female fraternity that slap is good but the truth is that they use it to hide ugliness rather than to enhance their own beauty. Guys don't want girls who have plastered their faces as if they were using Polyfilla on the moon. We just don't. Of course we want the girl to look nice but even pretty girls put too much cake on.

Let me take this further. Imagine a girl in a shower or a swimming pool. Her hair is wet, no slap in sight. That's when you know if she's really pretty or not. And that's when it matters, not when she's dunked her head in a bowl of Yves St Laurent like she was bobbing for a fucking apple.

My mother once told me that 'ugliness is only skin deep' and she is right, just because a girl is perceived as pretty doesn't mean that she is a nice person – met plenty of those, gorgeous but fucked up - or that she fits your template as a potential lover, but like in the animal kingdom we have all been programmed as to what is beautiful and what isn't and that's it. We'd rather be seen with a babe than a bag of spuds.

Of course, apart from the obvious beauty business model (wide eyes, symmetrical features, waist-to-hip ratio of

0.7 – Marilyn Monroe, Sophia Loren, Audrey Hepburn and Kate Moss, whoever she is) - men do have different preferences. Some like tall girls, some short, some fat, some thin. I like traditional beauty but she has to be a good person, and nice, and preferably not an FUD, a fucked up divorcee.

I dated a really beautiful girl once. More of her later too but walking down the street with her on my arm felt amazing. Her body was warm, great curves, she smelt fantastic, and I wished a busload of my mates were there to see me with such a catch but she was so fucked up, so selfish and limited in her sexual desires and experience that in spite of her beauty she wasn't for me. I was and am too old to fuck about playing games and this girl was all games; week one, sensual and oral sex, phone sex and seduction, the next ice and withdrawal. Week two, presents, an all over massage, copious amounts of sex, selfish in her case. Third week, no commitment, fear of heartbreak and rejection. For fuck's sake, all I wanted was to date her and to be her boyfriend. I didn't want to marry her. My theory is you have to know someone first. Now there's a breakthrough ladies.

FOUR

Against my better judgement I did the Internet dating thing. Desperate times, desperate bloke; apparently one in four relationships start on line these days. Maybe not on Shaghappy.com.

It really evolved from a chance meeting with a girl in a pub late one night after a big sesh. I'd been out for four hours on my own, a real Billy no mates, heavy on the pop, playing the game, looking, a lion on the savannah searching for an antelope to sink his teeth into when up walks a girl and she puts some music on the juke box which was just by where I was standing. Well placed, eh? I asked her what she'd chosen, why she was wearing such a stupid hat and what the occasion was: a birthday. We had a bit of a dance, nothing more and then she fucked off at about one in the morning.

I thought nothing more of it until the following day when I was trawling an Internet dating agency and who should I see but the same girl, the photo pretty, her eyes as wide as her smile, the photo not revealing her curves, her cushioned arse, not a bad thing, her sense of humour and the aura that she created, fun, frivolous, flirty. At the time I thought I'd chance it so I subscribed and filled out all the bollocks of detail that they wanted (star sign, hobbies, inside leg measurement etc. Bizarrely they don't mention sexual proclivity, which you'd think would be quite important, wouldn't you? I mean if the girl's into bondage and you're not then it's a non-starter from the set up. Ditto if he wants her to piss on him in the shower and she doesn't fancy it much. Never seen the attraction in that one. If a bird I pulled said 'will you piss on me?' my next words would be 'piss off'.)

So after paying my dues I emailed the girl and waited for a response. A few days later she replied saying that she enjoyed meeting me but she wasn't up for a relationship so soon after splitting from her ex. Her details were on the site by mistake; she'd forgotten to remove her profile. This was the nicest way that anyone had ever told me, 'fuck off you fat fuck, I don't fancy you.' I knew she was lying about removing her profile or the desire an need for a relationship. I think that rejection cost me a month's fees.

There were two more incidents from the web. I trawled the sites, saw plenty of familiar faces, and then I got an email. I checked her profile, she sounded okay, looked okay, a touch mousy, must have been the ears, teeth and block of cheddar in her hand, 39, with a teenage daughter (threesome in the making?) and she loved my profile so I wrote back telling her about myself, that I was an unemployed writer, recently divorced. Never heard a thing back. I think my job spec didn't match the size of her purse.

Another was a hoot. I met a girl at a party, big, black, pretty, older than me and she kept eyeing me up from across the room. She glided through the crowd, approaching, smiling and said hello, a pretty good starting point if you want to meet someone new and interesting and a potential lover.

'I've seen you before haven't I?' she quizzed. Not an original opening line but an icebreaker nonetheless. I mentioned the pubs and clubs I'd been to recently and after five minutes she had a 'eureka' moment.

'That's it! You're on that dating site,' she beamed, pleased with her recall and smug and satisfied and pleased all in the same moment. Embarrassed (why?) I joked along with her, telling her I'd not seen her profile and that I'd not had a lot of interest.

'Anyway, now that you've met me,' I said, 'just give me your number so you don't have to email me through the site.'

'What the fuck makes you think I'd want to email you?' she cackled.

Three tries, three strikes, talk about rejection.

I told Dan and Billy and they pissed themselves. In truth, so did I.

The following day I checked her profile out on the site; she was older than me, seven or eight years, no wonder I'd not seen her photo (blokes always look for a younger girl) and to be honest her photo didn't do her justice, just as Billy had said. She was far prettier, nicer, a good strong personality but having thin sliced her, and talked to her I'm pretty glad she didn't email me. I cancelled my membership to that site on the spot.

FIVE

Everyone knows that men and women are wired differently physically and psychologically but you wonder if a woman ever thinks about what the motivation is, why a man wants a woman, a lover, a partner or a wife in the first place?

There are a multitude of answers but does a woman ever think about them when she takes that step towards a relationship? Let's face it, motivations can be quite primal, most people like company, most people like sex, and there is nothing wrong with one-night stands as long as the sex is consensual but do women really go out on a date knowing what the guy thinks or what he wants? Girls, does he want to make out with you because you are beautiful? Or available?

Or in the same bar? Or because he hopes you give great head? Or because you are the only choice? Flattering, isn't it?

The men who are thinking about love and a potential long-term partner are few and far between. Men say that they are on the pull; that normally means sex, it doesn't mean that they are looking for the mother of their children. Girls are on the pull too but they are a little smarter because whilst eye-candy is high on the list and they are looking for sex too they are processing the man through their own internal computer in relation to the long-term. Could he father my children? Will he look after me afterwards? Has he earning potential to provide for his family? Will we stay together forever?

Once I pulled a girl late on a Saturday night. Let's call her Lois Lane to my Superman (get over it, it's only a line). I'd been in one of my regular bars for a couple of hours, a narrow room full of revellers, party animals, single blokes looking for company, hen groups using it as the start or the finish of their night, rugby types, friendly faces behind the bar, the jukebox playing, everyone singing along to The Boomtown Rats, Neil Diamond, Queen et al. It was raucous fun and there, close by, were four girls just reaching the end of their night out. We were all pissed.

As a single bloke this bar was a godsend, a sanctuary for likeminded folks. On this particular night I was Billy no mates again, no friends in sight, nothing to do, lonely, not on the pull per se but like any single bloke ready to play the scene that was in front of him.

After talking to a group of lads and girls I made a throwaway comment to the group of four girls and she turned her shoulders around towards me; I was sitting, she was standing. She wasn't the one I'd been eyeing up, that was the blonde in the bright red frock, low cut, but she was pretty, mid 30s and a glint in her eye, probably a mix of opportunity and Bacardi and coke. As she checked me out she approached and I offered her my left hand, which she took.

Before she could blink I had pulled her close to me and she was soon sitting on my left knee.

As I kept her balanced and comfortable we chatted, drank more and she quizzed me about my availability and my job. Basically, are you married and have you got any money? Are you worth following up? I gave her my business card and after a quick glance we were then snogging for England, public bar, early hours. Her friends pretended to ignore us but I guarantee that at least one of the three was getting horny watching, another jealous and another embarrassed. The kissing went on for fifteen minutes or so before she was ushered away into a taxi. I left too getting a smile and the thumbs up from the doorman, an old friend.

So was I out for a shag? Was she? Or something else?

The next morning I got a text from Lois Lane, she still had my business card, and after some text tennis I rang her and she agreed to come round: 'I'm doing nothing...unless there's a better offer.' We agreed to meet in forty-five minutes, enough time for me to tidy up a bit, take some headache pills and have a shower. Girls prefer a clean guy.

As soon as the door was closed we kissed, taking it slowly, me shaking, out of nerves, I told her, not alcohol poisoning, the more likely. She was cautious and wanted to take things easy – I know some women that would have just ripped my clothes off – so we did take it easy and it was nice, I enjoy kissing, and eventually I undressed her, carefully, no rush, unbuttoning her pristine white blouse – don't you just love that, the unbuttoning? - and then I removed her bra, the audible gasp when I kissed her nipple sent a real tremor of pleasure through my body as well as hers.

When everything was over we got dressed, the lounge still buoyed by the early afternoon sun and the aftermath of orgasm and we stood and held each other again, her head seeking comfort against my chest and heartbeat. Mentally she was beating herself up.

'I don't normally snog strange men in pubs in public . .
. I haven't let anyone do that for years . . . we were very
intimate . . . what must you think?'

What did I think? I think that I played the opportunist,
wanting some company and that she wanted some comfort
and she took the sex. Did she ever call again? No. Why not?
I don't know. Perhaps she wanted to look after the kids on
her own? Perhaps she was ashamed of her wanton desire?
Perhaps she didn't see me as a long-term viability? Perhaps I
hadn't matched the initial template of provider and protector
or maybe she wasn't looking for anything more than that
afternoon?

Female motivations do differ from men; for women to
have sex there has to be something more than just a pulse –
a bloke would have sex with a stranger at the blink of an eye;
a woman would never do that, so the studies show. But
women are remarkably similar. This issue of being alone is a
major one, women crave companionship, fun, friends,
someone to share a bag of chips with, someone to cuddle,

and of course there is the passing of time, the ticking clock, the maternal drives to have children. Empirical data states that most women have kids between the ages of 28-32 so if she gets to 35 the warning signs are like sirens during the blitz, the Countdown clock hurtling towards Armageddon. But do women settle for second best? Men they don't like? Men they tolerate because it's better than nothing? 'I just want a husband?' Even if he does beat me...or if he is a serial philanderer? I want someone to make me happy. But if one person is responsible for your happiness then that person is also in the position to be responsible for your unhappiness. So often do we rely on external influences to make us happy rather than loving ourselves for what we are, accepting our talents, accentuating our plus parts. Surely happiness comes from within? Surely happiness just is?

Let me elucidate a little.

'I am so unhappy.'

Impossible. How do you know?

It doesn't exist. Happiness is a state that can be created, it is a conscious decision to decide what makes us happy and what makes us sad. We think we all grieve in death. Some cultures don't because they have learned to act differently. Of course we can be pissed off? Angry? Yes. Disappointed? Yes. Hurt? Yes. Unlucky even. But these emotions are created by events where you decide on the impact. Most people who are unhappy are more likely to be the victims of misfortune and circumstance or just guilty of applying the same techniques to the same situations, getting the same results.

Let me put it another way. If you achieve a dream then you tell yourself to be happy. A beer can hit a spot. So too class As. So too orgasms. Chocolate gives a buzz. But they don't make you happy. A new car doesn't bring happiness. It's nice for a week and then when you have to clean it; it's just another fucking motor. Happiness just is.

To finish you wonder just how many women are actually in love with the man they share their life with. Or are they 'in lust', 'in convenience', 'in like', 'in better than nothing', 'in the doldrums', just letting life muddle on, a life lacking in passion, an emotional vacuum because they are surviving?

SIX

I don't know many couples that are actually in love with each other. I know that lots of people say 'I love him' or 'I love her to bits' but I really would question the validity of such a statement. They might say so to reinforce the relationship, feeding each other's egos, affirmations are very powerful, but...call me cynical...all it probably means is that 'thank God I'm not on my own'. Many relationships are born from necessity rather than emotion; it's why so many flounder and why there aren't enough divorces in the world. It's why there are so many affairs and why an average marriage lasts about eleven years. We really ought to be taught how to break up especially if it's going to happen regularly.

If you know that you are in love you know how it feels, you know that your gut feels empty whenever she's not there, you know that your physiology changes as soon as she walks into the room, you feel nervous, elated, edgy and high as a kite all at the same time. Psychologists the world over say that this condition, 'limerence' is its official title, can last between a year and eighteen months. If you're lucky this might stretch to three or four years. What they don't say is how many people it actually impacts on.

So let's go back to the reasons that men want to be in a relationship and see if these examples are scary or acceptable. As part of my research I recently chatted with some men in the pub and on the phone.

One, in the construction industry, wanted someone to look after the kids and the home, to cook his tea on a Friday night and to guarantee a shag at the end of the night.

Another said that having a girlfriend was 'sex on tap'.

Further questions brought out the response that it was convenient having a girlfriend. It meant he wasn't on his own, not lonely, better than nothing. And, 'at least I got a shag.'

I have read that without a partner men just go through the motions of living, they need a partner to complete them. None of the men mentioned this during the discussions.

'It was commercial common sense to move in together. Two incomes, one mortgage.'

'I fucking hate being on my own.'

'The perfect Friday is food, beer, shag, sleep.'

'I love women, I respect them...I've been around the block a bit but I am always honest if things aren't going well...but I do believe in love...and if there isn't any the relationship is pointless.' None of the men mentioned this during the discussions.

None of the men actually said the following either.

'I want to get married so that I can have kids, that I can be seen as a decent person, a married man...and so that I can shag anything else as and when the opportunity arrives.'

But serial philanderers wouldn't admit it to themselves let alone anyone else.

Let me throw a curved ball into this one. I got married. I wasn't in love but I think I loved her, two fundamentally different things, but the relationship was based on lust and alcohol; we never had the conversation about what I wanted and what she wanted.

These days it would be different.

'I have found a woman who is stunningly beautiful, intelligent, talented, educated, warm, funny, caring, with a massive heart, a soft touch and I feel elated every time I am with her. I hate not being with her, I miss her smell, her taste, her presence, how she complements my personality, and I would love to form a real long-standing relationship with her.'

How do you find a girl like this?

SEVEN

There is one truism about dating; you have to be ready, prepared, and you won't find a future lover if you're stuck in front of the telly every night on your own masturbating like a wild baboon. Have you ever seen a tame one?

It's a simple approach really. Tidy the house, clean sheets, clean towels, make sure the bog is presentable, dust a bit, shift the wash basket, get some wine in, and condoms, put all your paperwork away, bills and letters, she doesn't want to know you've been corresponding with hundreds of women, turn off the PC and tablets, get the music ready, sort the lighting, S, S, S, make sure you wash your cock and arse properly just in case she fancies a play with your perineum or massaging your prostrate, clean kecks and socks, glad rags (remember lads birds don't often take to you if you are dressed like a scruffy twat), brush your teeth, floss, little bit of splash, few bob in the wallet, sprinkle yourself with magic dust and charm and head out.

But to where?

Billy, Dan and me didn't really get very far; there was no great solution. As the women at home were probably asking the same question (easy answer girls, get involved with spectator sport) we still hadn't a clue where to find eligible bachelorettes. Where do all the good girls go? Between us we started to list potential hotspots where sober, educated women could be seen.

- Seminars – on a subject you are interested in.
- A book club.
- Charity dinners.
- Museums.
- Art galleries.
- Music recitals.
- Training courses.
- Self-help groups.
- Lobbies of posh hotels. (This was later scrubbed because we guessed that most were full of agency girls and tarts.)
- Book readings.
- Council meetings.
- Public gallery in the Crown Court (stretching a bit here.)

- Pop concerts. (Eh?)

- Any function where there is a chance to have a drink and a biscuit afterwards.

- Trade fairs.

- Become an extra in TV or the movies – get yersen an agent!

- Dog walking in the park (stretching again).

- Anywhere where there are nurses. One of life's great certainties.

- Join a movement (CND, am-dram etc).

- Join Weight Watchers. (Doh! All those fat birds!)

- Join the W.I.

- Do The Alpha Course.

- Weddings – I even pulled at my own wedding.

- Singles' Events.

We sort of agreed that the above list, far from finished, encapsulated a style of person that certainly me and Dan would be interested in, but it was all still ethereal, if that's the right word. It all looked and felt a bit flimsy. As well as that we agreed that we shouldn't go to these events or places because we had to but because we wanted to. And it would be wise to check up on the events prior, what age group was likely to be there, the men/women ratio, and the cost though we thought that paying a few quid for a reading from an eminent professor, or to a charity, was perfectly acceptable. And as Billy had said when messing about...we thought it was even better to go in twos and threes rather than on your own. Being Billy no mates with no foil or straight man was just about the same as having an arrow above your head with 'lonely' or 'loser' emblazoned in bright red on it.

And girls do like to be hit on by two guys at the same time, giving her a choice.

Then one day, it all changed.

EIGHT

It all happened by accident, or fate, you decide, when me, Dan and Billy saw an advert for a dance class in the free local weekly magazine. We passed the mag around, each of us digesting the details, silent until we all looked at each other.

'You must be fucking joking,' Dan said with genuine scorn. 'Prancing around a dance floor like some gay twat...no chance...you must be bonkers...full of fucking grannies and widowers...'

'All up for a shag,' said Billy.

'Might be your age group petal...'

'Cunt.'

'None taken.'

'None intended.'

I interjected.

'What sort of dancing is it anyway? Ballroom stuff? I learned to Waltz when I was eighteen but hated it...had to hold hands with a girl...at that age, I was just too young for that sort of thing...can't remember a step now. A bit like when I was five or six having to hold hands with Alex Gedney at Primary School. She was lovely but I was way too young.'

'You got her number? That would sort you,' prompted Dan.

'Would I be out with a div like you if I had?'

'Hey, this could be it,' said Billy running the movie in his head, pictures streaming into his consciousness, a veritable video, full colour, big sound, music, bounce, laughter, fun, and ...'Women!' he said gleefully. 'Holding hands! There must be more than the Waltz anyway...Dan, check out the website, I'll give them a ring.'

And so we did.

The dancing ranged from anything to everything: Waltz, Quick Step, Ball Room Tango, Jive, Rumba, Cha Cha Cha, Slow Fox Trot, Viennese Waltz, Samba, Argentine Tango, Social Fox Trot and Salsa. And then some extremes: Lindy, Swing, Meringue, Son, Mambo, Bachata and Kizomba, the latter turning out to be the African version of the Tango but with added free groping; it is not pretty.

Round at Dan's we clicked on the Internet on his new Mac and quickly found some video clips of dancing. Most of it looked bobbins, to be honest, contrived, blokes in tuxes, birds in posh frocks, all a bit formal, false smiles, fake tans, numbers on backs, no fun really, but there was a lot of women in the films, dancing, watching and who looked like they were keen to be there.

Maybe there was some mileage in this one?

And then we did something totally unblokelike.

Having watched a few clips of Salsa - world championships, from the movies, one with a bloke with one leg and a crutch (I kid you not) - we went to HMV and bought the 1987 dance film blockbuster 'Dirty Dancing' starring Patrick Swayze and Jennifer Grey. And like three mutant teenage girls we sat and watched the film, something a bit thin on plot, character and great lines, but full of fantastic music, some great dancing and some sex (girls would call it romance.)

Okay, let's put this into perspective. The film took place in 1963, a pretty good year, in the US somewhere, in New York's Catskill Mountains, the film, apart from the establishment, featured young, thin people, some Latinos, the hip and the trendy, and that ruled the three of us out straight away. Anyway, surely dance ghettos like those in the film didn't exist over here? If they did they were well hidden.

And the girls that danced the dirty dancing (obviously good looking) looked to be doing it willingly, actively positive, gyrating, seductive, sexy, on a real burn of sensation. If those girls existed over here then I didn't know them or where they hung out either.

The whole entity was seductive...Salsa, Mambo, Dirty Dancing...was that the way forward?

Billy rang about classes and got the details. And then the informant, presumably a teacher, or D.I. (dance instructor) as they like to be called, said that as well as local classes there were events all over the country, international, and that the ratio of men to women was normally 60/40 or even 70/30. When the informant clarified that this was women to men we were totally and utterly sold, especially when Billy was told that at some dance conventions there were over a thousand people meaning six hundred women, or seven hundred if you were lucky. Even if you just played the numbers there must be one person who would pass muster enough to reach the finals of my own audition.

It seemed like the perfect opportunity to shed the coyness of Britishness and to get down and do it dirty. And we did.

Over the coming years we went to classes, once a week, sometimes twice, sometimes more. We learnt New York style, Cuban style, Mambo style and Salsa tap steps and we took in videos and DVDs, anything to improve technique, even the smallest detail. We made notes, compared them, taught each other, challenged each other to improve, improvised, invented moves, copied other people and we visited conventions at home and abroad and became thoroughly imbued in the culture of the dance world. It was addictive, the music positively beat for your heart, the trumpets, the drums all adding to the drama.

We got good.

Very good.

And thankfully there were girls.

Aplenty.

NINE

I was at work recently when my pal Andy mentioned that a friend of his, who is a girl, had asked him to go to a Salsa class with her and he asked me what I thought. Andy is married with a young family; I'm not really sure how the invitation arrived or was made but after a brief description of what happens at Salsa classes and dances Andy was given the unequivocal advice of an expert. Don't go!

Of course there would be an explanation. I told him not to go with this girl but to go with his wife instead because I know what Salsa and Salsa classes are about.

When Dan, Billy and me first started we were like rabbits in headlamps. We hadn't got a clue what to do, we were in awe of the class prior where it looked like the world champions were on display and we were all shocked by the flagrant openness of the intoxicating sexiness and closeness that took place in public. It was like Dirty Dancing but better. It was aspirational. But it didn't seem to be something you would or should be doing with another man or woman if you were married or in a relationship. Surely this dance wrecked marriages?

Which is quite ironic because apart from a few couples that did turn up together the class was full of single people and divorcees, all looking for a partner. This is the absolute truth. Of course, there were people there who could dance, and went to dance, but they went for the company, the beer, the music and the chance to find a potential lover. One or two, of both sexes, were there on the look out just for sex. I was at a convention once, hitting on a pretty girl when she threw into the conversation that she wasn't into casual sex. I asked her if she wanted some very serious sex. Her laugh prevented the need for an answer. I am usually shit at pulling for a one-night stand and this just highlighted the fact.

So the first classes were full of virginal touches, the awkwardness of being with a total stranger, holding her hand, touching her body, sometimes bare skin, introducing yourself, trying to remember every name, hoping that your breath didn't smell, or your body, and that they associated the shaking of your hands as nerves not the bender that started forty-eight hours before. And there is that excruciating moment when the instructor asks you to find a partner. Experienced dancers know that it is perfectly normal to go through this routine. The shy, the nervous, the unconfident find it a terror. How do you pick? The closest? The prettiest? Some people just don't move, hoping that someone approaches them, removing any stigma or inferred intention. Some almost positively hide. Others rush towards their prey. I go for the best dancer.

But whether they acknowledge it or not most of the people at the class, obviously looking to fill time, in a sense, but most are on the pull. Most want a partner. Most see it as a serious breeding ground for relationships. And it is. Of course, there's the odd groper, but most are on the look out whether they are young, free and single, recently separated, divorced or in a shit relationship and they come from all walks of life – doctors, nurses, architects, teachers, lecturers, NHS staff, self-employed people, plumbers, builders, engineers, social workers, retail people, bankers, factory workers, receptionists, recruitment agents. Anything. But all on the pull. Even when they deny it.

TEN

To wank or not to wank, that is the question.

I set myself a tough task. Do I whack a quick one off before I go out, a sure sign of pessimism, or do I really set a stiff test, put on some porn and then see what happens? And if I do have a wank now it is inevitable that I will pull later and what would be the point of that with both barrels recharging. Shit, what a dilemma. People think that being single is easy.

You see, if I was happily married I wouldn't be contemplating going out let alone having a swift hand shandy. I mean, that's what the wife is for isn't it? And I don't mean that in a derogatory fashion; sex is part of the deal.

Here, let me throw this at you. You've seen porn, right? Well, what's all that about? They don't kiss much – I love the intimacy of kissing - the bloke is always hung like a horse, she licks him all over, her licks her all over, he pounds away not worrying about any structural damage he's likely to inflict, and then, just as he's about to come he takes his cock out of the last orifice and wanks all over her, either her tits, her back or her face. Inevitably spunk goes in her mouth, up her nose, in her eyes, definitely in her hair and she's not impressed that she's got to wash it again before the next shoot.

So what is it all about? You spend all that time charming a bird's pants off, you get that magic when she reaches for your belt buckle for the first time and then YOU wank YOURSELF off! What's the point of her being there? Surely she should be the one doing the wanking or the sucking or whatever? Not you. I mean, that is her role, isn't it? Or am I just being stupid? Is it just that these films are made by blokes who are into subjugation and belittlement? If they are they are seriously missing the point.

Anyway, I decided to keep me pants on and I got the bus into town to the local Salsa pally to see what the night would bring, forever optimistic that I could find someone to have a good dance with, someone to click with, or to find a potential long-term lover.

I say pally with reservations because all this place was and is, is a bar, two floors, no dance floor downstairs (tables and chairs moved to accommodate), two small dance floors upstairs, not enough room really, and if the numbers were good you'd struggle to see the teacher if a class was in motion.

This bar is typical of most that you find in any city, a theme bar, a name that the marketing guys think will attract custom, 'Cuban Spice', happy hours, cheap pub grub, cocktails, and once a week, a Wednesday, it hosts an independent company, Salsa This or Salsa That, same the country over, in the belief that the classes will bring revenue. It's pretty ruthless, if it doesn't generate enough cash then the theme will be changed.

It's a popular misconception that dancers drink lots of beer: lots plus beer equals money. They don't, not unless they're at a convention but beer and Salsa aren't the greatest bed friends. Too pissed and you lose control. And most dancers drive to the venue and have to get up the following morning to go to work. That said, if there are fifty to a hundred punters paying a fiver each and drinking two or three soft drinks a night then it's better than nothing. Midweeks are quiet in most cities; give the punters a reason to go out, why not and see if it works. If it doesn't the Salsa pally will quickly become a sports bar, a pool bar, Quiz of the week, a lap bar or a fucking bordello.

ELEVEN

When I walked in I paid my £4.65 for a pint of gassy, Spanish nay Cuban, tinny lager. Four pounds sixty-five friggin' pence! Continental rates. Since when did these fuckers have the right to charge so much for such shit beer? Then I paid my £6 to enter the 'dance emporium'. Emporium? It's just a room. There weren't many there. I clocked the heads, Billy and Dan right at the far side of the room, watching the floor, conspirators, checking for dance talent, offering each other an educated critique of the dancers. That'd be slagging them off then.

There was that Karen who I was with at a late bar last Saturday. Let's call her Karen Saturday, five two, mid twenties, size ten, auburn, shoulder length hair, perky butt, full lips, soft jeans and a mauve top, nice chest, works for the local authority. Last weekend we were in the same bar with mutual friends, a late bar, a post midnight refuge for the lost, lonely and drunk. We did some really close stuff when we were both pissed and it could have turned out to be what my mate Ski calls a two-pairer, that is two pairs of boxers or pants, whatever you prefer, one sticky pair and one pair of clean replacements. Anyway, she was hot was Karen, but pissed, and I remember caressing her tight arse with a stray hand or two, beautiful it was, but my guess is that sober she'll be a different story. She nodded at me shyly when she saw me. Told you. A disappointment and immediate rejection.

Over to the right was Curly. Tall she is Curly, good looking, thin, looked after body, super bright if not a tad serious, an orphan, age conscious, midriff on show, on the pull after a recent relationship went tits up. I hope she's not giving him one, the grey-haired old fucker she's dancing with. He's called Baz, thinks he's God's fucking gift to cool. He's not. He's just socially ignorant unless he wants your money – he puts on dance events - bit of a twat really.

In the middle of the floor was the Italian, from Milan she is, oozing class, every bloke salivating, even me. Tall, pretty, dark hair, almost pageboy, the confidence of a Baracca horse, nicely made up, well-cut clothes, she married an English bloke but that went tits up too. I don't know if there's a queue for her or whether she's bothered but it might be nice to have a bit of Continental. (I know one bloke who wanted to shag a girl from each of the countries in Europe but that's another story.) That said, the Italian's probably a proper church going Catholic, and that doesn't bode well for the bed stakes, all that sin and all that guilt.

Arlene's at the back, fat little thing that smokes too much. She wants to fuck me. I don't want to fuck her. End of.

There's Lisa, over there on the right, the face that launched a thousand wine bottles, she is in advertising, freckles, a glint hiding her nerves. She saw me and came over with her bright smile and cigarettes. What is it with these birds? All fucking fag ashes the lot of 'em. I won't say it's like kissing an ashtray, well just the twice, but it is. Disgusting and I don't care if it's Sophia fucking Loren or

Madonna, if you smoke you've no chance with me. That is unless you want to give up. Quickly.

(Here, let me digress one sec. I hear they brought out a new Madonna doll. When you wind it up it goes down on Barbie and Ken gives her one from behind. LMTO. Laughed me tits off when I heard that. Chubby Brown I think.)

But girls who smoke really ought to think about it. It is a well-rehearsed cliché, kissing an ashtray, but that too is a truism and a major turn off. I once approached a Dutch model in a bar on her second Woodbine of the night. 'You are so beautiful,' I said, 'but you've no chance with me.' I looked at the fag in her hand with disgust. She probably thought I was an English prick. Either way the message would have got through.

Anyway, Lisa cuddles me and I feel her ample breasts push into my ample chest. Lovely. But I've no chance. She's too young. Well, she's not. She just thinks she is. And that's me fucked then. Or not, as the case may be. But she's great is Lisa, talented, gifted even, a real performer, but another with low self-esteem after an abusive relationship. Her bloke kept slagging her off, saying that she was ugly, telling her to wear jeans to cover her legs because they were unsightly. What sort of a twat of a boyfriend is that? And why put up with it? Sort of defeats the object. She is really pretty and she has a big heart.

On the dance floor I spied Jenny with the glasses, Jenny Glasses. Five eleven, short blonde hair, pretty face, flat shoes, university educated, married, divorced by thirty, doing the rounds, searching, nice dancer except her hands are a bit heavy. I don't mean she's got big hands, I mean that to dance Salsa finger tip control is vital and if the girl grabs too tight or too much then it makes leading her more problematic than if her fingers were full of empathy. She's dated a couple of the guys on the scene, I don't know to what extent and I think she's courting with a bloke from Birmingham now but I could be wrong. I wonder what she does behind those glasses? I do know that she drives a small car, which must be an issue for a tall bird. And the car is a three-door job. That's just another name for a fucking death trap, especially for the poor fucker in the back. Jenny Glasses is a definite maybe.

Cliff Richard was there too, a good looking middle-aged guy, straight, well-tailored, semi-retired, nice clothes, bit of charm and savvy, a flat up the posh part of the city, has a posse of girls wherever he goes.

Next to him is big Nev in his new black t-shirt. Don't know much about Nev except that he is big, normally wears a white t-shirt and that he also has big feet on which he wears standard issue brogues rather than bespoke dance shoes. He looks like he could be military. Probably drives a truck and looks after his ailing and aging mum.

Most of my posse weren't there. What a pisser. But there was that graceful blonde, Katy something, who I dance with, slinking well with her boyfriend, Terry, tall, macho, solid. He's a good lad and she's lovely, a good combination. When I first danced with her I was terrified because I was crap and she wasn't. That was three years ago and now I can strut with the best of them so she's not a problem. She has great eye contact when you dance, good body shimmies but she does try to second-guess a bit. Princess Grace is her moniker but let's hope she doesn't drive her car the same way.

Sat down was another Karen, Karen Monday, sweet girl, nice chassis, great demeanour, soft complexion, good dancer but she's married. Bollocks. She's bound to be. Some guy got lucky there, except where was he whilst she was out gallivanting? Anyway, she's safe with me. Never date birds who are married or in a relationship. Not knowingly anyway. About 5' 5" she has a real tempo and is fun, I think that's because I take the piss and she likes a laugh, and she likes me too. It's not against the law to like people. Not clever to date them though, the married ones. Anyway, I only see her once in a blue moon so that's really a non-starter. Best just to enjoy the night.

Next to her was Eliza, tall, black, curvy, heavy chested, glasses, butt out. They seemed to be chatting under the music and they both waved. I blew them a kiss without using my hands.

Back to the dance floor I spotted Bobbin' Robin. He's called that because that's how he dances, up and down, up and down, up and friggin' down, and it's not really that conducive to Salsa. He knows the steps, and I'm told he leads well, but he just goes up and down, up and down, up and friggin' down, so much so that you think he's going to bob the fucking roof off. For the uninitiated Salsa is predominantly a forwards and backwards dance, there are circles too but steps aren't marched and it is definitely not an up and down dance.

Bobbin' is divorced, an insomniac, at times a male escort, tall and thin, crisply ironed shirts from Burton's or John Collier, The Window to Watch, and he recently turned down a trip to a Salsa fest because, he says, his girlfriend wouldn't let him. If his girlfriend knew that he was trying to get into the Italian's knickers do you think she'd let him do that too? I'm hoping the Italian has more taste.

And that was it, quick hello to the boys, we don't socialise a lot at these gigs, too many girls to occupy us, and then over to the dance floor, a dance here, a dance there, a look around at all the ethnics' skills, steps and styles, not all great contrary to common myth, time watching the dynamics, who's feeling who, who's all alone, who doesn't want to be and who's so fucking aloof that they'll be alone for the rest of...until they get off their cloud. It was dismaying to see that Bobbin' and the Italian were getting closer, arms round, and all that. Surely he's not giving her one? The bastard! In fact, the bastardesse. What can she be thinking? Jealous? Me? Never!

Three hours later I left, pissed and on my own. Lisa asked me how much I'd had to drink. 'Not enough,' was my reply. She'd better have not been judging, going all AP on me, Alcohol Police. Cheeky fucker, I never ask her if she's up to forty Woodbines a day, do I? We all have our vices; if that's what you can call liking a beer. I do like it, it's fucking lovely, but I can go without it I want to. I've done months without. I mean, I don't wake up in the morning and crave a swig of vodka. But I love beer, its taste, its myth, its place in our culture, its impact and when you're low you'll take every escape you can get.

I got a cab home and the cheeky cunt of a driver tried to stitch me up. A fucking chancer. He laid it on about how his meter was bust and that he didn't know the normal rate. He wanted eight quid. I gave him seven and a half. And that included the tip. Cheeky cunt. When I got in I was starving so I cleaned out the leftovers from the wok, cracked some wine and put on some porn.

TWELVE

Last night was typical of the venue, 'Cuban Spice', all glitz and frustration and to be fair I wasn't really in the right mood to pull or to prospect. Sometimes you're not; I had things on my mind. I mean there were lots of girls there, some I knew, loads I didn't, but what was I there for? Was I looking for fresh blood, or old blood, or did I just want to hide away from reality for a while? Being pissed didn't help but perhaps that was my escape and to be honest this bar isn't my home venue and I can feel a little shy, left out and depressed under the fluorescent lights even with a belly full of beer.

Let me take it a bit further. It's not one of the venues where I learnt to dance; it's almost like playing football as an away game so it's a little out of my comfort zone. And the venue isn't full of pretty white boys like me looking for a girl. This venue is home to Latinos, Cubans and Afro-Caribbeans, men with arrogance born from their skin colour and their innate belief that it is in their soul to able to shake their butt and strut their stuff.

Now don't get me wrong, I am not racist. I have some great black friends, Tuts, Vinny, PJ, JP, Eliza, Nigie, to name but a few, but there is something undesirable about the blacks that go to this venue. Maybe it is their arrogance? Maybe it is the way that they treat women? Not always positively. They see skirt as their birth right. And women are there to be had, to be used and abused accordingly, a lower caste that should be either cooking or fucking. If ever you've seen a

Cuban dance with a girl whilst he is chewing gum and being more into himself than the girl then you'll know what I mean. Does treat 'em mean really work? Do these blokes really play hard to get? Does being so dismissive get them hard? Some Hispanics are the same, all about me.

There are common myths that all blacks have big cocks and can dance. I can't vouch for the first but I can the second. It is not true. Yes, there is a natural non-Britishness to the way that they move their hips, not being scared of gyrations or public intimacy but that doesn't mean that they can dance. They might think they can and that confidence oozes from their steps but are they technically any good? Do they have a large repertoire? How is their timing? Their lead? The softness in their hands? Most of the guys I watch aren't great, black or white, most are limited in their ability and step-portfolio and most don't buy into the essence of the music and the dance. They don't get the big picture. And I really don't buy into the no eye contact dismissiveness.

Maybe the problem I have with them comes back to me just being a typical alpha male, maybe it is just pure jealousy, maybe it is all about pulling? For some reason white birds are fascinated by black men. Perhaps they all just long for some black cock? Maybe they think that the myth follows into the bedroom? Or to complete the myth, the gun cabinet?

But I digress. If all someone has to be to be perceived cool and a fanny magnet is to be black and turn up at a Salsa gig with girls thinking he can dance and wiggle his hips a bit maybe I should just black up like Al Jolson? Surely that would resolve the situation? I know that the Black and White Minstrels once blacked up for a radio show. True that.

I felt a right twat the next morning if only metaphorically. More's the pity. Done by a cabbie, no pull, no wank and everyone thinking that I'm a pisshead, which last night, let's be fair, wasn't far from the truth.

So what to do? After a thought it was into the bathroom.

Ten minutes later Dan turned up and we chewed the fat over last night, tonight, and the weekend, Easter. Fuck, Easter hurts the arms doesn't it? But sales of timber and nails always increase. Dan went for a lash. He's a big lug Dan, big, polite, funny, rude, smart, brash, to the point, a great dancer, lovely company if not a bit fucked up. That's what a shit marriage does for you.

'Hey you, you dirty cunt, there's some spunk in the bathroom sink!' he shouted for all to hear. That was just me and him.

'What do you want? I replied and giggled. 'A fucking straw?'

He walked back into the lounge and threw the Domestos and bathroom cleaner at me.

'Well, what was I supposed to do?' I defended thinking that I'd cleaned it all up.

'Use some bog roll? A fucking towel? Or a hanky? Use your fucking brains you dimwit. What if I'd been your mother?'

'I'd have been taller and less talented.' He scowled with sarcasm. 'Do you want a sandwich and a coffee?'

'Only if you've washed your hands, yer dirty bastard.'

THIRTEEN

Over time Billy, Dan and me ventured into different dance classes like most people crawl pubs on a Friday night on our quest to find that long-term love partner, for me and Dan at least. That included travelling around and trying all the dances that we discovered a few years ago advertised in the local mag because, although our experiment wasn't exactly scientific, we did need to know if the Latin & Ballroom classes attracted the same ratio of women and singletons with the same mindset.

This was a slightly different scene, the average age higher (what is the average age of a divorcee these days? 35? 37?), more couples, teetering towards retirement looking for something real to occupy themselves rather than reality TV, fewer purely single women though some married women who wanted to dance braved the venues without their partner or husband because they wanted to learn or because they wanted to escape from domesticity for a while. For their men dancing was a strict 'no-no', a taboo, a non-British hobby, bad for their image.

Bizarre this one. I know that some men are shy and that they have been programmed to react negatively to dancing in a strictly homophobic manner but there is nothing gay about dancing per se nor anything bad about anyone who is gay. In the thirties everyone danced, in some countries it is part of lore for men to learn how to dance, but there is something that some men don't get. Maybe they secretly crave having the knowledge and the ability yet their bodies are convulsed with fear. Maybe it's just the public perception; when you are dancing you are watched. Is it just fear? Of being on display or of not being able to do it in a room full of peers? Some people won't shit in a public loo. Some won't dance in a dance hall. For me, it was and remains a Godsend.

The night after the pissed exposé I went alone from the Ballroom pally to the Salsa pally, a new Salsa pally, this time a room in a bar, a working men's club, where an estate agent would describe the venue as intimate. Others would call it tight, a small dance floor, restricted space, few chairs and tables, obviously a cheap hire if not free gratis.

Numbers were few, after all it was Easter, all obviously at church or watching videos of Robert Powell when he was Jesus rather than that nurse on Holby. Maybe not. All on hols with the family or out on the lash or taking that much needed break.

There was only one familiar face, Dan, studying everyone, teachers and dancers, learning, checking technique and hand movements. He doesn't miss much Dan, an astute observer, an expert in body language and eye watching. If you're unsure if someone fancies someone just ask Dan and he'll tell you months before the couple get together. Every now and then he might even orchestrate it. Shame he can't do it for him and me more often.

It wasn't for me to be judgemental. The class was full of beginners because it was a beginners' class but amidst the dearth of talent and experience there was one to watch: five three, dark curly hair, Jewish or Greek face, olive patina, lovely rose red top, black calf-length culottes, lace tights though they could have been stockings. Standing across the room from her I offered my hands, asking her to dance and she duly accepted.

'We've just been talking about you,' I whispered.

'Oh, have you?' Her eyes widened slightly, there was a blush to her cheeks, her neck reddened just one RAL number, her pupils formed larger saucers in the whites of her eyes. Had you taken her BP or pulse, both would have increased 10% or so.

'Yeah, me and Dan thought that you were looking lovely tonight.'

'Oh.' Another increment up.

'Yeah. Beautiful hair, nice cut, smart top, lovely culottes.'

'Thanks.' And another.

And then she took a visible gasp of fresh air.

Let's put this into context. We were all sober and she looked great, as if she was going out on the pull later, or indeed, as if she was on the pull in this lesson. But how many people in her relatively short life, at a guess, twenty-six, had ever said something so nice to her? Sober? We danced in a beautiful and controlled manner, like you do sober and it was fantastic. I took to her and she took to me or so I thought but by the end of the night I felt a touch out of place. The body language changed as the night closed in and I sensed that she's another who obviously thinks she's too young for me. Even though she isn't.

It was clear that her target for the night was the bloke teaching. He's younger than me, single, thinner, bald, and in her eyes a better catch though he probably doesn't earn more than his age, not a great cue. He's a bit of a player too. She doesn't know it but as soon as he's fucked her he'll be off after another little starlet looking for the hook up with the man in the spotlight. It makes you wonder. If he weren't the teacher, would she fancy him? And what would his line be? 'Nice tits?'

I knew a bird that had three tits. I suppose you'd call them a pair and a half.

I knew another who had five. Her bra fit her like a glove.

FOURTEEN

Saturday night at the uni in the next city, another Salsa gig, not one that I found overwhelmingly attractive, a last resort of a venue, when there was nothing else on at all and when you'd run out of razor blades so there was nothing left to slash your wrists with. (I knew a girl who did that once. Benevolently I called her Slasher.)

It was always busy, too busy at the uni, the dance floor was like a war zone at times, there were no windows so the humidity was akin to a rain forest, the clientele was a bit cliquey, the bar staff obnoxious, ungrateful of their opportunity to earn some extra cash, and it was usually at least a forty minute drive to get there and two days prior it wasn't even on the list, not in the plan, but when it came the options were one hundred and eighty miles on a Saturday with a dance or two hundred and thirty on a Sunday without, so it was a pretty easy decision at the end of it all.

The drive was fine but tiring so when I mounted the stairs in trainers, jeans and t-shirt it was hard going. I needed a sleep, a change of clothes and for someone to tell me that this was going to be a good night. Driving, it would be a beerless night, a chance to show people that I wasn't just a charming pisshead but also a charmer sober, and a chance to suss out things from a different perspective.

Nine quid lighter (nine!) I sat down and watched the Bachata class. The Bachata is a dance from the Dominican Republic that is best danced very close and the beat goes step, step, step, hip. Or you can replace hip with wobble, side thrust or a double shake or a tap. It is sexy as fuck and is best danced with legs entwined. A Bokke mate of mine calls it one, two, three, c-lit, and to see it you'll understand why. Shy girls don't like it, it is intimate, bodies collide, air is shared, and breath goes from lungs to ear. Single girls love it. From sixteen to eighty.

I was too fucked to join in and anyway sometimes it's good to watch. The Italian was there but Bobbin' wasn't. What a result. Perhaps they've fallen out already? Perhaps she's found out about his girlfriend? Either way she looked stunning, all in black, a tight top with a flower at her cleavage, ripe for the picking, and her skirt a little long, like she should be in a business meeting. Not conducive to drops or slipping a leg in between.

Her mate was there the Mexican, Gabrielle, shorter than the Italian but still five eight, plumper but not plump, a novice dancer and she obviously has comfort zones elsewhere. Pretty though, sensuous like only Latin girls can be.

Looking round there was a surprisingly nice mix. The lovely girl from Thursday, the one I'd complemented sober, tapped me on the back and we strutted nicely, her in another red top, this one showing some cleavage. Lovely.

In one corner there was Hartcliffe Harry, King of the Chavs, all blinged up, earring, white daps, six stone overweight, another the victim of a shit marriage and poor calorie control.

In another Curly sat, all alone. Baz the twat hovered like a shadow, clean-shaven so that his grey look didn't totally put off every bird under the age of seventy. Jenny Glasses was there with another posh bird. A nice treble sat together; let's call them tall, dark and blonde. They are all a good laugh. Johnny Mambo was hosting. Arlene and Eliza were there. Bandana Joe and his moll took to the floor. Some teachers did their bit. Some classy dancers posed like they were the best in the country. That's because they probably are.

It was hot, really hot, a three-shirt night, no windows, as mentioned, just two large fans and it wasn't enough. High heat, high humidity. It could have been the fucking Congo.

How many shirts had I brought? How many hand towels to dry my face? Not many people brought hand towels but it was the most obvious and sensible thing to do.

The posh bird came to me as the girls moved around during the class given by the Salsa superstar Robert Charlemagne and his oppo, the beautiful Pam. When the posh bird arrived my hands were shaking. It wasn't nerves just alcohol withdrawal, though bless the egotistical fucker, she thought it was her impact. We had a laugh briefly and then she fucked off to the next bloke. I didn't speak to her again the whole night which was what I called a result. Whilst you are polite and will dance with everyone sometimes it doesn't click. I pick up on the body language, the fear, the bravado, what really is going on in the mind and sometimes I don't like it. I knew she was going through the motions with me and I deserve better than that. She should be honoured to be sharing the same room as me.

The posh bird is called Jackie but I call her Belle. That's because her surname is Vue, her elder sister was born prematurely and is called Deja. Her youngest sister, who likes a different perspective, is called Unautre.

Way back last summer I thought for a moment that I'd pulled Belle but I found out in no uncertain fashion that I hadn't. Let me give you the scenario. She's five ten, size twelve, pretty, educated, moneyed and with a mouth that's worth kissing. She dances brilliantly if not a bit OTT but her least redeeming feature is that she thinks that she is the most important person in the world, the centre of the universe, even more so than one or two of the arrogant French fuckers that I know. Maybe this is just her way of coping with a low self-esteem and flagrant shyness. Maybe she's doing a Bono and still hasn't found what she's looking for?

On that hot night last summer Belle was wearing a long brown frock and whilst the Samba girls, dressed like extras from Chicken Run, shook their booty like they were hitting invisible cymbals, I joked the pants off Belle. Well, not quite. More's the pity. She laughed at all my gags, my shtick, my one liners, my semi-gallic shrugs and we danced, bought each other beers and by the end of the night I thought I'd found the mother of my next child. She wouldn't even give me her phone number. I've hardly acknowledged her since. Perhaps I should buy her a crowbar to get her head out of her arse?

It's funny watching her though. For all her beauty and style she is on her own a lot, she doesn't get asked to dance that much and she never pulls. Either she is already sorted with a boyfriend away from Salsa, she can't be arsed, she's a Lez, or she is just so friggin' choosy that mere mortals like me shouldn't deign to be with her. Well, here's a thought for Belle. When you're old and knackered and seventy, I want you to know and appreciate the following: you missed out on me. I was there and available and you messed up. Your loss Honey.

God, I am a bad loser.

All I want is a life partner. Is that too much to ask?

Another one that I try not to give time of day to is a groupie who hangs around with some of the instructors...just because they are THE instructors. Gets on my tits that. It's like birds shagging a badge at work. John Prescott comes to mind. She has the air of royalty without the substance to go with it and what's more she can't dance. I tried to tolerate her during the Salsa but it was horrific. Her timing was off, she didn't respond to leads and I was relieved when the music ended. Hopefully I'll never have to dance with her again. You might have guessed that she is off beacon as far as a potential lover goes too.

Jenny Glasses asked me to dance and she remains and always will be an enigma. She is a tall unit too and so far I have yet to dance with her in an unhampered, connected way. There is no emotional bond. Dancing is more fulfilling with an emotional attachment. Sometimes it takes years. It's best when it happens instantaneously. For the dance to work the girl has to buy into the bigger picture, that is what is happening for those three or four minutes. Listen to the beat, capture the flow, live the intensity, allow yourself to be encompassed by the mood, let your sex flow a little, take the moment for what it is, lose those reservations and enjoy. I'm not sure if she thinks I'm a bit of a twat.

Gladly, the highlight of the year so far, and worth the effort and entry fee on its own, I danced with Pam, the instructor, mid twenties, size eight, beautiful and black. The DJ played Marc Anthony's 'When I Dream at Night' and she walked over and asked me to dance. It's fine for girls to ask, it doesn't mean home and bed, it means, dance. When I asked her name she answered, 'Pam.'

'That's an ordinary name,' I said, 'but it's my favourite.'

She giggled and we danced slowly to the Latin balladeer, the one time Mr Jennifer Lopez until his life was determined by his cock. The beautiful JLo, children, plenty of cash, and he goes off and shags someone else. Not all well at the ranch then, maybe she'd lost her sex drive? Or it's about opportunity, surrounded by pretty, available talent. Or maybe he's just a cunt.

Four minutes twenty seconds later I knew that it was time to retire. I had danced most of my repertoire. It had been faultless, the leads were soft, the routine contained five drops each greeted by a giggling Pam, 'Go, Big Guy,' and moves that are called Guernsey One and Two, the duck move, swimming, a double spear – I invented that - and Katy One, Two and Three, amongst others. She was fucking awesome, a pure delight, and when I left for the night she kissed me on each cheek. Her personality shone through her dancing. If she lived locally I'd marry her and live happily ever after.

Always best to finish on a high.

FIFTEEN

I had a couple of beers with the Travolta twins a couple of days afterwards. I've already mentioned Dan and Billy. Did I not mention that, because of their dancing prowess, they were labelled Travolta? And that they were twins in a DeVito and Schwarzenegger sort of way? They're not really, given that Dan's a big lug and Billy isn't, and there's a few years between them, but they are remarkably alike, think the same things and both have an aptitude for performing, whether that's singing, dancing, telling gags and stories or acting. I've written to the BBC asking if they will audition them to be the next Doctor Who. Twins would really work in that role. The conversation was ribald and direct.

'So Dan,' said Billy, 'what happened to that radiologist that used to wank you off?'

Without batting an eyelid Dan said that they'd called it quits because apart from the filthy sex they hardly ever saw each other and she didn't really buy into the ethos of 'friends with benefits' as The Telegraph would describe it, or 'fuck buddy' if you read The Sun. A few girls went for it but most wanted some commitment. Anyway, Dan worked a lot and was dedicated to his kids and she worked a lot and was dedicated to her family and dog, called, wait for it, Rover. I kid you not. So it was always going to be a tricky relationship with diminishing windows of shagability and from what I saw from Dan's body language was that they hadn't really sparked enough for him to commit more to her. He didn't want to use her, that would be unfair in Dan's eyes, and so they agreed to move on.

'She's a lovely girl,' said Dan looking back, 'but I didn't think about her all the time like I have in the past with girls...but we did have great sex...quick phone call, twenty minutes later, full on.'

'Do we really need to know the details?' I asked.

'You're not getting any,' he said, 'but I will say that I do like a bird that isn't scared of sex and who knows all about the physics of it and all that...'

'Well, she should, she's in the fucking profession,' said Billy.

'Two certainties in life,' I added, 'death and nurses.'

'And taxes,' said Billy.

'It's not just that,' said Dan, 'yes, you're right that she should know about physiology and all that, but she wasn't scared of the processes, the results and all that.'

'You mean the outcomes?' said Billy and we all laughed our tits off. 'Or was it just the one outcome?'

'It was heartening her attitude...come where you like, she said...very enlightened...saved a lot of questions or refusals.'

'Better than that other great motivational speech that some girls give you,' I added, 'I'm not sucking it...'

We all laughed aloud.

'And she abided by the rule...if I have sex I am not going to make myself come, that's what she's there for,' Dan concluded.

'Have you got her number?' I asked.

The beers flowed and as we were talking about radiologists, well, two in particular, Dan told about how he'd got caught up in a fight a few years ago. When he got to the hospital there was blood flowing from his right hand where the teeth of 'the big cunt that I smacked' had dug into his hand. The teeth, he added, ended up on the tarmac. At the hospital reception the lady at the station, all straight faced, asked, 'what can we do for you lads now?'

'I've hurt me hand in a fight,' said Dan. 'There were four of them against two of us. It was pretty hairy.'

'And which hand would that be?'

Again we all pissed ourselves.

The other radiologist...over two decades ago...was tall beautiful, had the most amazing chest I'd ever seen and she tasted fantastic. It was a funny night, me and my pal Shaggy (named after Scooby Doo) trawled the wine bars along with the rest of sporting fraternity and just as we thought the night had blanked he approached through the crowd looking like Hugh Hefner, a girl on each arm. There was a pretty one and a tug. My ardour dropped until Shaggy admitted that the tug was with him and the brunette version of Barbie was mine for the night. I didn't have to do anything to pull her, Shaggy had done everything. Minutes later we all drove home in Shaggy's Ford Escort (he must have been five times over the limit – I'd recommend a retrospective fine or ban) and watched TV until my radiologist nipped to the loo. I exited the room a few minutes later and greeted her at the top of the stairs. After a quick kiss I led her to the master bedroom.

Here though is where the compatibility ended. I was delirious to know that she wore no knickers, one of life's great discoveries, but the jaunt was frustrating because as extrovert as she was out of bed, behind closed doors she obviously forgot that old adage that 'you can't beat a bird that joins in'. She didn't. We met once more afterwards to cement this incompatibility. She was beautiful with glamour model looks but history.

After the beers with the boys I wandered off home to check out my emails and some free porn sites that I'd discovered on the Interweb. Great name for it that, the Interweb. If you look you can unearth whatever you want on the Interweb and I mean anything. It really is easy, and with android phones in every home in the country, just a few touches away, whatever your age.

It'd be easier to tell you what I don't like. All that stuff with animals, no thanks. Pain is a no go, not even a slap on the arse. Vulgar stuff with puke and shit isn't for me. And birds that look like they've been forced into it, either by threat or money, no thanks. Sex is purer than that and is far better when everyone consents to things willingly. A bit like Dan's first x-ray girl. I don't like the gratuitous stuff either, you know, where there are plates of spunk involved, or champagne glasses. The bukkake thing isn't for me either. Where is the fun in that? Twenty blokes and one bird? It's all about submission and I just don't go there. Dogging? How sordid is that? Swinging? Not sure I'd have the bottle. Threesomes – two girls and me, pretty good. Three girls and me, Nirvana.

As I said, sex is purer than submission and is far better when everyone consents to things willingly.

SIXTEEN

Loneliness is a hard bastard.

Each time you think that you've conquered it and it comes back to smack you between the eyes.

The four walls of the lounge.

The four walls of the bedroom.

When it's just you and some sort of mechanical aid: TV, radio, CDs, DVDs, iPlayer, tablet, phone.

Even when there is noise you know that deep down there is just you.

It's okay to like your own company, to be able to cope with being on your own but that can soon fall over the abyss into loneliness.

I hosted a dinner party once, seven people.

The food was prepared, cooked, sorted, eaten. We had drinks, beer, wine, the occasional fruit juice. We played games, chatted, danced, messed around, flirted, pulled. And then, once the cabs had gone, when people had walked off, when the last car light had disappeared into the night, there was just me and the remnants of the party. From adulation to devastation in the blink of an eye.

That's a cheery one, isn't it? Let's move on.

Let me tell you about my friend Layla. I first met her when I began to learn to dance...she was the teacher.

Anyway, she's forty-three, about five three, blonde, sometimes, a dancer, she's had such a rough life...that she now looks like her mother... she's been married twice, one of the guys that she married was English, the other a Turk, that is, a bloke from Turkey not Llanelli. When that marriage failed she decided to live with another bloke...you guessed it...another Turk. Apparently she has a predilection for the swarthy look. Either that or she likes touching her toes. I did say to her that when this relationship fucked up there were only another twenty-eight million Turks to go.

Layla lives in Turkey and she was telling me about the local scene in downtown Marmaris...she spoke particularly about the Russian girls...the red tarts...because apparently a lot of them are into rimming...

I was driving up the M5 when Layla said this. I didn't respond. The conversation went a bit like this.

'You know what rimming is don't you?' she asked.

'Of course.'

'What is it then?'

'Don't know.'

'It's when the girl decides to stick her tongue up the bloke's . . .'

'Oh...what's wrong with that?' I interrupted.

'You haven't?' She was playfully disgusted.

'I didn't say that...have you?'

'I have not...why would I want to do that?'

'Perhaps it's nice...so I've heard...'

It's funny this one. When a guy is performing oral sex on a girl it is almost impossible for him not to be tempted by licking her everywhere and, if she doesn't object, fingering her there as well. The arse is an erogenous zone and whilst some girls don't like the finger option I've never known one complain about the pleasure they get from a lick.

So turn that on its head and ask the question, à la rimming, what about the bloke? An erogenous zone for the woman...and the bloke, so why wouldn't he want a girl to lick him there too? And what about the male 'G' spot rumoured to be found and inch and a half inside the arse, another erogenous zone. Some men are scared of their arse being touched because it's something that they have always thought of as a taboo or something homosexual. It's only homosexual if it's done by another bloke and it's only taboo if there isn't lubrication. If both parties have showered and are clean, then why not give it a go? Maybe there's a new sensation to be enjoyed? Here's a quote from Tracey Cox, popular sexpert.

Give Him "Analingus"

Oral anal stimulation that involves licking, flicking or inserting a stiff tongue into the anal passage and thrusting feels great (for both sexes, actually), because the area is highly sensitive and loaded with nerve endings. If you're worried about germs or STDs, or if you're generally squeamish, put a barrier between the area and you, such as a piece of plastic wrap or a cut-open condom. Lots of guys love this, but many are too shy to tell you. So pretending it's your favourite thing to do (even if it isn't) takes care of that without awkwardness: If you like doing it, well, he has to indulge you, doesn't he?

Anyway, me and Layla went on to discuss a new pop band . . . Layla and the Rimmers . . . and she was a touch surprised when I said that there was a goalie in the 70s called Jimmy Rimmer, Villa and United, brilliant he was.

You know you get to that point in a conversation? You know . . . the 'too much information' point...

Well, my mother and Layla were downloading sex icons from the Interweb . . . Remember, Layla is forty-three . . . and my mother is eighty something . . . she viewed it as if they were reading a red top newspaper together, just part of the normal day.

There was one icon of a large pair of boobs.

There was another of a girl giving some guy a blowjob.

I jokingly turned my nose up at them and went to the bathroom.

'Oh, don't be such a prude,' said my mother.

'I'm not . . . the good news,' I said, when I came back in the room, 'is that I think I know her.' We all laughed; I wish I did know her, you can't beat a bird with a healthy appetite for oral sex.

'Sex isn't just for the young you know,' added mother. 'I have a friend who is eighty-four who has a very full sex life...'

'Urghh Jesus H . . . what do they use for contraception?' I asked.

'Photos of you, you fat fucker.'

You couldn't help but laugh. Mother doesn't swear. I looked towards Layla who was all smug on the sofa, lapping up that I'd just been one-lined.

'I don't know what you're fucking laughing at,' I said to her, 'I know what you use for contraception . . . your fucking mouth.' She didn't deny it but I suppose there is another option open to her.

At the end of the night mother went to bed and as I said goodnight to Layla I told her that I was now going to bed to 'masturbate like a wild baboon'. I should add that I didn't . . . it was only a line. The next morning as Layla packed for her return to Turkey she said that if I started rumours that she was into rimming she would tell everyone that I was into masturbating like a wild baboon.

'Fine,' I said. 'I think I win that one.'

Talking of sex . . . let me tell you about Tunisia. My youngest brother . . . affluent fucker that lives in London . . . took my mother to Tunisia on holiday. They were on the beach, reading, when he blurted out, 'mother, I feel that I must tell you . . . I've just read . . . for the first time . . . a homosexual sex act . . .urgh.'

'That's funny, she said, 'so have I.'

He didn't know which way to turn.

'But that's nothing . . . when you've seen it on a video, reading about it is quite harmless.'

It's true that. I was once sifting through the videos at my mum's house and lo and behold there, in an unnamed box, was '101 Great Cum Shots'.

I know . . . doesn't bear thinking about.

SEVENTEEN

Morag is Gaelic and stands at 5' 8", bobbed brunette of hair, full lips, trim, always dressed in pastels and fluff, rabbits and rainbows, pinks and silvers, her soul soft, a teacher with a penchant for Schnapps. Billy always thought I would end up with Morag.

I went for a dance with her.

She is scared of me. Not in a physical sense, I mean, I'm soft as shite me, but she's scared nonetheless. You see, we have a bit of history. Nothing too serious just that I like her and am not scared of telling her and she likes me but is scared shitless of saying so. She's one of the birds known in our circles as 'waiting for Brad', you know the type, very fussy, looking for the perfect physical package, above everything, the six-pack, soft skin, a metrosexual, a man who cares about himself, monied, OHOC – own house own car – and the personality. The girls waiting for Brad are renowned for not putting out too often either. Can't beat a bird with sex drive.

Now don't get me wrong, I don't have a problem with shallowness, well I do actually but I won't go there yet, and it's okay not to be promiscuous, but sometimes you have to be more proactive for things to work. The problem gets worse when Morag has had a bottle of wine, or two. Her reservations disappear, she becomes more physical and she doesn't mind close contact. When we dance our bodies touch, hand to hand, arms, legs entwine, her chest squashes against me in a comforting way, but more than the normal gyrations it is the look in her eyes that give it all away. Her eyes are saying 'take me'. But when she sobers up her eyes say, 'I was just pissed and it didn't mean anything.'

Her denial is interesting but I guess I know why she's like that so it's not a problem. Let me put it straight. Morag and I could easily get together, we both know that, and that is what she is scared of. You see, Morag has been hurt in the past, engaged for three years and then, poff, nothing, and she is more than aware that I could hurt her in the same way.

You see, I'm riding a crest of a wave at the moment, offers from a few girls and I've refused a few and it seems that I might be turning into a bit of a player, something that I would never have foreseen, ever. This dancing lark works. It is easier than the entire list that Dan, Billy and me created, you can almost get to pick and choose, in the main, from all the girls on the dance circuit and on the Friday night cattle truck although the latter react to your look not your dancing ability, charm and personality. I mean, how can people converse in a club full of showboating peacocks when the music is blasted out at a hundred decibels? Not that I am flagrant, I mean, I'm still as lonely as the next fucker, but I do all right and this queers my patch somewhat. From wanting to find a potential lover now I sometimes feel like the only cockerel in the chicken run. And I like it.

Normally I date once a quarter, maybe once every other month and I've even been known to walk away from some women. So that is what Morag has to compete with and she has made a choice to say, 'fuck it, I do like him, but if he's going to tart himself about with all and sundry, just like he does with me, then fuck him. When he calms down I might be available.'

She's very astute is Morag. Time will show that she didn't find Brad but a nice fella who looked a bit like ET. They are now married with child.

EIGHTEEN

Just thinking about Morag made me think about the porn I watched recently . . . well, last month . . . well, last week . . . well, last night . . . well, this morning . . . oh fuck it, you've guessed, it's on there now. What I've noticed is that loads of the birds on the films have fillings and more and more have tongue studs. Morag is pierced in eight places, four and three in her ears and one in her . . . tongue.

I've never snogged her or any bird who has a tongue stud for that matter so I don't know what it feels like tongue to tongue but I did once chat a bird up in a club in Gloucester and she said that she had to take it out when she gave her boyfriend a blowjob because of the pain that he felt. Bear in mind that I'd known her for a full three minutes. Another girl I know assures me that there is no pain involved at all. Just a different kind of pleasure. I am willing to act as a guinea pig for this trial and will suggest it.

One thing I've also noticed in my study and research into the availability of hardcore porn on the Interweb is, going back to rimming, that there isn't actually that much of it that goes on in conventional movies. There's plenty of blokes licking birds' arses and giving her one up the Gary. And there's plenty of specialist sites, so that I'm told, and there are gay sites too though they are a strict no-no for me. But when the bird is giving the bloke a blowjob there's plenty of cradling of the bollocks, an occasional lick across the nads or even a nad suck, but very little else. And you wonder why. I have a mate called Jack who has been a bit profligate in the past and once, whilst in the sixty-nine position he told me that he stuck his tongue and finger up the bird's arse. Sensing she'd been given a green light she reciprocated and he didn't like, or so he says. Perhaps they should have used some oil?

NINETEEN

I need to mention the lovely Morag for the last time for a while just to give you an impression. Morag hangs about with her best mate Tamsin. I know, stupid name but there you go. She's sweet though is Tamsin, funny, nice personality, a live one, a bit of a shaker, works in retail. Nice tits too.

Well we were watching a band. I was sober, driving, Tamsin was driving and Morag was on the vodkas, not that she can drink many. The music got going and Tamsin and me had a little dance. There wasn't much room but we managed and we were the first to get up and have a go. That meant that everyone was looking at us. I didn't give a toss about that, as you can imagine, and neither did Tamsin. We strutted and rocked and it was pretty good. When the song finished a blonde girl, half my age, nice chassis, smoker, so off the list, turned and said, 'wow, you two were great...I'm jealous...we'll have to have a dance later.' She was talking to me, I should add, not Tamsin. Tamsin smiled at me and she said, 'fucking hell, that was quick . . . you've pulled.' I smiled nonchalantly and eyed up another stunning blonde on the same table, taller, younger but also a smoker. She's off the list too. Anyway, Morag seemed put out. Till then she'd been cold, reticent and backed away. Now I don't like that. I mean, what the fuck am I going to do to her? Give her a Dracula bite on the neck?

When the band stopped at the end of their first session Tamsin went to the bar and I sat down. I motioned for Morag to sit down and again she was like a friggin' iceberg and she stood up a while, two or three yards away. Eventually she sat down and Tamsin came back with the beers, my second and last for the night. Them two got talking and this girl walked over towards us on the way to the loo. Five eight, pretty, nice body, mid twenties, in fact better than pretty. Surprisingly she stopped and bent down to talk to me.

So, who was she? Apparently she dances in the same hall as me on a Monday in a class before mine and she recognised me so she came to say hello. I thought that was it but I stood up, chatted to her, there was a bit of body contact, hand to back, chest to chest, and I thought that I'd pulled again. Just my situ. A young bird who'd had a few beers. When the young bird was in the loo Tamsin smiled at me again. 'You are a fucker, aren't you? You've pulled again.'

'Story of my life,' I said.

Morag watched it all unwind, the girl came out of the loo and went back across the room from where we had some eye contact. I think I could be in there. No, don't be so fucking dull. What would she find interesting in an old twat like me? As the band kicked in Morag and me danced and there was a total transformation. Having seen the competition Morag responded in kind, close, tight, physical. Lovely. She is a strange fucker.

As for Tamsin she's a filthy fucker. The lead singer picked up a mouth organ. 'That's not a mouth organ,' I said, 'it's our Monica.' I know, old gag, but you've got to know your audience. Without a blink Tamsin replied, 'Well he can put his organ in my mouth anytime.'

Can't beat a bird who plays hard to get.

TWENTY

I've found a website where people can upload video clips of themselves shagging. The category that was the most interesting was the Turkish section. Whilst there was no mention of the red Russian tarts and their rimming there were plenty of titles like 'Turkish Threesome', 'Hot Turkish Sex', and 'Turkish Couple Having Fun'. I crossed my fingers that I would come across Layla at it with one of her Turkish minions. Sadly it didn't happen. I did though get an email from her showing a cartoon of four skeletons sitting round a table and the captain read, 'women waiting for the perfect man'. I'd have changed it to 'Waiting for Brad'. I did browse for a while but never came across anyone I knew. There was one bloke and girl that I've seen around who I'm told did webcam sex if you paid enough cash. He's a bit if a tit so I'm glad that I don't have to conjure with that image.

Anyway I got a shock tonight. I saw Bobbin' Robin without the Italian at 'Cuban Spice'; I was there with Dan. That could mean they aren't together. Hopefully. But that wasn't the shock. The shock was what Dan showed me when he pointed out the couple doing the teaching. One was the normal head honcho, black, bald, thin, high as a kite on enthusiasm. But the girl was a fat bird with an attitude problem, thinks she's Ginger fucking Rogers. She's not popular, a bit plug (ugly) and I was seriously fucked off to see the fat fucker being used as a teacher. I mean, that will surely put off all the blokes from dancing? It is a given that the female teachers should be half decent to look at and have the figure to go with it, and the elegance, and the class. But not here. Well, would you? With her? I mean, I know she's lost weight but even at an uncomfortable size twenty you just wouldn't. I'm told that she's trying to get her face on the stamps of the realm. That's the only chance she's got of getting a lick.

Whenever you hear the word 'knowingly' you almost always know what is coming next don't you? Upstairs at 'Cuban Spice' Dan was talking about his theory of morality and as a single bloke now, having been minced by the Family Law courts, he said that he won't date married birds or birds in a relationship. Knowingly. Well this puts me in a dilemma.

There's this bird I dance with, Ava, tall, beautiful, sexy and a nice dancer, now. She likes close dancing, she likes me and we have a great laugh. She's a divorcee but she has got a bloke. Now I don't know him at all but that's not the point though it does beg the question, where is he and why isn't he here with his girl? From another marriage she has got other kids. Now I know that given different circs I would love to get it on with Ava. But I can't now, can I? Not according to the world according to Dan.

I laughed and joked with Ava one night and she jokingly said that, 'You do what you can get away with.' Now was that an offer? A come on? Or just a line? Would she really want a bunk up with me? A secret tryst? Tryst! Posh fucking word that. But I can't, can I? What happens if the bloke finds out? How does he feel? Do I want to be the one who fucks up someone else's life just for a bit of sucking and fucking? Would I be able to look him in the eye if it was all secret? I do get consumed by guilt, old school thing. Could I really be that two-faced twat ruled by my dick? I know, I know what you're thinking. You're thinking that she wouldn't be up for it if things were all hunky fucking dory back at the palace. And there are plenty of blokes I know who wouldn't give a toss, nail it and try to nail it again. Well, I think that Dan has a point. It doesn't matter what the stats say – 75% of married men are having an affair and 46% of married women are at it too – it's pecker in the pants time.

TWENTY-ONE

Dan has been in the doldrums recently, which is a strange saying, don't you think, because the doldrums itself, per se, has fuck all to do with this phrase. Most folk I know interpret the doldrums as someone being miserable and down but it's not at all, it's more about stagnation. Dan has been stagnating; he's now in fucking freefall. Ripped of all self-respect, no or few material belongings, a friendly drinker turned into a piss head with no respect for himself, up to his tits in debt. Recently he met Annie and he told me a tale.

Annie's a posh bird who lives the other side of the city, rangy, thin yet curvy, soft skin, a smoker, in a weird relationship where they were trying to work it out. In the mean time she got on with her job, social worker, she cultivated Ganga in the airing cupboard and she was very, very, very fond of wine. And she was best mates with Laura and Nige, a couple that Dan befriended on his lonely trawls of late night bars, a couple he introduced me to a while ago. They were fun, smart, grown up, and in love with each other.

Nige rang Dan and invited him to the pub where he and Laura gave Dan the SP on Annie. It was Laura who spelled it out in words that were music to Dan's ears. 'She needs a right good fucking seeing to.' Well, let me ask you the obvious, who fucking doesn't? Annie's thirty-six and wasn't getting plenty and Laura explained a little about her, educated but reserved, a bit like Morag, dances better after a few vodkas and hates exhibitionism. Dan, on the other hand performs when a fridge door opens and the light comes on. He doesn't need an alcoholic stimulant to dance publicly. Anyway, Dan's a charmer and he fancies his chances with anyone.

On the afternoon of a Barbie, Nige made the call that changed Dan's day.

'Mate, get fucking down here! It's a cert.' Had Dan been able to see Nige's face there was so much joy conveyed that you'd have thought that it was Nige who was going to get his rocks off.

Dan rang me and, to help him along, he is a ninny who needs help sometimes, I went with him as his wing man. Girls love having the attention of one man. Two is fanfuckintastic.

Everyone nibbled as they ambled round the garden, wine and beer slipped willingly into the afternoon, barriers disappeared, the sun and warmth loosened reservations, inhibitions and restrictions.

And in walked Annie, serene, her mind in the clouds, a fragrant sky blue blouse knotted at her midriff, very seventies, the touch of alcohol on her lips, her mouth broad, eyes sparkling, her body needy and expectant.

To me, it felt like a set up, Laura and Nige playing Cilla the fucking matchmaker, a genuine blind date. I went on a blind date once. She turned up wearing dark glasses, carrying a white stick and being pulled by a Labrador. I know, old gag.

Here's another. What would you get if you crossed a bat with a lonely-hearts club? Lots of blind dates.

Anyway, Annie is introduced.

'Nice to meet you,' said Dan, 'Laura told me you were beautiful . . . how could she undersell you?'

Yep, at first I was thinking bucket and puke but he delivered the line so smoothly and warmly you knew that he meant it. And so did this Annie. And she just melted. Strange thing with beautiful women, they have the same ego as ugly birds and still need to be told that they are beautiful. They're insecure fuckers on the old QT. Nice tip that. When you're sober always target the beautiful girls at a dance. Ugly blokes think they're out of their league but if you walk over to a bird and say that they look lovely it's almost a guarantee for a hand down her pants.

Just digressing a tad, here's the best chat up line of all time.

'You fancy a coffee?'

'I don't drink coffee.'

'I haven't got any.'

'Brassed Off,' Ewan McGregor to Tara Fitgerald.

Compare it to this.

'Nice legs, what time do they open?'

'Fuck off Paddy.'

Something with Peter Kay.

Which reminds me of a time when I went to see a customer. We were standing on the doorstep of his office when the postman knocked on the door next to his. This bird opened the door with a towel wrapped around her tits, obviously straight from the shower.

'Lovely,' I said, 'I didn't recognise you with your clothes on.' The girl signed for her package. 'Go on,' I continued, 'give us a twirl.'

'Toss off you fat cunt,' she said and shut the door. Direct quote that.

Fucking hilarious. How could she call me fat?

Anyway, back to Dan and Annie. They met up again a week later at a pub on another date organised by Cilla the fucking matchmaker. Dan was wary and for the first hour he was unusually boorish, insensitive and totally not interested in Annie. Everyone was pissed apart from Dan so he tried to catch up and then spent the last hour before last orders engaging Annie in very close and intimate chat, something that he did only after a warning from Laura who looked across and mouthed, 'what the fuck are you playing at?' Dan knew exactly what he was doing. Alienate the target by ignoring her and then hit her with both barrels.

As the pub ended Nige and Laura disappeared back to hers and Dan and Annie went to find some food within walking distance. Their quest was fruitless so Dan suggested his flat where he'd done a curry earlier. After a long snog in the middle of the pavement he took her hand and away they went. When they arrived the thought of food had dissipated and there was only one thing on both their minds. Annie stayed over, so Dan says, and the following morning she uttered those fantastic, immortal words, 'are you coming back to bed?'

When she left four hours later Dan was sated, Annie was sated and she headed off back to the other side of town. 'I'd like to do this again,' said Annie on exit though they hadn't exchanged phone numbers or email addresses. Dan knew that it was a one-off, that she really did need a good seeing to, that she had had it, him too, and she was off to tilt at the windmills in her mind.

TWENTY-TWO

Dan caused a bit of stir last night. No, not because he had a jump with Annie; all it took was one text message and a misinterpretation and that was it, send for the SWAT team, James Bond and Our Man Fucking Flint. You see Dan is rehearsing a couple of routines with one of his posse, a girl he calls ZF, short for Zipless Fuck, because that is what he'd like with her, you know, a full frontal, no holes barred, unattached, zipless fuck. No commitment, no relationship, just a one off bunk up. Dan fancies her and she fancies him but the circumstances aren't quite right for anything to happen, so Dan says.

So these two practice every Wednesday and Dan tells me that it is one of the highlights of his week. ZF hasn't done much ballroom but she is a quick learner and she loves dips, drops, lifts and anything that involves contact. Dan's like that too and it makes teaching her easier. There is a real spark, some natural chemistry and they could get it on, even though she's engaged. Funny thing is, her fiancé has seen them dance together and he doesn't mind. Pretty decent of him really but it does beg the question how many blokes know how their bird dances with a bloke? Sometimes it's more sensual dancing than it is for the bird and her bloke at home. I mean, I dance close, hands everywhere legitimate, hips moving suggestively, mouths close together, breathing on necks, an occasional kiss on the cheek, a hug, an arm round, a pat here and a stroke there. Is it any wonder that some blokes get jealous or that the dance world breeds sex and relationships?

The answer is to learn to dance, mate.

Anyway, yesterday ZF texted Dan to say that she couldn't make it to today's session and he replied back.

'I'm just going to throw myself off the bridge then, such a penalty for just wanting to dance.'

When he showed me this morning in the office I looked at it and it was pretty innocuous but ZF took him at his word and panicked and texted him back.

'Ooh, don't do that . . . what are you on about? Jumpers make an awful mess.'

Thinking she was playing along with his humour Dan replied.

'Will avoid the bridge then . . . will check drawers for barbiturates instead.'

And Dan thought that was the end of it and he went back to his DVD of Sidney Poitier in 'In the Heat of the Night'. A minute later the text alert sounded on his phone and it was ZF who really had got the wrong end of the stick.

'Surely nothing is so bad you have to do that. Keep your chin up mate. If you want to talk, call me. I haven't called you as I'm a bit worried.'

When do you call then?

And then he got a text from Layla in Turkey, crapping her pants about his jump to oblivion. And then he got one from Morag. And then the phone rang and it was Layla having palpi-fucking-tations. Dan explained the missed gag and then he texted Morag.

'Don't panic, misinterpretation of humour.'

Then he rang ZF and chatted for twenty minutes.

What a fucking fiasco. Perhaps ZF had been on the sauce? Perhaps Dan had. Talk about a mountain out of a fucking molehill.

Silly twats.

TWENTY-THREE

There's a bird at a club I go to called Connie. Tall, blonde, blue eyes, smiley mouth, kissable, nice tits, comforting arse but another young one at just twenty-five.

'I don't have time for a bloke,' she said, as I gently quizzed her about her lifestyle.

Some birds don't have boyfriends because they don't put out. Some are still virgins at thirty. Others, as mentioned, are waiting for Brad. Others won't tell you either way. Some are just too fat or too ugly or both. The rest of the birds who don't have a bloke are lezzies so I asked Connie the obvious.

'You into birds then?'

'No.'

I would have said, 'am I fuck!' and protested more but Connie has class. She explained that she didn't understand lesbians or homosexuals and that the business of one of the birds taking the male role was strange and bizarre.

'Why is there always a stunner and a biffer?' She asked with genuine incredulity.

Only a true lez could explain that to you. Me, like most blokes, I don't really go for the lesbian thing though if a bird is bisexual then that's cool, especially if there's a threesome on offer. How fucking sexy is that, snogging two birds at the same time? That nearly happened to me once. I was up north out with two of the lads, Nocker and Loopy, and this tall blonde, well-stacked and flat stomach came over asking for a light. This is a common icebreaker used by both sexes until smoking indoors was demonised so I knew that we had to hang on to her, now she'd made the first move. I didn't have one but the lads are into chokers so I blagged a lighter.

'This gorgeous girl needs a light, Nocker, sort her out, there's a good lad.' And he did. She stayed and had a chat and then her two mates came over, a redhead and a brunette. Well, from where I come from three into three is a good equation so we hung around for a couple of hours and all got pissed. As the night wore on, the blonde moved away and I bagged the redhead. The brunette was talking seriously to the other two and then Blondie came back over to me and

Red. And then Red and Blondie started snogging right there in front of me, full tongues. Fucking fantastic. My own live sex show. Sadly, when it came down to the crunch Blondie backed off 'cause she was married. Gladly Red didn't.

Another time, in the same bar, about six months before Loopy and me had pulled two chicks. When we walked into the bar I saw these two and gave Loops a twenty quid note.

'You see those two birds over there...get 'em a beer, I'm off for a piss...I'll be back in a minute.'

This he did and when I came back, after a short dance, I bagged the tall good-looking one. Good night that.

I found out a month later that one of the girls had won the National Lottery three months before. Go on, I know you want to know. Two point eight fucking million. Go on, guess. Yep, you're right. The millionairesse was the one sucking Loopy's nads not mine.

Well, truth be told, we also found out more, later.

She hadn't won the lottery. Her ex had. She caused a stink wanting half and he acquiesced.

Anything for a quiet life.

TWENTY-FOUR

Dan's charm and dancing skills make him popular with the girls. There is a mixed bag. There are those that think he is safe because he doesn't normally mix dancing and shagging, those who want to dance with him because he has such class and grace on the dance floor and those that just want to fuck his brains out. But for relationships to work there has to be an understanding as to what each partner wants and the timing is critical. Most men can move from girlfriend to girlfriend without batting an eye; indeed many plan it that way, they always have option two and three in the pipeline. But if you've just come out of a shitty marriage the last thing that you want to do is to get involved again with someone else. It's really a terrible balance; you want to be with someone who cares for you but you can't commit because the fear of facing the fleecer for a second time is still very much at the forefront of your thoughts. That's where Dan is.

Loneliness has done for him too.

The other way to frame this balance is to think about the physical needs, the emotional needs and the plug to the loneliness. Everyone needs a shag, a sexual release. At times it feels right to satisfy that with a one-night stand, an evening with an escort, an hour with a prozzie or a quick hand shandy.

But that doesn't help with the need for an emotional connection. And if she just fucks off into the night then you're back to square one again, on your fucking tod sat watching the goggle box.

Sometimes I watch him and think that he's so nice he can't be on his own but anger is a strong emotion and the girls who know him sense it. He's not angry with them but with his ex and the system. He's still good company but most women are scared off by this underriding rage. Some aren't and Dan has learned to have some very adult and mature conversations about what he wants and what he doesn't want.

I don't think he is the male equivalent of 'waiting for Brad' . . . what would that be? 'Waiting for Angelina?' It's just that now he has a lot of choice his selection has to be spot-on, it has to be someone who can dance, but from a personality point of view there has to be a real chemistry and click for her to be singled out as someone special. One thing that Dan isn't is a coward.

Let me add meat to this one. Most men want just anyone; I've already said that but they are emotional cowards and Dan isn't prepared to compromise his emotions just for company. There has to be that real spark, more than just loneliness.

So whilst Dan isn't ready for the long-term, unless something special happens, the timing with women is vital too. If a woman has been in a shitty relationship for six years the last thing she wants when it all goes tits up is to get into another in a big way even if she is greeted by her own equivalent of George Clooney, Rosemary's lad. Some might want to fuck around a bit, others might just want to avoid the rejection factor but the last thing they want is hassle, physical, mental or emotional.

Single parent women are terrified of being exactly that; single. Without the dual incomes, or one and a half to protect her and her offspring, you'd have thought that most women would be looking for a partner and they do, as mentioned, out of necessity. It is emotionally wrong and there must be a better way for them to survive.

It's because of this fear that women tolerate such shit and set their targets so low. I know one girl who's had three partners in the last twenty years, one that she married. The big mistake that she made was that she hadn't really got to grips with the motivation of each, why they wanted to be with her, and by accepting their situations it just caused her trouble in the long run. Getting the selection of a potential lover right is vital. Her first was 'in convenient with her' and she thought it fine to get married even though he never admitted to being in love with her and vice versa.

Do you really need real love for a woman to be married and have children?

With the second they were 'in lust', always going to die off after a couple of years, and with the last it was 'quite quick, in convenient with her'. Her insecurity at being on her own fuelled three doomed relationships. Had any of the three actually been 'in love' with her the chances are that she would have stuck to that one man even if she wasn't in love with him. If two people are 'in love' with each other there is far more chance of the relationship lasting any desired length.

Let me make one point here; I am not judging her or her male friends I am just explaining the dynamics. It's funny that when relationships don't work, when there is a divorce, it is inevitable that someone somewhere will say that 'it failed'.

When were we programmed to believe that living in the same house or not with a member of the opposite sex for ever was a success or a failure?

TWENTY-FIVE

One of the talking points with the girls is Dan's aftershave. Sometimes he walks into a dance hall and he is followed by this waft of male perfume, 'Rive Gauche' by Yves St Laurent, 'Pour Homme' by Yves St Laurent or 'L'Homme de la Nuit', also by Yves St Laurent. 'Ooh, you smell nice,' they fawn. 'Lovely aftershave.' Some of the girls even turn their head when he walks in. And if he's there first, they know because they can smell his trail.

Me, Dan and Billy were in a bar when the young, gorgeous barmaid made a quick statement.

'Mm, someone smells nice.'

'That would be me,' said Dan without blinking. 'All the girls tell me that. It's because some aftershaves blend naturally with some people...this one does for me.'

'Yeah, he's got the latest aftershave all right,' said Billy. 'It's called Toilet Duck.'

Three of us laughed. Dan sat there and waited for the moment to pass. He knew that sometimes a riposte is unnecessary. There would be other times for revenge.

The conversation moved on quickly as Billy ordered more beers and then our mate Bryan walked in looking worried. Bryan is a non-dancing car salesman, new cars mainly, commercial fleet stuff, not second hand. I've known him twenty years; he's a good lad. In fact he's one of the best.

'All right lads?' He looked towards Billy. 'All right Bill, get us a pint mate. Lads, I need your help.'

'What's up mate?' I asked.

He whispered, 'I think I've got a dose...'

'Haven't you got to shag first?' asked Dan.

'Some comic you are.'

'Chicken pox is it?' continued Dan.

'You got a dose Bry?' asked Billy walking over to the table balancing three pints. You should get an O B fucking E for doing that. Services to equilibrium and alcohol retention.

'Think you should say it a bit louder, you noisy fucker?'

'You shagged some old slapper?' offered Dan.

'No, your missus wasn't available.'

'That's a surprise,' said Dan. 'She always used to be...I was in a taxi once and I asked the driver to take me to a house where I could get a blowjob for a tenner. He took me home.'

We all pissed ourselves.

'No,' said Bryan, 'I've got this red ring round me cock...'

'I had that once,' I said. 'Thank fuck the doctor said it was lipstick.'

'Yer all fucking hilarious, aren't you? Look I think I've got a dose...what shall I do?

'Yer been to the doc's yet?' I asked.

'I can't . . . it's a bloke.'

'You want it to be a bird?' asked Dan.

'Well, you ain't got that much choice mate,' I continued. 'Don't be worried . . . doctors don't like it any more than you do . . . though maybe the nurses at the clinic enjoy it a bit . . . '

'What do they do?'

'Swab . . .' said Dan, 'so I'm told.'

'Shite,' said Bryan.

'That's another story,' said Billy. 'I love my doctor,' he said. 'Well I ought to love any bloke who's had his finger up my arse . . .'

'I hope that when you get down there that it's a girl you know...in uniform,' I said. 'I am reliably informed that two of the girls in our dance classes are sex therapists down at the clinic.'

Now that conjured up a picture. My God, what a picture! Dance hall . . .

'Where do I know you from?'

TWENTY-SIX

At the next beginners' class me, Dan and Billy helped out. We do it sometimes to suss out the chicks but more likely we're looking for dancing talent. The beginners we dance with either shit themselves because they're dancing with quality or they just melt and feel totally secure. Having been a beginner it can be daunting until you get that Eureka moment when it all falls into place. I was like that with the Samba and the Quick Step and then one day I just knew the mechanics. Just like that.

Some girls were whispering.

'Fuck, there's a lot to learn,' said a brunette hottie to her two girlfriends as they waited for the next instruction.

'We're doing everything we've learnt in the last twelve weeks,' said the teacher.

'Bloody hell, he'll be telling us there's an exam at the end of it all next.'

I moved closer.

'Only an oral,' I said.

Two girls gulped and the other tittered. That's her in line for a shag then. Give it six months.

As the class finished the supposedly better dancers filtered in though to be fair most of these fuckers weren't much cop either. Only bravado and a false sense of ability stop them from moving down a class. That's birds and blokes.

There's one that hasn't completed the loop. Mickie, short for Michaela, doesn't dance much with us. She thinks she's too good but she's hard work to dance with, a bit heavy, tries to lead, always a fucking arm wrestle, and she doesn't like the close stuff either. Given that she's not exactly built like JLo this is a surprise. Maybe she's trying to protect her image or the sanctity of her marriage, which is another surprise given that I know that she's had the odd dance shag here and there.

I taught Mickie how to dance once and a few weeks later I bumped into her in a club. I was pissed and she doesn't drink so that wasn't a good start but I said hello with some enthusiasm and I kissed her on both cheeks, and then at the end of the dance I kissed her again. I thought nothing of it till the next time I saw her at a class when she blanked me and waved a finger.

'No kissing!'

The moment left me bewildered. What the fuck was her problem? The following week, at the start of the class, she offered her cheek with reservation and I pecked it. She nodded patronisingly implying it was all right. As we left, the class done, the bar beckoning, she offered her cheek again and I licked it from her bottom jaw to her eye. Unimpressed and angry she tried to karate kick me as I ran off. Fucking hilarious. Pompous little fucker.

A week later I was at a bar – I know, umbilical cord – and she dropped her knees to the back of my legs to get my attention. I bought her a beer and I asked her gently what her problem was. Better to get this resolved if we're going to be on the same circuit for the next thirty years.

'How many times did I kiss you?'

'Seven.'

'Seven?'

'Yeah.'

'Open mouthed?'

'No.'

'On the mouth?'

'No.'

'Did I rip your clothes off with my teeth?'

'No.'

'Did I kiss your shoulders?'

'No.'

'Did I squeeze your butt?'

'No.'

'Or your tits?'

'No.'

'So, I just kissed you on the cheek.'

'Yes.'

'Thank fuck for that. For a minute I thought I was a serial killer.'

TWENTY-SEVEN

I heard on the grapevine that Morag has been dating an old boyfriend, the very same boyfriend who decided to shag one of her mates when she was on holiday, two thousand miles away. Now it's not for me to say but ain't she being a bit fucking stupid? As much as I play the field sometimes I am always faithful and never have more than one bird on the go at the same time. Fuck me, there's me getting all righteous . . .

There's a lot to be said for the honour and dignity of fidelity but this twat that Morag's tied up with, let's call him The Pup, wouldn't know either, even if they smacked him in the face. The Pup is younger than Morag and frankly he could be a teenager given how he acts. Immature, smarmy, loves himself, another who thinks he's a fucking stud. Billy and me think he's a cunt.

I think you're getting the drift that he's not popular, The Pup. Well, any bloke that fucks someone else when his bird is away on holiday is a bit of a twat isn't he? That said, why did she go on holiday without him? Not destined for longevity this one.

The bird that he shagged was a lot older than him, old enough to be his mother. So what is this? Fucking Oedipus? Or just a good ride on an old bike? Sure enough she'd be grateful at her age.

And what the fuck was she thinking, 'Morag's away so I think I'll fuck The Pup'? What sort of selfish cunt does that make her?

Why Morag likes him is beyond comprehension. Who knows what goes on in the mind of a woman? If I were Morag I would be wondering what goes on in the mind of The Pup. Why did he shag this other bird? Why did he ditch Morag and stay with the other bird? What did the other bird have that Morag didn't? What did she do that Morag didn't?

This could be a clear case of sexual incompatibility. We all know that birds like shopping and blokes like sport. That's a genetic given. Get a bird who's into footy or rugby or cricket, or all three, then it would be best to just marry her.

But if she doesn't like sport the relationship would still be okay. But in the bedroom it's totally different. You both have to have a similar appetite. And similar afflictions.

Let me take this further. If the bird doesn't give head then the bloke has to tolerate this or find someone else who does, if that is what he likes. If he doesn't like oral and she does then she's had it, or she hasn't, more's the case. If she's scared of spunk and he likes facials it only breeds tension. If he's into anal or rimming and she isn't there's more reason for fallout. You see the drift of the discussion? So why did The Pup ditch Morag? Perhaps the fucker is into S&M and all that bollocks? If that's the case Morag's well out of there. But she still acts like a fucking teenager pining for the cunt.

TWENTY-EIGHT

At the Salsa pally Billy, Dan and me bumped into Frankie, a lawyer with a black belt in karate, who we had known for a while since he'd been shagging an Irish bird from the class. Both are Scorpios, set in their ways, inflexible and as a result that relationship had come to a close so he was available again and he stood there salivating like a dog on heat. Another that craved company come what may, he was genuinely interested in finding the love of his life as long as he got to audition a few on the way.

'Did you hear,' said Dan as we all watched the dancing, 'that my ex has been diagnosed as bulimic?'

'Sorry to hear that,' said Billy.

'Yeah, the fat fucker just keeps forgetting to vomit.' He cackled like an old woman and we all laughed and looked at him. Was he getting happier? Just on cue we spied two fat birds on the dance floor surprisingly popular with the male fraternity.

'Sperm is very calorific,' said Dan. 'That's why blokes go for fat birds on the dance floor.'

'They are not fat,' said Frankie, ignoring the line. 'Cuddly...the blonde is really pretty.'

'Hey,' I interrupted, 'isn't that the fat bird that blew you out last summer Frankie?' She was five foot tall and the same wide.

'I think you'll find that it was me that blew...'

'That's bollocks Frankie, she told us,' said Dan. 'She said that you blagged a lift home, you had a snog and she ditched you because you were a shit kisser. Nice to see a bird with taste.'

'Do you fancy her then Dan?' asked Billy, a man with a penchant for the larger lady himself.

'I prefer 'em taller and prettier,' Dan replied, 'and when I know they've actually got feet.'

'So how come you targeted the fat bird Frankie?' I asked. Was she really his pin-up of choice?

'She would have done for the night.'

'Nice to see such high standards,' I added. 'What about her mate then Frankie . . . they're like bookends those two.'

'That depends if I can get my arms around her...'

'They say that she dances four or five nights a week,' I said.

'Don't fucking look like it,' said Billy.

'I hope she's got a spare blouse as well as fresh Danish pastries in her bag,' I said.

'Got to keep that physique up somehow.'

'I actually like big women,' said Frankie, defending too much. 'And little ones.' He'd been with birds in Paris, Berlin, Salt Lake City and Sarajevo.

Once the dancing kicked in I sat down and sipped an orange juice as the others danced. Billy and Dan were on fine form. Frankie did what he does best, basic moves and lots of stopping to re-start when he made a mistake and was off time.

Billy dances with a certain style, he remembers steps, leads well and is not shy. Moves flow from him like an electric energy and at times he can get very close, comfortable for some women, not for others, though the women that don't like it don't dance with him. Their choice and loss. Tonight he danced with a teacher, the Italian, two doctors and a number of beginners, Billy being benevolent yet calculating, looking for potential new dancers to add to his posse.

Dan was in his new shoes and he flowed, girls queuing for the privilege but Billy explained that this was nothing to do with dancing even though Dan is in the Premier League. Billy has a theory. Once a guy gets laid he walks with a certain swagger, not arrogance or aloofness, but there is something natural after a night of shagging, a chemical release, a smell, a scent or something that birds pick up on.

It's a bit like lions on the savannah. First there's the kill, then the feed, and then he wants some hot sex with a slinky cat and he gets it, no queuing outside a nightclub for hours (what the fuck is that about?) for the King of the Jungle. And once he's had sex the other lionesses flock around waiting to bag some of the big guy's action. Well, it's like that for humans too. Women subliminally scent the aura of procreation and they want some.

And Dan had definitely been on the savannah.

TWENTY-NINE

Dan had pulled again, seemingly without trying, but maybe it was him that had been pulled? Some women do that. They pretend to be just a casual acquaintance or a mate and they invite you somewhere where there's a group of people. 'We are going...do you fancy it?' And then, during the course of the event, be it a birthday, a gig, a picnic, a barbie or just a night in the pub, they make their play. Beer plays its part, so too the dynamic of who sits next to who, or who is bagged to help someone, for example, check on the burgers or mix cocktails, but with stealth the woman pounces. It's either a pre-planned move – 'oh, there's just the two of us now' or 'shall we go and get some chips?' and then the opportunities just open up and the guy might make what he thinks is the first move.

'So there I was,' said Dan to Billy and me, 'and I gave her the old alternative close . . . you can come back to mine if you like, you're too pissed to drive. You can choose then . . . you can either sleep with me, on the sofa or in the spare bed.'

'And she bought it?' I asked incredulously.

'Lock stock and both smoking barrels,' he said with an air of nonchalance.

'So you fucked her? Good lad,' congratulated Billy.

'You could have got her a cab and sent her home,' I offered.

'Would you?'

Fair point.

As for me, I've had my fair share of savannah too though not as much as I would have liked. Being with different women is fine but it's a repetitive process; if one doesn't fit the bill then on to another, in search of the Holy Grail, that affinity that could lead to commitment, fidelity, a soul mate, a lover, a friend and a life companion. As you might have guessed I've had to say no to some girls, to let them down and reject them – it's not you it's me, laff me fookin tits off – but it has worked the other way too. Even the

King of the Jungle doesn't get it right every time, even though he wants to.

There was this chick, let's call her Kitten, new to dance who I decided to help. I do this, from one girl to another, leading, cajoling, coaching, ensuring a smooth transition from one level to another and in doing so you can find out quickly who can dance and who can't, but you also find out who has the potential to become one of your posse. A bit of dance grooming.

Well, Kitten is a big chick with bright eyes and dark hair and she'd remind you a bit of Snow White without the dwarves. From the first moment that we met there was an instantaneous click, a mutually positive thin slice, instant attraction, sexual chemistry, pure electricity that would have boosted the national grid. We went to one dance together, excluding all others – that was popular – and then a week later she came back to my place on the premise of work. We talked over plans and projects, forecasts and budgets; the atmosphere in the room was like a firecracker waiting to go off, sexual tension more than abundant. Legs brushed, arms and hands, eye contact was intense and a kiss was a blink away. Clothes would have hit the floor faster than a boxer taking a dive. It didn't happen, I scratched my head for weeks and then I met her in a pub and asked her what was going on. Nothing was the answer. Well you could have fucking fooled me.

Months later I bumped into her at a barbie and she was hanging around with some hirsute orang-utan who spent his days swinging from one tree to another chomping bananas and nuts. No he wasn't black. English-Greek, I think. I haven't seen Kitten since. She's probably left town or fucked off to Borneo with the ape.

THIRTY

You'll have heard the saying, 'There's nothing as under-estimated as a good shit'? Well there is also 'nothing as over-estimated as bad sex', and that is doing it, watching it, or reading about it, as, coincidentally, I just have.

Let me give you the scenario. This guy and girl, both mid twenties, have been playing hard to get with each other on a business trip to Ireland. During the course of a formal evening they have a couple of drinks, they dine, drink wine and a brandy nightcap and then they share the lift before departing to their respective rooms. Just before she gets out he giggles, '2602 . . .'

Minutes later she knocks on his door, a clear buying signal and he lets her in. After some shy jostling he kisses her. She doesn't kiss him, he kisses her, making all the moves, all the running as sexual equality disappears out of the window. He undresses her, she asks for the lights off, something not unknown even for the most beautiful women who are scared of their own shadow when some guy wants to rip her clothes off with his teeth, but the light from the stars and neon signs filters through the curtains, enough for him to enjoy the faded feast, his brain appreciating the visual vista in front of him.

In command and lead mode the guy kisses her, grinds against her, touching all over, kissing her nipples, her belly and then he lowers himself between her legs.

'What are you doing?' she asks.

I suppose it would have been the wrong time to reply, 'guess?' but I reckon that is as close to a cold bucket of water on your ardour as you can get. Our hero, battling on against sexual naivety and inexperience, carries on regardless in the hope of convincing her the integral value of oral sex. He kisses her, laps her and teases her until he feels the crescendo of orgasm power through her body. He doesn't stop and the sensation repeats itself before she pulls his head away. Inwardly pleased he retraces his steps up her body only to be greeted by the words, 'don't kiss me, you smell and taste of me, don't kiss me'. Fetch me another bucket of cold water and a certificate to award to 'selfish twat of the night'.

I don't suppose there's a universal answer to this conundrum but I don't know many women who don't like the taste of themselves whether they are giving head after penetration or whether they are licking fingers, the bloke's or their own. Now there's a reason to never go out if you're a woman. Put your fingers inside you and then lick them dry. I used to be all macho about girls masturbating during sex, like no, that's my job, but now as long as I get to lick the fingers too it's a fantastic turn on.

Anyway, back to our intrepid hero, unsated, wanting his own orgasm. She hardly touches him, he applies a condom at her request and he fucks her, she doesn't fuck him, a kissless, soulless fuck. In the post-coital 'do you want a Woodbine moment?' she admits that she used to fuck his boss, a married bloke with three kids (why do women do this? What gives them the right to sleep with a married man? Why the lies and deceit? Why can't women just say no, not until you're single?) Our hero, disappointed, angry, jealous and resentful sends her off packing to her room for a cry.

I'm sure that the guy was disappointed by his experience; I'm sure that the author wanted the reader to feel just as deprived. I did. There is nothing worse for a guy to be greeted by a girl from the Starfish R Us School of Sex. I guess the female equivalent is the one-minute shag she has to tolerate when he comes home pissed from the pub demanding his conjugals before collapsing asleep pleased that he'd had his shag.

THIRTY-ONE

I want to develop the theme a little, why the girl didn't join in, why she wanted the light off, why he had to make all the running. The explanation is obvious and one that engulfs everybody at some stage of their life. Put simply it is all down to sexual fears and let's start with men's fears first.

When I grew up I was taught that boys didn't like girls, it wasn't a macho thing to do and even when you're playing kiss chase in the playground someone somewhere was shaking their head saying, 'no, no, no, go and play footy with the lads.'

I'm not sure where this total discomfort comes from, I don't know if it's the same the world over, but during the 60s and 70s in Great Britain there was nothing but embarrassment associated with being with a girl after you were seven or eight years old. You didn't hold hands, you didn't talk to them much unless it was telling them to shift and you certainly didn't kiss them. It was total conditioning and programming. And it applied to showing softer emotions too. Boys could be angry and alpha male but never cry. Feelings were for girls. I remember a girl falling off her chair at school when I was about fifteen after I'd told her I'd just finished reading 'Love Story' by Erich Segal.

And then puberty kicks in, you get a tingle in your groin and suddenly you want to reach out at the lumps and curves that suddenly appeared on the girls at school. Do you remember that? Breaking up in July, coming back in September, and seeing the metamorphosis in the girls in your class? Where did all those bumps come from?

But here comes the killer, you want to but you haven't got a clue how to and this can either take seconds or a lifetime to learn. How do I say hello? How do I impress her enough for her to want to go out with me? How do I know if she likes me? If we go to the pictures who pays? What's the protocol? Do I hold her hand? Or put my arm around her? And what about kissing? How do I kiss? Do I practice on my arm? Or on the wardrobe mirror? And what next? What are the rules? What does she expect or want? When is it okay to touch her body? To undress her? And what happens if she undresses me?

With experience, time, research, investigation and practice these things can be resolved and confidence grows but that's not the end of it because then it becomes a question of all things physical. Am I good looking enough? What do I look like without a shirt on? Naked? Unaroused? With a steaming erection? Does it matter? What if I don't want her to see me naked? And why should she? And if she does, what then? What does she expect me to do? And how do I do it? What about premature ejaculation? Ohmigod, I'd die of embarrassment, a failure, ashamed, if I came within seconds of her touching me or on primary penetration? Or as soon as she takes me in her mouth? And what if she hasn't orgasmed? Or doesn't? Jesus, all this is so complicated.

Let's take kissing as an example? Some people, men and women, are crap kissers. It might be that they don't brush their teeth or that they don't floss but more than likely it's just down to crap technique and the fact that they have never been taught, or learned what to do. Do I open my mouth? If so how wide? I kissed a girl once, she opened her mouth wider than the Mersey tunnel and for a moment I feared for my head, let alone my mouth. And how much tongue do I use? I knew a girl once who was snogged in a bar by my mate Brendan. 'Why does he kiss with his tongue?' she asked aghast. I had to teach her. Another kissed like a sheep. Don't ask me how I know.

So you can see why there is fear. I guess it all depends on how you were brought up and in what era. If you were liberated in the 60s maybe you have a different view on nakedness than say a strict Presbyterian. If your parents walked around the house nude then you might do the same.

In Nordic countries it is normal, so I'm told. But if you're not used to communal nakedness then being stripped and clotheless with one person is going to take a huge amount of courage.

Having good body confidence is born from what we as individuals believe is the acceptable norm; it is our judgement, our picture of our planet. Am I too fat? Too thin? What about my belly? Who is going to judge the size of my genitals? And why?

This is the same for girls. I was dating a girl once and she said, 'and you haven't even seen me naked yet,' almost petrified but her body was fantastic. Another asked, 'so, you like my body then?' wanting an affirmation. I told her that I loved her body. I did. Gorgeous.

For men, all with egos, performance is important but how do they know if they have been 'good in bed'. What is the gauge? Ten seconds instead of five? Ten minutes instead of five? The number of his orgasms? The number of hers? Has he taken long enough in the build up or has he been the proverbial bull in a China shop? Is she left in second gear whilst he has gone from fifth to reverse?

Worse than all this is the anxiety caused by the conditioning of a certain era that having pleasure through sex is morally wrong and that sex just wasn't for enjoyment. To have an orgasm with someone, so that they could see your pleasure, was just an episode of cataclysmic guilt even if years later you discover that it is totally normal. It just wasn't allowed. For someone to see your face at the moment of ejaculation just wasn't done. Such is the power of programming.

THIRTY-TWO

Ah, girls . . . girls, girls, girls. Worries, worries, worries. Fears, fears, fears. The pressure that women are under is immense, again conditioned by time and place as to what is acceptable, as to what they should be, how they should act and how they should look, a lot media and sales driven. Whatever anyone says there is a preconceived picture of what is beautiful and what is not and if you don't fit into that mould then that's just they way it goes. But if women look close enough at their male counterparts there aren't that many Adonises either so in terms of being a sheer beauty, girls, stop worrying.

It's funny isn't it? The most insecure women in a nightclub or at a party are normally the beautiful ones and it is predominantly a result of their beauty for beauty can hide a lack of intelligence, warmth and personality. Beautiful women crave being told that they are beautiful just the same as pretty or plain girls crave compliments for their real qualities.

Sexual confidence isn't just about beauty but it is about the acceptability of how a girl looks with her clothes on and without and the lesson for girls here is simple, similar to the lesson for men. Make yourself presentable, don't use too much slap, dress as nicely as possible, brush your teeth and relax. Being naked is different but if a girl is body conscious a healthy diet and exercise are obvious options but most men who date women aren't thick. They know who is beautiful and who isn't. And they know if a girl is thin, fat, pretty or plain, and they accept it for what it is. As much as a man might crave Miss World on his arm he knows that it's not going to happen so he accepts a woman as she is.

I know a bloke who was your archetypal 'tit man' yet he married a girl with a 34B cup. 'Tits can never be big enough,' he used to say; yet there were obviously other attractions for him with his wife. And as I have already said men like women of different ages, sizes and colours.

Sometimes a man has a 'type'. Me, for example I like tall women, pretty and beautiful, educated, smart, funny, caring and loving who share my sexual tastes. I don't like excessively fat women but I don't mind cuddly. I once joked to a friend (girl) that I only dated girls taller than 5' 7". 'That's me out then, I'm only 5' 3".' She was visibly gutted and these days I rue that missed opportunity. I didn't even know that we were on a date. How dim can you get? But for different circumstances I would have dated her because my first predilection in terms of taste is that she has to be a nice person. Rules out a few that I know but not her. And she was gorgeous too.

So girls, your fears are only ingrown. Men know what bodies look like. They know they differ in size and shape. They know what fat looks like and they know all about breast and nipple size and pubic hair, or the lack of it, so your job is to be happy with you.

I was once with a girl and I undressed her in the lounge. After a while we decided to move to the bedroom and once we'd stood up she went to put her knickers back on. 'What's the point?' I asked. 'You're going to take them off in a minute.' She was so concerned about walking around flashing her arse and fanny. She kept them off.

Another once commented on the light being on. 'I don't mind...I love looking at your body,' I reassured her. She didn't so we dimmed the lights but each subsequent liaison took place with the lights on. She figured that if it was okay for me then it was okay for her.

Women are very similar to men in terms of gaining sexual experience; we all have to start somewhere yet women are as concerned as much as men about being undressed for the first time by a partner. What will he think of my underwear? My breasts? Stomach? Legs? Do we keep the lights on? Is it okay for me to make the first move? Is he a good kisser? What will he look like naked? Can I drop to my knees and fellate him before he even touches me?

And similarly when things hot up the questions flood out. What will he do to me? Is he an experienced lover? Is he a virgin? Will he be any good? What should I do to him? When should I do it? What if he wants to do something I've never done before? Or that I don't like? And what does he expect me to do to him? What is allowed? If I want him to fuck my arse how do I make it happen?

One girl I talked to said that she never decided before going out with a bloke what she was or wasn't going to do with him on the date. She was experienced and had tried out many different sexual experiences: oral, anal and she even had one guy piss on her . . . without prior warning; she didn't like it at all . . . unsurprisingly. But she never knew until she was actually with the guy as to whether she would suck him off or massage his prostrate and encourage his reciprocation; she just followed her gut instinct and did what she felt like doing.

But she has the advantage of experience.

Trust is a major issue for women. Is it the right thing to do to invite him back to my house? Is it safe to go back to his? What happens if he doesn't get his own way, if I am non-compliant? What if he gets forceful? Angry? If he condemns me to accepting what he wants? It can be scary. Just shows the importance of rapport and trust.

Women also have to be able to cope with the guy too. As much as she may be worried about her own look and performance she is always worried about his. Will he be too big, too small and what if he comes too quickly? What then? And what about her pleasure? And what if his humping is too slow and she wants it fast? And what if she wants to be licked and he won't? (I read once that Cybill Shepherd introduced Elvis to cunnilingus. He said that he didn't do 'that'. She said he did. And he did.) And what if he wants to and she doesn't? You don't know if you don't try but compatibility is vital. Knowing each other's body takes time. So too knowing your own.

There has been a sexual revolution in the last few decades. It is now legal for women to enjoy sex, not just to be the reproductive agent of the species. It is allowed for women to have orgasms, to want to try new things, to use sex toys and to masturbate. The guilt has gone, girls are allowed to make the first move, to demand what they want and to enjoy sex. Which is great news for any man with an open mind and a liberated spirit.

My advice to all girls is to practice a lot . . . especially with me.

THIRTY-THREE

Why don't I ever see anyone I know in a bookshop? Because no fucker I know can read. Well, it's the same with porn really. How come I don't see anyone I know in a porn movie, or on Youtube or Youporn? I know loads of people and watch my fair share of porn so how come there's never a familiar face? It's almost like the nightmare scenario of you walking into the STD clinic to be greeted by a girl that you know.

The amateur films are fascinating and they literally show the world what a big fucking bunch of exhibitionists and voyeurs we all are, even women; most girls I know like watching porn too. Best to do it together. If you are genuinely inquisitive as a person these films are like going to a dance class. You can learn moves, positions and techniques just by studying though I don't think you'd ever get a grant from the local education authority. That said I understand there are classes in The States where girls can learn how to give the perfect blow job. I'm not sure whether they practice on dildos or the real thing. I'm sure there would be plenty of volunteers.

Sexual compatibility is vital if a relationship is to remain strong and to flourish and both parties have to understand the value of sex for each other, it means different things at different times, and people need to agree how sex fits into a relationship. Sex drives may differ. Preferences too. The easiest way forward is to talk about it, openly, honestly. You might want to start with a blind tick list, if there is any embarrassment, or talk on the phone – girls love talking about sex on the phone, ring them when they're in bed – but sometimes you can't get the right pleasure unless you tell someone what you like and what you don't.

A mate of mine was talking about how his girlfriend was giving him a hand job and every minute or so she kept on asking, 'am I doing it right?' They had been together for ten years and she was still asking. By now you'd have thought that she would know the techniques that he prefers or that they would have discussed it, but it seems not. If she was cooking him eggs she would have asked how he liked them and he might have even showed her how to do it so why should sex be any different? Save for the British coyness that envelops this land.

The one that makes me laugh is when the girl holds the bloke's cock as if it were the best China, finger and thumb only, pinky finger to the side like she's having tea with the local vicar. Some guys might like this technique but if you ever studied physics you would know that this wasn't the most efficient way of generating the required increase in blood pressure to maximise the performance. Ever heard a song 'It's all about the Base?' My mate Tamsin says that gay blokes get better sex from their partner because they know exactly which buttons to press.

THIRTY-FOUR

Talking of Tamsin she was in cracking form yesterday when we had lunch together. Married once – 'got the fucking t-shirt, love' – now happily divorced and dating we chewed the fat: who was doing what to who, whether him and her would work, why she is single, why he is having an affair etc. Like a newscaster Tamsin spread the word. Morag is back with The Pup, Gill and Joan have been speed dating, Helen pulled on holiday, an Italian, Steve and Steph have split up, Joanne got caught by the cleaner at work giving the boss a blow job, Sally's back on her own, and Tamsin admitted to having a lesbian snog with Jackie from Leeds. It was a lot to keep up with. And why the lesbian snog? Apart from the fact that Jackie is stunning.

I bumped into Morag at a Salsa class later and told her that it would end in tears. 'What would?' she asked with a quizzical look on her face.

'Chopping onions,' I answered.

I felt a bit sorry for her really; accepting that your partner is a philanderer is a tough call, some would say stupid, a waste and never the foundation of a quality relationship. Why would she want him so much? Did he just have a big cock and loads of money? Was that it? Was he father material to her unborn offspring? Fuck knows. But it will end in tears.

At the class there were thirteen men and twelve girls including the woman teacher. Dan sidled up to the male teacher.

'The numbers are even if you dance the lady's part Tom...statistically, as one in ten men are gay, there should be at least one bloke in here who wants to dance with you...though I should say, it's not fucking me.' Tom blushed and giggled at the same time.

Dan does this sometimes. He's a comic, he makes people laugh, he drops in comments with such precision and timing that it's almost impossible not to laugh. He is irreverent and rude but he gets away with it calling it shtick.

Later he was chatting with Norris The News.

'She's got a lovely arse that one over there,' said Norris, 'so has her sister . . . '

'At your age you'd better ask if their gran is available.'

'Cheeky fucker,' Norris smiled, no offence taken.

'You see Norris, me old mate, what you've got to do is work the strategy.'

His eyebrow raised as Dan continued. 'Sleep with the mother when she's forty, book the girls in for when they're forty, and target their daughters for when they're twenty.'

'Yeah,' he said, 'but there's a problem there . . . I'm forty now and when the girls get to forty I'll be fifty-five, so when their daughters are twenty I'll be seventy-five...'

'Well there you go, something to aim for.'

THIRTY-FIVE

As the months go by Dan, Billy and me are all planning and looking forward to a weekend Salsa festival oop North, by the seaside, a trip we make annually, the chance to learn, learn and learn, to be awestruck by some of the best dancers in the world, to dance to the point of exhaustion, to drink to the point of overflow, if you fancy it, and it is the chance to fraternise to your heart's content, this is where there will be over five hundred women. Surely there will be one who is single, eligible and available. For those looking, both men and women, this was a genuine opportunity to meet people in a friendly environment, a chance to chat without the humdrum blast of a night club, where people aren't judged solely on their peacock status. It is a chance for personality, charisma and charm to win the day.

Last year I met Sharon

I was shagged out, it was late on Sunday night and we'd been on our feet since Friday night with small gaps for sleep and food. We'd danced like our lives depended on it, the right balance of beer and wine, not loaded, and the vibe was buzzy, higher than octane, dances became more expressive, closer, dirtier. 'Ooh,' one girl cooed in my ear, 'you don't dance like this at home'.

And she was right; it's all about context, you know, the atmosphere, the music, the lights, the expectation, the attitude, the feel. And when that's right your head goes into a different plain, your brain zones out, and suddenly you are surfing, not a care in the world, the only important things in the world, you and your partner, inhibitions disappear, the tempo is perfect, the mood grabs you and you grab the mood. This was when I met Sharon, 5' 5", blonde, sometimes, size 10, wearing a black one piece flashing her arms, cleavage and thighs, seriously sexy.

Sharon had seen me dance and she came over to the edge of the dance floor and grabbed my hand. She didn't take it, she grabbed the fucker and she tried to pull me towards the heaving, dancing bodies.

'Whoa,' I said, 'slow down, I've just danced four on the trot.'

'Whoa, nothing, you're fucking dancing.'

And we did though it was closer to dancing fucking, every move tight, limbs entwined, mass gyrations, no fear. The four minutes passed quickly, I pecked her cheek and went off for a beer only to return, to her surprise, to her table. I took the chair next to her, put my arm around her, pulled her towards me and my left hand settled just underneath her left tit. She didn't back off; she just got comfy.

'So, you haven't got a girlfriend or wife here who's going to get in the way?' she asked as she hid the wedding band on her left hand.

I looked around. 'Not that I know of.'

'And I presume we're going to dance again?'

'No.'

'Well you can fuck off then.'

I squeezed her a little tighter. 'I'm not going anywhere.' And again she snuggled closer, my fingers subtly cupping the bottom of her tit. She leaned over and kissed my cheek and ear.

'So,' I said, 'what are we having for breakfast in the morning?' It was just a line, a tease, she was married.

'We! When did we become a we?'

'Just thought you might like breakfast in bed...'

'What sort of a girl do you think I am?'

'My scrambled eggs are legendary.'

She leaned forward, kissed me on the cheek and whispered, 'next year.'

THIRTY-SIX

So, was Sharon looking for a potential love partner or a shag or just a bit of flirting? Maybe all three, but she knew that this convention was the perfect medium for her and others to test the water, to see what was on the market. Not all the men (or women) would be single but she could satisfy her own needs, whatever they were. One wonders if people are actually checked out at conventions for singles only? Bring your ID and your Decree Absolute. Because we all know that men will shag anything and that if someone asked them if they were single they would lie their tits off. I don't know which sex is the bigger liar, but if a bloke says he's single it's always worth never believing him.

I met Ali at the convention too, Ali from Somerset, tall, narrow at the hip, heavy chested, sultry, exotic, erotic, a girl I had met four months prior at a local Salsa gig and I hadn't forgotten her. Sometimes that happens. But she was memorable, the way her eyes burnt, how she felt in my arms, her softness and her one green eye and her one blue eye.

So, me, Billy and Dan entered the main hall at the convention on the first night and we settled at a table with the girls from our town, a dozen of all ages, sizes and abilities. Dan went for the beers, we changed our shoes and then, like a general overseeing the battlefield, I stood up and did a recce, familiar faces, pockets of annual acquaintances, mild electricity in the air, anticipation as powerful as an aphrodisiac. All the girls in our group were itching to dance but during my recce I did a double take of this beauty not three yards away and as soon as our eyes met I walked towards her, bowed gently but still looking straight into her eyes and asked her if she wanted to dance. She accepted and we strode towards the floor.

'I've danced with you before,' she said, her arm in mine, my date for the night, well, for the next four minutes or so.

'I know . . . Wednesday night . . . August 25ᵗʰ . . . you're Ali from Somerset.'

'Crickey . . . how would you remember that . . . you're Paul aren't you?'

'No . . . he's my brother . . . do you know him?'

The dance that followed was better than August, closer, more intimate, we had both improved. Ali bought into the intimacy of the dance as much as I did, her body gyrating, her head thrashing, her shock of hair spraying erotically, her pupils dilated, her pulse high, sweat permeating onto her long, figure hugging dress.

Back at the table there was a typically male response.

'You two looked like you were fucking,' said Dan, all matter of fact.

'Calm it down a bit, eh?' said Billy. 'There's chalets for that.'

'You,' I pointed in jocular fashion, 'are telling me to calm down? Pot and fucking kettle. Fuck me, it must have been filthy.'

It was.

I danced once more with Ali that night and then I didn't see her again until the next afternoon when we'd arranged to dance together at a Tango class. Her natural welcome was as warm as ever and soon, with the full backing of the instructor, we were dancing chest to chest, a leaflet between our torsos. If it hit the floor we were too far apart. I led her through rock steps, side to side, forwards and back, simulation, intensity, and then an occasional drop, her hips forced against mine. All in the name of dance. When we'd done I kissed her four or five times on the mouth, our tongues brushing lightly and then she backed off.

'Easy Tiger!'

I wish girls wouldn't use such stereotypical put-downs. The hurt is bad enough.

Okay, it was embarrassing for a nanosecond but what was I supposed to do? The vibe was so intense and frankly it was the same for her. I wasn't trying it on like some perve, it just felt like the natural thing to do at the end of such intimacy.

Later, on the Salsa floor, we danced again, I apologised again for the kiss and we agreed there would be no more of it. And I thought that was that, but fuck me, what happens? There we are in the middle of another routine and she kisses me, full tongues and tonsils.

'That was you!' I joked. 'Don't let me stop you from doing it again.'

THIRTY-SEVEN

'Who are you?' I asked in a frank and open fashion to the girl taking the money at the Salsa pally. 'Where have they been hiding you?'

She smiled, unsure but glad of the compliment and she looked at the bag I was carrying; it held my shoes, towels, shirts and water.

'I'm Terri. Are you moving in?' she asked.

'Bit soon isn't it, I don't even know you,' I said as I paid and moved away.

Terri was sultry, curvaceous and a total stranger. Given the amount of dancing that I do I'd have thought I'd have met her before but no and apparently, according to Dan, she has been on the scene for years, married to another dancer.

'Lucky him,' I said.

'She was my first dance teacher,' said Billy. 'If it wasn't for her we wouldn't be here tonight.'

'Or our mums and dads,' I added.

It is rare that a room is lit up by such a smile and such a personality but that is what happened here. There was just something about her. We'd thin sliced each other; there was an instant attraction.

Inside there was a live band, body heat and the need for the Sirocco to cool us all down but there wasn't what I was looking for. Normally you get a lot of familiar faces on the Salsa circuit and I was hoping to catch up with Ava.

Remember her? Tall, beautiful, intelligent, soft eyes, tender hands, a real pleasure to dance with and to be with. We like each other a lot but she has a bloke.

There was a feeling when I spoke to her last time that she wasn't happy at home and that she was looking for some action, be that company, someone to go to the pictures with, someone to fuck senseless or someone to love. I followed Dan's mantra of not dating someone in a relationship knowingly but there was a tingle with Ava, like the start of a cold sore. Crap analogy and nothing personal Ava, honey, but you know what I mean.

And two conversations sprang to mind. Janneau is a sixty-eight year old opinionated Frenchman, divorced and remarried, retired and one of life's real good guys.

'If you fuck her it's not rape you know...she has wanted to as much as you. And anyway, you'll be sixty tomorrow'. Meaning that life soon passes by and that opportunities are there to be taken and not ignored. (I know a legal company called Carpe Diem and I rang for an appointment. They couldn't fit me in for a fortnight.)

The second conversation was with Ava herself. 'If a girl in a relationship gets involved with another man it is her choice and she must be ready for any consequences.' There was little wonder that I was looking forward to meeting her again but she wasn't there. What a pisser!

By the bar Mickie the Lick was there with a stunning looking girl, one I'd never met before, mid 20s, posh was the first word I thought of when I saw her, size 8, come to bed eyes.

'Mickie, how are you...who's this? Your daughter?'

Mickie scowled and introduced Sue who I kissed on the cheek. They ignored me the rest of the night.

Belle was there too looking lonely amidst her friends. As she cooled I playfully dabbed her down with a towel as if she was a boxer in between rounds, her forehead, her shoulders and when I reached for her back she politely took the towel from me.

'To be honest,' I said, 'you might as well take your top off and put on a clean one. You can borrow one of mine.' With this I held up the towel as if to block everyone else's view. She looked at me as if I was the hired jester for the night. To prove the point I dipped my fingers into my pint of cold water and I flicked the spray on to her face. This time she laughed aloud. Is it me or is something happening here?

Curly came into the room, her ragged hair hiding her pretty face, her slinky hips rocking gently to the vibe, her skin-tight cut offs needing no belt at the waist. Dan danced with her, Billy too, she was surfing high on the moment and there was no sign of the grey-haired old fuck who'd been stalking her. Probably couldn't get a pass out of the old peoples' home.

By the wall was The Runner and Moira from Ireland his lift for the night. I say lift because she was driving; she wasn't his ride. They sat in the corner like they were at a Darby and Joan club, him loafing there with his pipe, sipping his pint, her with her knitting and rum and pep. They didn't talk. Every now and then they would dance and they'd return to their seats and still they didn't talk.

I saw Dan dance with her, The Runner looking on, studious and envious, a man with a dilemma. He has all that money can buy but he hasn't got what he can never buy: style, charisma and charm. When he dances he bends over a touch, knees bent like a primate, his eyes empty. There is no soul and Dan has it in spades.

THIRTY-EIGHT

Dan upset Connie last night with what can only be described as a brilliant one-liner thrown in at the wrong time to the wrong audience. Oops! The practice room was full but it was hot and everyone was fighting for a window, a fan or the air con. Everything was going well, the girls circulating from one man to another, practising with different people is vital to developing your techniques, and when Connie got to Dan they both smiled, he cuddled her, kissed each cheek and squeezed tighter.

'Hiya . . . wow, you smell nice,' she beamed. She does that Connie, she really does beam, her pretty face and smile illuminate any room she enters.

'It's YSL . . . Rive Gauche . . . it seems to blend well with my natural pheromones.'

Whilst I was thinking that if anyone else had said that he would have come across as a right tosser but I knew that Dan was deadpanning it, ready for the crunch.

'What's the perfume you're wearing Connie? Toilet Duck?'

I reckon that's the closest I've seen Dan to getting a knee in the nads or a poke in the eye. She wasn't impressed; it was the first time she'd been able to afford Chanel. During their dance Connie nearly cracked Dan in the face with her elbow, accidentally, and she smiled through grimaced teeth and left quickly after. Oops indeed.

In the bar later Dan was unperturbed by Connie's departure; he knew she was on earlies.

'I see Morag's back with The Pup then,' Dan said to me, Billy and Tamsin. 'Silly fucker, beyond redemption. What sort of bird tolerates "adultery"?'

'A desperate one?' I offered.

'Maybe she's in love?' Tamsin offering a female perspective.

'Even if you're in love you still don't put up with that shit. Once a serial shagger always a serial shagger . . . you allow it once and that's it then, he can do what he fucking likes,' Dan opined. 'I've seen it so many times...he goes home, lies his tits off, she's happy as Larry and then he does it again on the premise of "what she don't know won't hurt her" and does it till he gets caught. Then he cries his remorse, she forgives him, and they don't live happy ever after. It's never the same after an affair. There's no trust. And what's her option? Kick him out?'

'Sounds pretty logical to me,' I said. 'The courts are designed to fleece the shagger and support the suffering spouse. You can't live a relationship without trust, honesty and respect.'

'When I found out,' said divorcee Tamsin, 'I cut his running shoes to pieces with the garden shears and left a note telling him that he's lucky that it wasn't his bollocks. Then I changed the locks and divorced the cunt.'

'Go Tammy! Go Tammy!' I cheered like a pom-pom girl. Sometimes it's invigorating when a girl uses the 'C' word. Dan tells me that it was his ex's favourite word; in that case not pretty, not pretty at all.

'Anyway,' said Tamsin, 'before we start auditioning for Oprah...Morag went to Manchester with Patrick last week...so maybe she's testing other waters away from The Pup?'

'Patrick? O'Dawes? The cake maker?' I asked.

'Yup,' said Tamsin.

'Fuck me!' I said.

'Is that an instruction?' asked Tamsin with a glint in her eye.

'Who the fuck's the cake maker?' asked Billy.

'Her stalker,' said Dan. 'He decided that the best way to charm himself into her pants was to bake her a chocolate cake. He took pots, pans, ingredients, the full fucking Monty to her house to bake her a cake.'

'I never thought of getting a shag like that,' said Billy, musing.

'Anyway,' Tamsin interrupted, 'he's keen and she's not.'

'Not?' Dan asked. 'Chocolate cake? Manchester? Valentine's dinners?'

'Perhaps he's just a casual fuck?' offered Tamsin at the height of her devil's advocacy.

'Is he bollocks,' we all three chorused together.

'I thought she was waiting for a prince to come along?' Dan asked. 'White charger, steed, joust, lance, the full kingdom shit. She wouldn't fuck the frog for the sake of it?'

Tamsin took a drink and kept schtum.

'I've never fucked a frog,' said Billy.

THIRTY-NINE

When I was asked why I was there I replied that I was 'just passing'. It wasn't the truth but that wasn't important. I had a plan.

The room was large with high ceilings and nice lighting but one look at the dance floor and Fred and Ginger would be turning in their graves; it looked like it had been assembled from a cheap pack of Meccano. Need to be careful out there.

On the periphery was a lot of talent, most flashing off cleavage or with tight fitting tops, one benefit of the hot weather, and a couple of girls came over to say 'hello'. That was nice. But I was beginning to scan the room and then she walked towards me, the reason for my guest appearance.

Ava.

She was on her own, that is, no bloke, so I held her closer, slightly longer and I kissed her twice, once on each cheek, each time slightly longer and slightly closer to her mouth. She didn't back off.

The class passed quickly after that and I moved towards Ava to dance. We luxuriated in each other's company and at the end of the first song we just carried on dancing. At the end of the second we just carried on. After the third she took a breather and went for some water. She sat down and I pulled a chair close to her, close enough to touch her leg or arm, near enough to look straight into her eyes and handy enough to talk into her ear. And then we chatted uninterrupted for an hour, an intimate conversation about love, life and romance, reality and dreams. I think it was this night when I actually fell in love with her. I had found my potential love partner but there was a caveat, a savage, brutal and coruscating caveat. She wasn't available. Even now as I write I can feel my stomach churning at the thought, my physiology changing, my blood pressure rising, my desire escalating towards the top of its Everest.

A smiling face disturbed us. At first he looked at us both, then Ava and then me.

'Could I drag her away from you?'

Returning the smile and then looking at Ava I answered. 'You'd better ask the lady...you'll find it's her choice.'

They danced.

Four minutes later we resumed our conversation at exactly the same point that it was broken. We chatted some more, danced once more, a slower, intimate and soulful dance, and then, as the music died down I walked her to her car.

And then I kissed her.

FORTY

I drove home that night and I cried my heart out. I couldn't believe it. Here was this woman, beautiful, intelligent, talented, warm, caring, her life a dearth of love and affection and there was me ready for the first time in my life to commit to someone on a major level, that is, with my heart and my soul. It is fair to say that I have 'liked' some girls I've been out with, and maybe I have 'loved' them, whatever that means. Did I care for them? Enjoy their company? Miss them when they weren't there? And I had been married. But this had never happened before. As soon as we drove off that night I missed her. I craved her. I wanted to share her space, her life, her heart. And it fucking hurt. It hurt so fucking much. My whole body ached for her. And that was why I cried. As well as her being unavailable.

I beat myself up for years about this. Do you decide who you fall in love with? How do you fall in love with someone who isn't available? How do you decide who you fall in love with? If she is in love with you and you aren't with her, can you make yourself? I know that there are obvious matches in the game of love. If you scored a girl out of ten on looks and then you scored her partner they wouldn't be far away from each other. Classes seldom mix. Races too. An upper class bloke rarely dates a working class girl. A thick bloke rarely dates a clever bird. A girl into saving the whale wouldn't date a Japanese harpoonist. Someone polite wouldn't date someone with the social graces of a shrew.

Opposites attract as long as they complement each other. But why Ava? Why indeed.

What I really loved about Ava, apart from what my innate sixth sense was telling me, and more of that in a minute, was the way in which she looked in to my eyes when we danced. I know it's only a small thing but in a different age it would have launched a thousand ships. Her eyes sparkled into me, their shining hiding an inner turmoil, veiling years of a love vacuum, burning with desire, enflamed with a message. And that message was simple: I need your love, love me please.

Looking back in hindsight I don't think that anyone had ever been 'in love' with Ava before. I know that she has had relationships, some that have lasted and some that haven't, and the main reason that they hadn't endured – notice I haven't used the word 'succeeded' or 'failed' – was because her men were never in love with her. Relationships of convenience aren't geared towards quality and longevity. Likewise those based on lust or a shared love of hedonism.

My sixth sense was spot on that night. If you are spiritual in any way or believe in Karma then there is a theory that people arrive in each other's lives for a reason, like an angel, when you need them. I needed her and she needed me. In all her years love had been a spectator and never a participant in her life and it scared her. She had loved and lost and it hurt. It does. But it isn't the losing per se that hurts, it's the deceit, the lies and the distrust. It's the fact that you can't have what you had, and by that I mean the ideal not the man or the woman. Being in love is better than being out and when you are out of love you crave for that intimacy, the common bond, the shared goals, winning the fights and battles together, struggles that add to your collectiveness. You crave that person to complete you, to be there in your hour of need, the person to resolve all the problems, to take some of the strain, the person to make your life worthwhile, someone to value you for what you are, someone to be a witness to your life.

My sixth sense has a self-esteem monitor and it triggers with most people. There's a song playing now as I write: 'Baby, I'd love you to want me'. How apt. We all want to be wanted, to be needed and to be valued. Ava was shorn of that. She wasn't desired because of who she was. She was desired because it was better than the bloke being on his own. She was desired for her beauty but not her complete person. She was an abused partner mentally and emotionally, taken advantage of. For years. And this just nips away at the self-esteem, day-by-day, week-by-week, until, one day, there is none.

And me? I have confidence and a strong self-esteem; I know what I am good and bad at and I don't need a trophy or a rosette to confirm it. And I am emotionally courageous these days; I wasn't always. If I like someone I say so. If I don't like someone I usually keep it to myself. Why disrupt someone else's life with your views? I have learned to be positively honest.

Following my own break up and fight against authority - a fight I lost heavily, but it was worth it even if the odds were so stacked against me. I'll tilt at a windmill with the best of them – I was never in a position to let myself love for the fear of repetition of what happened before. It was denial at its best. Don't do it. Think of the pain. It is a shocking place to be, lonely and fearful yet desperate for affection and company. But in time my reserves of love built up and up and up, high to the point of overflowing. As Layla once remarked. 'You have so much love inside you. There must be someone out there for you.' And Lulu, a real love in my life added to this. 'You are too nice to be on your own; you are such a good man.'

So when I met Ava something must have happened and given way inside of me. I had love in spades to give and she needed it as much as a diver needs an oxygen tank. It really was the most natural synergy I have ever seen.

That night . . . just looking into those eyes . . . those eyes that said 'help me', 'love me', 'take me'. So I had to work out how.

FORTY-ONE

Dan was getting frustrated with his search for a lover because he was finding too many barriers in the way of a fulfilling relationship, some that he created and others that were the product of circumstance. Dan wanted to date, he wanted to bed, but he found that most of the women who he was interested in were problematic.

Let's put this into context. As I have already said the dance scene is full of single girls looking for a partner. So is Dan but he's starting to get a reputation as a bit of a dance tart, Monday with one girl, Tuesday another etc till the end of the week. He never lies about dancing with different girls but along with the dancing there is an assumption that he is adding to the dancing with bedroom activities. He assures me he isn't, for what it's worth. And on some nights he can dance with ten women, miss five, these get huffy until he charms them over, but he's a bit like I was B.A. (before Ava), he hasn't found a girl worthy enough to drop the rest of his posse because there is an inevitability that as you spend more time with one girl you spend less with the others.

It's a dilemma that only he can overcome. If he wants the benefits that being with one girl brings then he has to be prepared to forego the other delights. Girls like that. They all know that men are driven by sex. Most women are prepared for that; they like sex too. But afterwards if you want more sex then you have to offer more too, more commitment.

On the other side of the coin there is what we call the 'window of shaggability', that is when is there time to spend hours between the sheets with your selected lover? For many people quality sex is spoilt by normal life.

Let's take a look at a couple of examples. Dan knows one girl, single mum, two kids, works full time, sometimes gets a baby sitter so she can go dancing. If Dan is invited back to hers what happens then? It's not the greatest aphrodisiac worrying whether the door will open when she's on her knees licking his nads. 'Mummy, I've got a headache...mummy, what are you doing?' Even when it's in the bedroom there's still the chance that little fucking Jemima comes barging in saying that she can't sleep because of the monsters under her bed. What mum would lock the door?

So when can they commit to quality sex? When the kids aren't there? How often is that? How can time be engineered to be kid free? Of course, there maybe times when the kids are with relatives but how often can you make that happen? 'Ah, Aunty Sue, take the kids for the night can you, I need to give Jackie here a right good seeing to.' Doesn't work does it? And what if there are no relatives? And they can't exactly bunk off work for a quickie at lunchtime can they?

The ideal time to get together is the obvious one, after or before a dance – did that once and everyone commented on how relaxed she was - or instead of a dance, a babysitter coping whilst you get your rocks off. But if it's after a dance you can't exactly coerce the bird back to yours when she has to get back to dole out the fifteen quid or whatever the going rate is.   No sleepovers.   No early morning oral.   Just frustration. I suppose the ideal situation would be to move in together, but that is miles away, light years.

One girl I dated lived in the same house as her estranged husband who was free to come and go as he pleased; he was still paying the mortgage. So you go over for nibbles and a snog and then you hear the car pull up outside. It's not exactly a case of in flagrante delicto but it just doesn't work as the ideal setting for affection. He was a funny fucker he was, shagging some bird across town yet still jealous when his ex wanted a bunk up. Issues? You betcha.

Another girl had three kids and her ex looked after them every other weekend. That gives a fortnightly 'window of shaggability'. Is that enough? Sometimes it has to be. But what if he plays the twat and pisses her about? Sometimes that window can go from two weeks to four. Acceptable? Straining.

So it's not all as easy as it looks. I know one girl who dated a bloke once and he moved in the next day. Rare but they are very happy.

The other thing that is preventative is the age gap because invariably the real single girls, the ones without kids, are either perceived as too young or too old. Me and Dan are both over forty. So young real single girls, say under thirty, aren't really going to date a bloke ten or fifteen years older than them. Some would but not many. The thirties to forties are probably still 'waiting for Brad' and you both know that that isn't you. Over forty but under fifty, and if the kids have left home, there is a shout, but over fifty? Don't know.

The Internet dating websites are all very age conscious where older men are looking for younger women and where people state their own age and the age of their target partner. If they are looking for someone between 30 and 40 what happens if you're 29 or 41?

There are plenty of girls that dance on the dating sites; any trawl produces results:

'Well, wood you believe it?'

'She's 33.'

'Nice photo.'

'Old photo.'

'I thought she was married?'

One girl I know went on a diet especially so that she looked photogenic on the Net. Another changed her age criteria upwards away from my target range when she knew how old I was. Made me laugh anyway.

As you can see the ocean full of talent is fast becoming a pond.

FORTY-TWO

Dan weighed up the odds still searching for his potential lover. Me too; I had to keep looking because as much as I had found Ava she wasn't available – would she ever be? - and even if she was available would she feel the same way about me as I did her? This hurt like hell. It gnawed away at my stomach. I don't know if men are supposed to feel like this. I don't know if any do. But I knew what had made me be like this. God, I wanted that woman.

Some girls are happy to move quickly from one relationship to another in spite of the pain of a break up or the atmosphere of acrimony that accompanies some splits. Sometimes the reason for the split is another bloke so they already have Plan B lined up. Women who are emotionally strong, who know their heart and follow it, the 'better to have loved and lost' girls, will make strong decisions and they will control their destiny. They will be alone if they want to be but they won't be single if they see someone they fancy, someone to date, someone to get to know better. They won't be fuelled by fear just possibility.

Of course, we all know of 'rebound', we all know of 'loose women', and we all know of women who just hate being on their own for emotional reasons rather than financial ones, but every now and then there is one that thinks clear enough will make the 'right' decision.

But what is the opposite? Women scared of a relationship because of the emotional turmoil and the pain? One girl I know said that she would never be beholden to another man ever after the sham of a twenty-year marriage disintegrated due to his continual infidelity, even when they were engaged. Women fuelled with anger and resentment? Women who will never date again, cocooned in the safety of their own world. I'm not sure how long this anger lasts. One girl I know looked at other couples, smiling, tactile, affectionate and at first she thought it would be nice to be like that. But then cynicism kicked in and she began to despise and hate the happy couples, the fools, not knowing what is around the corner, the pain that will engulf them at some stage in the future. What was the point?

Maybe she hadn't met the right man? Maybe the men's reasons for dating weren't strong enough to make the relationship work? Perhaps the needs of each person weren't being met because ultimately when the gloss of being in love/lust/like/convenience has worn off then it is all down to how each other's needs would be met, if there were mutual respect, selflessness and a total reciprocal devotion. Maybe they had nothing in common? Maybe he liked cars and she liked books? Maybe he was more into TV and the PC than her?

When people get together, married or live together, whatever, the dynamic is simple. There's the two of them. Relationship one. But if this relationship is ignored or belittled by either another person, a machine or a hobby then the future is far from bright.

Example A. Bloke works, comes home, eats tea, opens six-pack, TV, bed. Yikes!

Example B. Bloke works, comes home, eats tea, PC, bed. Yikes.

Example C. Bloke works, comes home, eats tea, she goes out. Yikes.

Of course people need their own space but couples need to spend time with each other, doing the same things, giving time to each other. In my relationship labelled a marriage my ex spent an hour a day talking to her mother on the phone and an hour every other day talking to her sister on the phone. Easy question? What about me?

I have heard women talk disparagingly about their men folk calling them another child to look after. 'Is baby not getting enough attention then?' And you wonder why men fuck off and shag someone else? This mutual goal of being together, working for each other, prioritising, enhancing the dynamic rather than destroying it is really the way forwards for a couple to survive. Both parties need to give, to bring equal effort to the party. Any slide can have cosmic consequences.

FORTY-THREE

So me and Dan still looked, me half-hearted to be honest, though Dan was torturing himself, hating the loneliness and the thought of compromise. He hated being on his own but he couldn't really give too much, such was his fear of what might happen. Funny that we're always scared of what might.

We met Louise, Patsy, Jane, Julie and Jackie, but two were married, one was too old, one too young and one just not right. It was like they were auditioning.

*

Louise, brash, young, heavy on the eye contact and big in the arse. If there was a remake of any of the 'Carry On' films, she would get a lead part given her penchant for double entendres, lascivious looks and filthy laugh. She used to be a tester of sex toys for Anne Summers. I asked her to dance.

'Come on Looby Loo, let's do it.'

'You think I use it?'

'Sorry?'

'You think I use it?'

'Sorry?'

'Lube . . . lubrication.'

It took me a minute to explain that Looby Loo was a character from kids' TV many moons ago.

*

Patsy used to sell cars for a living and now she administers in a doctors' practice. Another divorcee, nice face, we were at a Salsa gig when Tamsin produced some champagne and I had the last glass. Patsy wanted some so I took a swig, had the champagne in my mouth and I kissed her passing the champagne into her mouth. Sexy as fuck. Tamsin stood there as if she'd just been jolted by 5,000 volts. Hilarious. And Patsy didn't complain.

*

Jane, tall, Londoner, married, three kids, great, positive demeanour, pretty, wavy brunette, just starting out on her dancing career, hubby at home, festering in guilt and shame at the thought of being able to Fox Trot.

'You look absolutely lovely,' I said as I looked her up and down, toe to top. The sun had been out, she wore a knee length dress, cream with navy fleurettes, sleeveless, cut at the cleavage, a great balance of skin and cloth. 'Am I allowed to say that to a married lady?'

'You can . . . absolutely . . . in a house full of men I don't get to hear that sort of thing very often.'

'Well, I don't suppose they appreciate the effort you make?' I smiled and she blushed.

Men do this sometimes, the ones who aren't that clever. There are never enough compliments to fuel the relationship, not enough cuddles, not enough kisses, not enough warm touches. Yesterday I asked for a hug and got it. It lasted thirty seconds and it felt fantastic. I needed it; I guess she did too.

The thing that always surprises me is the men who aren't interested in their partner much at all, and the partner tolerates it. Golf widows have it tough unless they play or caddy. Cricket widows . . . definitely a game for the young and single unless the woman has an uncommon interest in the game and that specific community. And when I see a beautiful woman at a class or a dance, one I know is in a relationship and I make any comment where the underlying question is 'are you getting plenty?' but not always phrased like that I am shocked to find that Girl A or Girl B isn't getting any affection. And they don't like it. But they tolerate it.

*

Julie is a nurse. 'Have you sobered up yet?' Cheeky fucker.

'I did try hard to drink enough to make you look pretty.'

'You're a cheeky monkey aren't you?' she said as she smacked me playfully on the arm.

'Ow! That's assault . . . and I don't do pain . . . just pleasure . . . anyway, how did you know I was pissed?'

'It was after you danced to that fast track . . . the girl you were dancing with was panting a bit so you offered to take her pulse.'

'Nothing wrong with that.'

'No, except it was her femoral pulse in her groin, not the pulse on her wrist.'

Oh, yeah, I thought, I remember that now.

*

Jackie works for the BBC, researcher I think, medium height, curvaceous, not 30. Her top, perfect for the sunny day and warm evening revealed more of her ample breasts than it covered. Apparently girls don't want you to look at their tits or their cleavage, which begs the question, doesn't it? Why not wear a t-shirt or a sweater then? Why display them? Isn't that a contradiction? Men are programmed to look at tits, it's God's way of ensuring the survival of the species. We danced.

'Nice top,' I said.

'Thanks . . . but can you look me in the eyes when you say that instead of looking at my tits.'

'I wasn't looking at them . . . I was picturing them covered in cream, cherries and grated chocolate.'

'Oooooooohhhhh,' she said.

'Sorry . . . you did ask.'

FORTY-FOUR

Ava was bothering me. Well that's not strictly true, it was the thought of her that was bothering me; I just couldn't get her out of my head. I kept imagining what she would be like with me, giving a hundred percent rather than holding back, hiding behind her sham of a relationship, free from fear, unshackled, ready to offer affection. I wanted her to be with me. I wanted to be with her. But I knew, after talking to her, in a really intimate way, that she might not ever be available, physically or emotionally, and if she ever was, it could be years. I fantasised about walking down the street with her on my arm. And I pictured her astride me in the sack her bodied contorted with orgasm.

Billy watched my angst. Suddenly the fun had gone from the quest to find a lover. It wasn't supposed to be like this, was it? Why her? How come I selected her above everyone else? I could have just changed my sights and taken up with a plain Jane, safe, secure but ultimately passionless and worthless. And I wasn't going to compromise my emotional integrity and take the first girl on offer. A lot of men do that, the emotional cowards, but I'd rather be on my own than with someone just because it is with 'someone'.

Time was the key, a horrible thing to say and to understand. I could be dead tomorrow. We all could. So what point was there in looking at time? If we got together in our mid 50s we'd have wasted ten years, over twenty percent of our adult lives, wasted.

Billy told me to take it one day at a time because things happen quickly in this world. 'If she knows you are there, that's all that you can do,' he said. 'Be nice to her, tell her how you feel, and let her decide. In the mean time stay open to ideas from other women and if it feels right, go for it.'

'I can't,' I said dejectedly, 'it's not that it would be like cheating...but I would be comparing every other girl to her...and the ones that know that I like her...they'd know they were second choice.'

'Well, you have a choice. Either you go route one, tell her and be there, or you go route two, don't see her, don't chase her, don't ring her, don't dance with her, cut her out of your life altogether. Then, if she wants you, it's her move.'

'But how do I do that? How do I rationalise that in my own head? In my heart?'

How indeed.

Ava has had a few relationships, some bland, some passionate, but passion is a strong bedfellow of anger and she had opted for a safer option; her current bloke reliable, emotionless. It was a relationship born from convenience not love and destined to doom.

A decade or so ago I was going through a bad time. Some people close to me died and it fucked me up. I went into depression, helpless, nearly ended up at the wacky farm in a padded cell, and I was so close to it that one doctor feared I would harm myself. I just wanted to understand.

But it was this doctor that offered a radical approach to relationship management. He reckoned that part of my depression was caused by my fucked marriage and that to improve the situation to a tolerable level that I should satisfy my needs elsewhere. He cited French society, mistresses and wives, and he suggested that I took the same option. How I wish I'd trialled that option.

However, my guess is that Ava has the same dilemma, a life shorn of passion, attention, romance, honesty, trust, spark and chemistry. That can be a really lonely and empty place to be. Is that the space that I would fill?

So I decided to talk to her, to tell her that I hadn't bumped into her by chance, that I loved the connection we had on the dance floor and off it. She said that she loved dancing with me and she said that she thought Salsa was sex with your clothes on. I agreed but she breathed in again when I said that I wouldn't mind trying the opposite.

FORTY-FIVE

'You really are gorgeous aren't you?' I said.

'That's still six pounds please,' said Terri on the door again. It'd been ages since I'd seen her.

'What are you reading?'

'Chick lit . . . I haven't reached the bits with the sex yet . . . when I do I'll let you know.'

'You want to check out the well thumbed pages . . . they don't dance like this on Copacabana Beach do they?' I said as I surveyed the beginners cringing into a Samba.

'Ooh, have you been?'

'Of course, I have a villa there,' I lied. 'I'm due a return trip next month . . . you could come along and be the glamour part of the trip.'

'Shall I bring my husband?'

'You really know how to spoil a man's dream, don't you?' I smiled after catching her eye and sauntered off, leaving her to ponder. On the dance floor Dan was standing with Lola, the teacher, long-term partner of Tom.

'You okay?' asked Dan as Tom did a demonstration, Dan's gentle, comforting left arm circling Lola's back and holding her waist. It's one of the benefits of being comfortable as a dancer with touching women...a hug here, a squeeze there, take a hand, comfort a shoulder. 'You look tired . . . too much wet grass?' he proffered.

'Chance would be a fine thing,' Lola's mind wandering. 'No, just a bit tired . . . I haven't had a lot of sleep.'

'To be honest love, you wouldn't get a lot of sleep at my house either.'

She giggled.

'Too many jobs to do,' she continued.

'Me too,' said Dan. 'That said, I only clean the house twice a year…when I have visitors . . . did you know I don't drink tea or coffee? But I still have it just in case I have guests. Once a week I buy a pint of milk and then once a week I throw it out . . . no guests . . . past its sell by . . . but at least it's organic.'

Billy was watching The Runner. Me and Dan joined him.

'He's not really very good, is he?' mused Billy. 'Timing's off, arse out, chest forward, a bit like a Thunderbird model.'

'He dances like a fucking baboon,' said Dan, blunt, harsh, accurate.

'Who's that?' I had spied some fresh talent, five ten, brunette, figure hugging dress, striped like you'd imagine a Technicolor dream coat would be. Her olive skin blended beautifully with the dress.

'Maria, Spanish,' said Dan, the font of all knowledge. 'Married an English bloke, divorced, acrimony, I offered to be her counsellor.'

'Good idea Dan,' said Billy, 'with your history.'

'None taken.'

'You could pull her Dan . . . man of your charm.'

You could see Dan thinking about it.

I was thinking about Ava. I was wondering what sort of person she really was, would she have an affair, would she feel guilty about enjoying herself with me, would it be bad for her to walk in at home smelling of my aftershave. I craved time with her when she was comfortable, relaxed, not looking over her shoulder, being able to kiss her in public without her thinking that MI6 were watching her every move, when she could act like an adult not a school kid, embarrassed by public displays of affection.

And I dreamt about her too, one with her breaking up, another when she was sexually promiscuous and there was a queue, and one when I woke up next to her, her mane of blonde hair flooding the pillows, the sunlight catching her hair like a beam of celestial energy, wearing pastel yellow pyjamas. I wondered which dream will be her legacy?

FORTY-SIX

I was watching a porn movie. The girl, fresh from the school of subtlety said, 'I'm not putting that in my mouth.' She did anyway; it was a movie after all, not real life. In the next clip the girl said, 'not in my hair' but he did anyway, after all, it was a film, not real life. This adds a real dimension to the phrase 'suck it and see'.

The reason I mention it is that I saw Dan last week and he said that he might be getting somewhere with ZF, Zipless Fuck, one of his dance partners. The last time I'd seen her she had looked stunning in a full-length dark black dress and her hair had been groomed to perfection. She could have come straight from the catwalk and with hair like that you could really imagine her saying 'not in my hair' in mid throes.

Dan said that ZF had had bloke troubles and that she had texted him saying that it was an emergency so he'd rung. Was she pissed, lonely or did she just need a telecom cuddle? It's a quarter after one, I'm all alone and I need you now . . .

It appeared to be the latter; her bloke was out, not responding to calls and texts and she was sitting there waiting for him clad in just suspenders and one of his shirts, and she'd drunk two bottles of wine. She was lonely, miserable and she wanted her bloke home. For some reason he didn't want a relatively early night with a girl who, if ever you had to draw it, looked liked sex, pure, organic yet desperate.

'He doesn't even get turned on watching porn,' she said. 'I've tried leaving it on before we have tea and it doesn't work. He must be seeing someone else, or he's gay or he just doesn't fancy me any more?'

It was then, Dan said, that she started blubbing and talking incomprehensively in between sobs.

'I even set up some porn sites on his favourites' list and that didn't work either...'

'Perhaps,' Dan offered, 'you didn't hit his buttons. Why not talk to him about it? Set the mood for the night...candles...beer...soft lights...and then stun him with a pole dance? You did a course in that didn't you?'

'Six weeks...great for the upper body.' She had stopped blubbing. 'As long as the pole is firmly attached at the top and the bottom it's very safe. I could get one fixed up in the spare room.'

'I could give you a hand,' said Dan thinking he'd rather give her something else.

A few days later they met and as they cooled down after a dance Dan chatted amiably without any edge at all.

'Great dancing...you love the close stuff don't you? You know I'm an expert on reading people don't you Zed? I study them, what they do, what they say, how they react, their faces, their eyes. And I have a theory about you…I reckon you like me but you're scared of me . . . in the nicest possible way . . . a bit off limits . . . you won't come back to mine to watch dance videos . . . dance videos . . . even in the daylight . . . because you might not be able to cope . . . especially at night . . . a few beers, a glass of wine, a few dance moves and you know what would have happened . . . even though there is a spare room . . .'

'You are terrible, aren't you?' she said playfully. When she left she kissed him on the cheek and then on the mouth, just a while longer.

(Dan did this once with a girl. Once a week they danced and went for one beer afterwards. On the tenth week she offered to go back to Dan's to listen to some CDs.

'You know what will happen if you do?' he asked and they drove back in separate cars. Back at Dan's they listened to music, drank wine and went to bed, together but fully clothed. It was only the morning after when it all kicked off which for Dan was problematic. He'd been excited and erect for most of the previous night with no release, so he reports, and resuming such levels was hard work but he coped, a story he tells without any arrogance or bragging rights or without naming the girl. What a gent.)

Later that night Dan sent ZF a text. 'It's not illegal for people to like each other.'

FORTY-SEVEN

One way that men can get women to like them or even fall in love with then and vice versa is to offer a skill that he or she can teach; something that the man or the woman always wanted to do. My plan with Ava was to ingratiate myself into her life, to be the Mr. Perfect, someone who made her feel good, the only person who complimented her, opened doors for her, listened to her, charmed her, bought her little presents, understood her and valued her. I wanted her to go home thinking 'what a wonderful experience I have just had with that man'. I wanted to deliver pure happiness to her, and then to compare it to the humdrum of her home life in the belief that the time with me, the experience, the smells, the taste and the music, the memories were what life could be if she decided that was what she wanted. Having chosen Ava as my primary potential lover I pedestalised her, put her up there above all others, my goddess.

One of the key ingredients was that I offered to teach her how to dance and she accepted. Why? What was it in her psyche that allowed her to spend more time with me than with her bloke? What did she want? Just to learn how to dance? To feel my body? To accept my kisses and caresses? To create a land of make believe, a place to escape to once or twice a week? Was she just using me in a blatantly obvious way? Was I just her mind porn? Sorry, pawn? Was I being played for a mug?

I don't know the answer to that. I don't know if she is just the chief manipulator, the Machiavellian queen of the dance hall. Only time would tell.

Either way, I taught her to Tango and herein lies the next question. How, I fucking ask you, am I supposed to stop myself from snogging her face off and giving her one up against the wall after fifteen minutes of intensity, intimacy and passion that is the Tango? How? 'Cause I'm fucked if I know. What a sensation! The atmosphere crackled with electricity and sexual tension.

We did our usual class and then afterwards I commandeered a side room to begin the private tuition. The lights were low and I was nervous, not because I didn't know the moves but because I knew why we were really there. We both did. We were testing the water, seeing if we liked each other and I'd picked the Tango especially, feisty, passionate, sexy, simulation, sex with your clothes on, not as bawdy as Salsa, less erotic than the Waltz, but a truly sexed up dance. I taught a twenty-four-year old once and it really was hard for us both to not end up ripping each other's clothes off even though she was engaged. We didn't.

I talked slowly, calming my nerves, going through the hold, the timing, quick, quick, slow, which foot goes where, balance, tap steps and she picked up the dance really quickly the only absence being a modicum of finesse and elegance. With Carmen by Bizet flooding the room we danced, held together by Velcro, cheek to cheek, a fleeting kiss, a well-timed thrust or rock step, a perfect union and Ava revelled in the situation, buying into the dance and everything that it entailed. She was buying into me. When I looked into her eyes I could see real desire and we stared intently at each other for what seemed like an eternity.

FORTY-EIGHT

After some classes or dances me, Billy and Dan take a corner of the bar at the local pub and we chew the fat, dance anoraks, sober, smiling, charming, the antithesis of the normal clientele, the pissheads, the divorcees living in a vacuum, the nowhere else to go gang, the students, the chavs, the local mums out on a special, the fawning couples and the married blokes pretending to be single. There is little wonder that we are popular with the girls who tend the bar, students raising money to try and fend off loans, antipodeans on a year's break, the occasional Eastern European, all under twenty-five, off limits for us old gits. Well, we don't think so but they are on the look out for younger fare.

Hannah, from Inverness, an actress at the local theatre school, a redhead, originally from Dundee, size eight, beautiful face and a warm smile, bright, savvy and far more streetwise than I ever was at that age.

'Hey, Hannah,' said Dan, 'you're in the business aren't you? Could you get us three a gig? We want to be the next Doctor Who triplets…who are you? I'm The Doctor, I'm The Doctor, I'm The Doctor…simultaneous roles, what do you reckon?'

'You might have to sleep with the casting director…'

'What's her name?' Billy asked.

'Geoffrey,' she said and we all laughed. 'Hey, if you three play The Doctor then I could be the new companion.'

'The Doctor kissed his companion last week,' I said, 'I'm sure we could factor that into the script . . . as long as it's me first.'

Hannah gave us all that 'what are you like?' look and went to serve someone else.

'Well,' said Dan, 'that's scared her off . . . here, did you two see my Quick Step tonight?' Here we go I thought, the big lug's going to regale us with how many lock steps, spin turns and tipple chassés he did, self-indulgent stuff that normally puts us to sleep. 'It was fucking crap,' he said, surprisingly, and we all pissed ourselves, Billy laughing so much he had to grab his stomach. Humour does that, reverse humour, the bit you weren't expecting.

'I thought you'd given her loads of private lessons?' I asked.

'I have, but she was fucking awful, complaining about pain in her fingers and shoulder...never mentioned her fucking feet once...bizarre that...I told her it was old age and rheumatism...she said that she got younger each year and I said that was because she danced with me...but look at me I said, look how much I've aged since I started dancing with you?'

'Did she smack you Dan?' I asked, the three of us giggling like school kids.

'Nah, she knows I was only joshing.'

'I danced with that tall bird again,' I said, 'the married one...with kids...I told her to take smaller steps otherwise we'd end up in the fucking car park together...not a bad thing...that was when she slapped me gently on the arm and said "Oy! I'm not that bad!" It was only when she realised what I'd said...knee trembler over the bonnet sort of thing...that she blushed.'

'You weren't hitting on a married woman?' said Billy. 'You know Dan doesn't approve.' Good job they don't know about Ava, I thought.

'No, not hitting, just some light flirting...make her feel good once a week, that's my job . . . she makes me laugh . . . she concentrates so hard and when she gets it right there's that little grin and recognition in her eyes . . . that self congratulatory slap on the back, as if to say, "Yes! Got it!" I saw her in the supermarket last week . . . do you reckon she's stalking me?'

'No.'

In another corner of the pub there was a gaggle of six women just coming to the end of a midweek session and because I'd been sitting in the sheriff's chair, that is, back to the wall, surveying the scene for out of the ordinary action, I clocked that I knew two of them, dancers, who had used the medium specifically in search of a bloke.

One of them, five nine, size fourteen, bit chunky, pretty, clever, bounced when she danced, her version of going for it, had given me her number twelve months or so before, 'just for dancing'. Have you ever been so humiliated? I never rang. She wasn't a great dancer, a bit like life on a trampoline, and as soon as she pulled she was off the dance scene, until it all blew up and she re-started looking for another alpha male meets Einstein meets Rick Stein meets man at C & fucking A.

During one conversation I'd had with her she mentioned that I looked like her dad. Good thing? Bad thing? How many girls wanted to shag their dad? Please don't answer that, it is only a hypothetical question. When she eventually pulled we bumped into each other in the supermarket and she regaled me with the fact, she was so fucking proud that she wasn't single any more, it was as if she'd been awarded a badge that said 'I'm normal, I can pull, I have got a bloke'. No more stigma of being single.

For me I read it as her relief, a palpable, off the shelf relief. It also meant more space on the dance floor and no further threat to the light fittings with her bobbing up and down.

The other girl with her that I knew had the ignominious pleasure of being in the wrong place at the wrong time and I'd stood on her foot during a dance. As a result she had avoided me for two years, not even a hello. Funny girls aren't they? When it's their mistake they blame you.

I had this once with a girl who was due to pick me up to go to a dance. I was sitting on the wall outside the house, freezing, in the dark, on the mobile to fill the time and my lift was getting later and later. Eventually I hung up and rang her and she said she was on her way home. Why? I kicked the wall in frustration. She said she'd waited for twenty minutes, tried to call my mobile, got no answer, so she went home. She agreed to turn around and she picked me up. It transpired that she'd parked outside the wrong house, fifty yards away, but it still took fifteen minutes for The Tundra to melt.

Anyway, the girl with the bad foot, sparkly party dress et al didn't know as many steps as she thought she did and her body crumpled when my weight transferred onto her foot. My first thought was, 'what the fuck was she doing there?' The second was, 'I suppose you don't fancy another dance?' The third, 'no chance of a blowjob then?'

She was on the Internet dating site too, played in a local dixey band, and also disappeared off the dance scene once she'd pulled.

FORTY-NINE

It makes you wonder about some women doesn't it? They come onto the dance scene, try a few blokes out and then they're off. But what about the dynamic? Is it still the guy's job as alpha male to make the first move? In the Salsa world it is rude to refuse a dance so it is easy for men to ask a girl to dance and vice versa though the shy of both sexes still struggle a little such is our normal culture in this country. But the nature of the dance is such that there is plenty of body contact, mild intimacy, sometimes intense intimacy, and although some women just dance like that because that is how you dance Salsa there are plenty of occasions when the guy knows that the girl is interested and vice versa.

So what happens next? Does the girl get brave and ask the guy if she can buy him a drink, a sign of positive friendliness, something that rarely if ever happens in a public bar or a nightclub? Subconsciously, anyone who accepts anything from anyone is then indebted to that person. There is that programmed belief that once you have propped you will kop. Quid pro quo. If I buy her a drink she will remember it and will be friendlier and less resistant as a result. And it works both ways. As soon as a girl buys a guy a drink he knows that she is interested, level to be ascertained. So one wonders why women don't do this more?

Away from the sanctity of the Salsa pally do women ask for that dance? Or do they even say, 'Hello, who are you?' Have the genders evened out? Do women make the first move? Are they blatant about asking someone out on a date? Or do they just give off signals that dumb blokes don't pick up on for eons? Fertile female baboons initiate sex by waving their reddened arses in front of their male counterparts as a direct invitation. I'm not saying that birds should drop their kecks and moon but an unequivocal message would solve a lot of fucking about.

I went to a club once and I asked a girl already on the dance floor to dance. She simply refused. I really couldn't believe it. So I asked her again and the result was the same. I nearly reverted to the line of, 'Don't you know who I am?' on the lines of, 'But I Am The Finest Swordsman In All Of France.' But I didn't. All I wanted to do was dance with the silly fucker, I didn't want to marry her, but she just equated it to sex, not to the fact that I am a highly-skilled multi-dance specialist and that it would have been a great benefit for her as a novice dancer to enjoy the experience.

So are girls proactive? Or are they still the meek waiting to inherit the earth?

There is a lot to be said for female courage and emotional honesty. Do I fancy him? Do I like him? Can he be my friend? Will he be my lover? Can I be up front? Will he be embarrassed? Will it ruin our friendship? And if we date and it goes wrong, what then, surely that will ruin the friendship? And could I get hurt. Best go lie down in a safe box love...

Of course, it is a given that if alcohol is involved women become braver, they say hello out of platonic interest, and they engage with people that they would normally avoid, and of course, again, they may do things that they regret. I met a girl called Vanessa in a bar, we'd chatted a little before, but I hit on her in a big way, my hand on her back, my mouth close to her ear and I listened to her tell me about her job and her dreams. I empathised a lot, listened with intent, we both laughed a lot and every now and then I kissed her cheek, the side of her head or her neck. As the bar gently got pissed we got closer, me aware that eyes were watching for the next move and it came from Vanessa. She kissed me on the mouth and she tasted real nice even though I had broken a cardinal rule and hit on a smoker. Minutes later she went to the loo and I didn't see her again that night. Was it really that bad, kissing me? Obviously. I've only seen her twice since, once when she was out with a gorilla on a Friday night, and again in the same pub when I complimented her on her hair, something that I guarantee no one else had done that day. No hard feelings; she's probably at the zoo as we speak checking out her next mate.

There has to be a way for girls to have the courage to say hello or to be interested in someone. You don't have to want to marry the guy, just be interested.

Me, Dan and Billy talk about this all the time. We are genuinely interested in people, we ask questions, interview, even interrogate in a friendly way, because we want to try and understand an individual's psyche, and we are brave in the questions that we ask, direct at times, pushing boundaries and exiting comfort zones.

We do it because we like people; we like to form a portfolio of people's likes, dislikes, emotions, life experiences and motivations. We're not just after a shag; Billy is happily married and whilst me and Dan like to get some skin it isn't the be all and end all for us as it is with some men. We want to get to know the people in our world; they are mainly good people, some wonderful, others talented, all friendly otherwise we wouldn't tolerate them, and like most of us, lost souls searching for an answer that we hope we can find by being with someone else.

But how many women follow this same pattern? How many ask questions over and above 'how much do you earn', 'where do you live' and 'what car do you drive'? Not many. Is this because they are genuinely disinterested? Are they shy? Don't they give a shit? Or is it because they have the social skills of a pea? Could be why they are single...

FIFTY

'You can't just have anal sex you know . . . a girl has to prepare . . . there are things to be done.'

You couldn't make it up, could you?

We'd just finished a class, Terri had been on the door, worth the entrance fee on its own, and in the bar Louise was holding court with three girls and two blokes and they were talking about the pros and cons of taking it up the arse. Well, Louise and the two blokes were. The other girls looked like they'd rather be haemorrhaging.

'Don't forget I used to be a tester for Anne Summers . . . I used to test the dildos, toys, DVDs, creams, lubes, you name it.' Both blokes looked like they were ready for a wank, eyes bulging, glazed, saliva on the chin, that sort of thing. 'So, believe me boys, I know what I'm talking about.'

I'm sure that some of the people in the bar had come for a quiet night out and to talk about Eastenders, the footy or The Apprentice but instead they were caught up in the film script of Debbie Does Salsa.

The same night I'd danced with a girl and her mobile phone vibrated in her handbag just when the teacher was explaining a new move.

'I hope that's just your phone,' I said as she crimsoned nicely.

And so did the girl who used a Lypsyl just before dancing. She slipped it out of her pocket.

'For a minute I wondered what you were going to do with that,' I said.

The conversation about anal sex dissipated quickly but the racy nature of the subject continued as the blokes, all blasé and shock tactics, talked about erections, ejaculation, cock size, oral sex et al. Nonchalantly subjects like dogging, wife swapping, threesomes, foursomes and swinging were batted about as if we were talking about what was on the shelves at Tesco's and the price of chips.

Dogging and swinging got the main attention, dogging, public sex with strangers, down a lane, in a park, pre-ordained, agreed places, where there was an unwritten code of ethics and swinging, couples seeking sexual variety, predominantly at parties and private clubs.

Frankly neither does it for me. I don't mind sex outdoors, in fact it's quite liberating, but with some fucker watching, wanking away? No thanks. Sometimes the wankers are allowed to join in – car windows and doors open is the usual sign - but some couples just lock their doors, put on the dash light and do a little cameo. One guy I know who had never heard of dogging and who wanted a midnight shag

June 2019

236

in the local park was going down on his bird in the car with the door open when suddenly she froze and it wasn't because of orgasm. A stranger was in a cock's length of her lover and it looked like he wanted a bit of the action. Seconds later, after a mild rebuke ('fuck off will you, you twat!') the stranger walked off, disappointed . . . probably someone's family doctor that.

I read that doggers get a great rush of adrenalin at having sex whilst being watched or out in the open but it can't be safe can it? Even with condoms you don't know who's done what to who and with what . . . and lots of people don't use protection at all. There's a massive risk of oral herpes, STDs and HIV (Doncaster is the AIDS capital of the country; you have been warned.) I mean, each to their own but you wouldn't fancy being part of a queue would you? Sloppy fifths? Desperate and degrading? You tell me.

Swinging, studies show, is more controlled but again you have to wonder at the motivation, especially that of the women, over and above having a high sex drive, wanting to be promiscuous and to taste as many bodies as they can. For me it is as emotionless as fucking a prostitute but why do women do it? Do they like it? Are they coerced? Is it about the sexual fulfilment? Excitement? Fantasy? Hedonism? Boredom? Bi-curiosity? A fetish? To satisfy your bloke? (Not every woman buys into swinging, some women, unsurprisingly, just don't fancy the thought of their bloke getting his cock sucked by someone else.) Is it so that one partner can viscerally enjoy their partner's pleasure? If statistically one man in ten is gay, if one person in twenty swings, then take a look around your workplace and try and guess which one it is.

FIFTY-ONE

Dan has been worrying me and Billy. He's had some bad luck in the last few years but when he's out he acts like he's the richest (not), funniest bloke in the world (probably), not a care, he dances his socks off, he charms, he's attentive and although he gets a bit pissed every now and then you'd think his world was full of contentment, happiness and the secret to eternal youth. It's not; it's just a veneer, a mask, a shroud over his inner misery. I asked him in a rare bout of seriousness if he was okay.

'Not really kid. I need some money, some work, a dance partner and a woman . . . I'm sick of being on my own . . . it's a great principal but no fucking fun, me, the remote, the corkscrew and two hundred channels on the telly and nothing on, no one to talk to, no one to ring, no one to chat with, no one to share with. Bit of a pisser really.'

He explained that his life was full of frustration on virtually every front, even his dreams, adorned with journeys that never end, games that never finish, searches for people and finding no one, reading a book that never concludes. One dream specifically related to him trying to play golf. He said that he tried to put the ball on the tee and it kept falling off. And when it did stay on there wasn't enough room to swing the club. And when there was he couldn't follow through properly or the ball had changed into a flower. Or the green was full of people so he had to wait. This, he said, was the story of his life.

He pulled out a list from his wallet.

'Look' he said, 'these are the birds I dance with...the good ones...but are they really any good? In Salsa it's all right, we can freestyle, but ballroom's not like that . . . they have to know the routines . . . and bless 'em, they don't remember much these birds do they . . . even when I teach them privately . . . I train them up on the Tango or the Quick Step and then their boyfriend or husband or kids get in the way and I have to start again and train up some other fucker . . . I don't know why I bother . . . I'd be better off staying at home having a wank.'

'Well,' I said, 'maybe a girlfriend is the ideal dance partner? You need to find a bird that's as passionate about dancing as you are . . . someone that's into you too...and I reckon you've solved two problems in one hit.'

'You don't think I know that?' He wasn't being churlish or lippy; Dan's a bright guy and even he can pick up the 'right in front of your face fucking obvious', as he described it. 'Have a look at this,' he said, producing another piece of paper, this one showing a table that he'd drawn to highlight his chances of pulling in the near future. There were five columns: the day of the week, birds I fancy, married/with partner, birds that fancy me and potential, this last box containing nothing but nils. 'Look at that,' he said. 'Eight birds that I fancy . . . and I don't mean shag . . . that would be nearer fifty . . . and seven are partnered up and one thinks she's too young.'

'Yeah, but look at the list of the ones that fancy you,' I offered trying to cheer him up.

'Doesn't matter a fuck does it? No chemistry...you can't operate without a connection can you? No spark equals no future. Some of these women are just looking for anyone . . . someone to fill the armchair with . . . a boyfriend . . . a husband . . . and I don't have a problem with that but there has to be chemistry. Listen, I could date 'em all, bed 'em all, but that would be false wouldn't it? What's the point of that? And if you say loadsashags I'll chop yer fucken nads off . . . I don't just want to have soulless sex, not just for the sake of it.'

There'd be women reading this now clapping and cheering at such gallantry, something that they probably thought never existed but Dan is like that and since my real connection with Ava I was in the same boat. I wasn't interested in anyone else, only her, and the girls knew it. But when would we ever get together? If ever? Could I get her to a dance convention? On her own? Away from her bloke? She still lived in domestic purgatory and she wouldn't ever leave. Could I engineer time for us somehow? Would she be willing? What about her sidekick? Could I get her on her own? When was I ever going to see her? Relaxed? At ease? Comfortable? Would it ever happen or should I just bite the bullet, suffer the broken heart and move on?

On that happy note I went to get us both some Valium.

FIFTY-TWO

I was surfing the Net, the dating sites and I came across a girl I know, another dancer, Barbara Finn. Nothing unusual in that I can hear you say and you'd be right but this bird has got a bloke, I'm sure of it. Surely she wasn't on there looking for someone else whilst still dating someone? This would be crude and Machiavellian in the extreme. I know that some people forget to cancel subscriptions and leave their profiles for all and sundry to see but chasing new partners whilst still with someone in such a brazen fashion? Extraordinary.

Her profile was deep and complex, her hobbies many, honing in on spirituality and how the bloke of her choice would have to love her horse too. Jesus, how do you compete with a horse? What was really funny though was that she lied, no, not about her age, but she said that she was a light drinker. Light drinker! Well, what a load of bollocks that is. Whenever I see her out we have a competition to see who can get the most 'wankered'. Technical term that. She also omitted the fact that she was famous in a casual way.

The next time I saw her she was with Dan in a bar and when he'd nipped off to the loo I broached the subject in a subtle manner.

'I thought you and Gerry were an item?'

'We are . . . tricky patch.'

'Website?'

'Bit of a laugh.'

'Since when have you been a light drinker then?' I said.

'Okay, I'll change it to...except when I'm out on the lash with my pisshead mates.'

She's all charm.

When Dan returned, relieved and cheery from the night, we talked about dating, girls and chat up lines. There is a popular misconception about chat up lines, that is, that there are those that work and those that don't. This isn't strictly true. I read that Neil Strauss in the book 'The Game' used card tricks, magic, hypothetical questions to break the ice. These are fine when you are talking to dimwits but a bird knows when she is being hit on and most don't want it and they don't value it when it happens at one in the morning just because a guy is feeling horny, lonely or both. I've said before that most women want to talk to men, to be valued as a person not just a sex object and they crave contact with sober men not the desperate and the pissed.

I once chatted to two girls outside a pub. They'd been singing, choir practice, and there was a quiz on in the pub, one with a picture round, so to break the ice I asked them to help. A genuine, sober approach, a ruse really, and we hit it off very well. As is, one was married and one wasn't my type, not the married one, but the approach worked.

Neil Strauss taught people how to pick up girls and one opener was what he called the ex-girlfriend question, about jealousy and honesty and 'could I have your opinion?' Well, most girls have thoughts on exes and they feel valued when asked what they feel so it is obvious that this approach would work. But is it any better than saying, 'Hi, are you having fun?' Or 'Hello, you enjoying yourself?'

There is a chat up line that psychologists voted the best ever.

'Hi ladies, my mate just gave me £20 to get you a drink, so what are you having? Time to fill your boots.'

This is all about disassociation. The guy offering the money isn't there so the fella talking to the girls won't be the rejected party; his mate will. The girls have no pressure to judge their benefactor. And they get a free beer. Win, win, win.

The lines that women cringe at are normally the lines that men cringe at:

'Will the keys to my Merc fit into your handbag?' Thanks for that one Dazzler and no, she wouldn't have been interested had you been driving a Citroen 2CV.

'I bet you were a stunner when you were younger.' Dan.

'You don't sweat much for a fat lass.' Mike Harding c1978.

'Just think how good you'd be if you lost a couple of stones.' Chris Scire.

I'd first met Barbara by chance at a party that I'd been invited to by my pal Charles. I hadn't got a clue who was going to be there, what the party was for or what the address was but I got a cab to the street and followed the music. Inside there was booze aplenty, butlers in the buff – blokes acting as waiters wearing nothing but a pinny, not a pretty sight – and loads of girls in party frocks. Is there anything nicer than birds frocked up? I felt like I'd gone to heaven especially when the music started; I could dance with anyone and everyone.

Charles, keen to see me showcase my skills, introduced me to a number of girls and I led most through a dance, they clearly hadn't done much more than handbag-disco stuff, and then I was grabbed from behind by this brunette who claimed to be a Salsa dancer. She was and that was Barbara Finn.

We danced well, pissed and flirty, up close and dirty, and then, as happens with Salsa, most of the time, we just pecked each other's cheek and disappeared into oblivion, well me to Charles' where I fell asleep with my head on his kitchen table. One of my proud moments. Barbara now uses that story as part of her repertoire.

'I met Charles the other night and said that I'd been dancing with you . . . who . . . the bloke who fell asleep on your kitchen table . . . oh, him.'

FIFTY-THREE

'So, are you always on the pull?' asked Jan, she and Christine were having a drink before a Salsa gig. I'd surprised them by buying a bottle of Chardonnay and approaching their table with three glasses. I poured.

'Jeeze, is that what it looks like?' I asked.

'Obviously.' They both smiled, one a thirty something, the other a generation older, related, possibly, friends, yes.

'No . . . not really . . .' I defended slightly thinking that I was always assessing the possibilities and who was available, but not pulling, not all the time trying to get into the knickers of the next chick I talk to. 'I do like women though . . . 'nother glass of wine? But just because you're looking doesn't mean that you're pulling does it? I watch women all the time, how they hold themselves, what they wear, their mannerisms, if there are signs that they are happy, single, married, whatever . . . it's better than watching blokes . . . supermarkets are good . . . especially the girls who buy Listerine, a small bottle for her handbag . . . sorry, that's a bit rude . . . but you can tell a lot about a girl from what she puts in her shopping trolley . . . if she has pets . . . if she's a veggie . . . if she's an alki . . . the family girls. There was one girl who bought one of everything . . . one apple, carrot, bread bun, sausage, pie, yoghurt, orange juice and the guy at the checkout said, "you're single aren't you?" "Yes," she replied, "how do you know?" "Because you're fucking ugly."'

Jan and Christine burst out laughing shocked by the sheer rudeness but loving it in an illicit sort of way. After ten minutes I took a glass of wine, left them the bottle and I went into the pally with only one thing on my mind.

Throughout the course of the night I danced with ten or eleven girls, good ones, bad ones, young ones, old ones, slow music, fast music but my heart wasn't really in it. I mean, I was okay, and I did my usual stuff, dancing rather than showing off, the two facets often confused and misunderstood, but I needed a lift for the night and it came when Ava entered the room, beautiful, her face made up just so, hair cut short like the mane of a lioness. I gulped inwards, my physiology totally changed without warning, butterflies attacking my stomach, knees weak, atremble, fingers jittery, akin to the vertigo I get at heights, looking down . . .

We danced and it was like driving a Rolls Royce with power steering and I told her so, Ava proud to take the compliment. God, she felt good. The DJ played a Bachata, the dance from the Dominican Republic, the dance that is almost dry humping, legitimate, grinding, acceptable, legs entwined. Given that I will never be able to take this girl out to dinner or to lay there chatting after a gruelling fuck fest this was a pretty good alternative.

We did a move that I think is technically called a fallaway in ballroom terminology but this was a move drawn from the beaches, fuelled by rum, sun, sex and sand, not from any formal textbook. The girl's legs are straddled over the guy's right thigh, she takes her weight on both and she drops backwards, rolling around, right to left, the guy pulling her closer to his knee to aid her balance, her groin taking the full thrust of his leg, her pubic bone masturbated, no hands required. The girl can feign orgasm, throw her head back as if in mid-throes, she might not be faking, but there is little wonder that this move is popular with the ladies. I did it with Ava, her hair cascading, eyes closed, revelling in the moment, passion, absorbed, absorbing.

When I watch people do this move I am normally thinking something totally different than everyone else. I am watching the guy's technique, how much he bends his legs, what he does with his arms, how much he thrusts his hips, not something that men are taught to do very often. And I watch the girl and wonder where her head is, what she wants from the move, the dance, if it is just a dance, an escape, a fantasy.

Others watching, beginners, the staid, the English, well you're not sure if they are shocked, jealous or envious. I did a vox pop with the following results:

- That is beautiful dancing
- That's a bit raunchy
- They're dancing a bit close
- I wish I could do that
- What the fuck is going on there?
- Is he grinding upwards with his thigh?
- Is she pushing down onto his thigh?
- Do they know each other?
- Does he fancy her?

- Does she fancy him?

- Are they shagging?

Let me take you back a few decades to youth, fluorescent lights and tentative teenagers. When you saw a couple getting it on at a disco during the last dance and when you were on your own you had that empty feeling and you just wished you were the one on the floor snogging the face off some sultry beauty. I think that's what most people think when they see this dance and this particular move. I'm sure that word will filter back to Ava's bloke.

Later, over a beer, we discussed the pros and cons of a local teacher with a bit of a reputation as a Lothario.

'He was okay,' said Ava, 'but I don't like beards.'

It was then that I stroked my beautifully shaved chin, stared right into her eyes and said, 'that's good then.'

She pissed herself. Maybe this does have some miles after all?

FIFTY-FOUR

Every three months or so the class timetable changes in one particular dance school and what this means is that there is a fresh influx of new talent, or new girls, more's the point. The bored housewives, the divorcees and the single girls decide that dancing is for them and that maybe they'll get a pull from the clientele of men, newcomers too, and experienced stagers like me, Dan, Billy Not Available, and Frankie the Lawyer.

Frankie isn't around all the time because in his search for his 'true love', as he calls it, or 'any bird that can tolerate him and his fixation with anal sex', as we call it, he pulls, tries the girl out, and he so desperately wants it to work, and invariably it doesn't, so he's only about for one reason. Him and his latest squeeze have come to an impasse and he is on the prowl again. It is all very cyclic. When he is dating he devotes himself to the cause, he lives in isolation with his new catch, occasionally trophies her at dances and then, when it goes tits up he hibernates for a few weeks, licks his wounds and then comes out fighting again.

Girls don't understand men very well and some don't even try. It is true that many men are 'sexual automata' as described by Leonardo da Vinci, that is that they have no control of their cocks and what they do with them (some men do, I was faithful for seventeen years), but here's the crunch, men have feelings and men get hurt just like women do; men die from broken hearts too.

I know, tough one for women to get. Men hurt. Look at me and Ava. The lack of success there rips my stomach to pieces. 'I'm crying inside and nobody knows it but me,' said The Tony Rich Project (1996). That's the truth and now everyone who reads this knows. Frankie is the same. We can all take a bit of rejection, a girl who won't dance with you, won't date you, won't kiss you, because you can always find one that will, but men do get emotionally involved. They want someone who wants them; we all want to be loved.

The reason I mention this is that men rarely admit to this process. Okay, some men stay married for forty years and are very happy. But what happens when she decides that she 'doesn't love him anymore', when she finds someone else 'more sexy', when a girl becomes an ex because she has chosen some else instead of you? Of course, it might be the bloke's fault – inattentiveness, takes her for granted, no romance, selfish, etc - but the rejection cuts men to pieces. Yes, another partner may be around the corner but feeling discarded, de-selected, ashamed and fearful are difficult emotions to stomach.

Some men find de-selection really hard to take. Did you know that 13% of all homicides committed in this country are by jealous, jilted or rejected husbands, killing the wife? Statistically women initiate most separations and divorces. For the sake of their safety, keeping the issue away from 'I've found someone else' might be a lesson to be heeded.

FIFTY-FIVE

There's one girl I know who has lived in a crap relationship of convenience for six years and the reason, even when she had nothing in common with the bloke, and even when she didn't really like him, was that she was scared of the upheaval, the financial split and the house move. Nothing else. She just didn't want the hassle; in fact she was engulfed with fear as a result. Surely being alone would offer freedom? Spiritual enlightenment? Sanctity? Value? To me this is a really sad compromise and a waste of her life, let alone his, both living a lie, both bored but tolerant, her faithful and dutiful, him adulterous and flagrant. Surely she is worth more than that? The only person who can tell her . . . is herself.

Another recently separated girl on the scene doesn't want another relationship 'ever' because so many have failed. 'I'm no good at relationships,' she confided. 'They never work, and the only common denominator is me.'

That was true. It wasn't her though, I counselled, more her choice of partner, and never having the conversation about what they wanted from the relationship in the first place and if they both sang from the same song sheet. I'm sorry to say that this conversation rarely takes place because people are scared that their dreams don't meet. And what then?

Of course there are moments at the end of a relationship when negativity sets in; I was angry for years after my split and I wasn't ready for a full on relationship but had I met someone who I fell in love with on the steps of the Family Law Court I would have embraced the union head on. My friend Chrissie did this. I saw her on a date in a pub. He moved in the next morning. 'Life is too short not to be loved,' she said. 'And it's too long too . . . to live in a shit relationship . . .'

Chrissie put a lot into perspective; she laid the cards firmly on the table.

'Look,' she said, as I got comfortable and listened, a great trait to have, knowing when to listen. 'Look, I am a divorcee, I am single, I work, the bills get paid and there's little mortgage and I do okay. The kids are at university so I decided it was time to wander the prairie looking for a companion, a friend or a lover, whichever happened to be around. I took up dancing, met some nice people and then there was one guy who stood out for me, same age, good looking and friendly, he made me laugh, and in seconds I knew that I fancied him and that he fancied me and so we started dating.

And do you know what he does to me? He makes me feel fanfuckingtastic, that's what he does and that's why we live together. He cooks, washes up without asking, he hoovers, polishes, irons, cleans the bathroom, leaves the seat down, he makes me a cup of tea every morning, if he has to leave early for work he puts his clothes for the next day in the spare room so he doesn't bother me, he buys me little gifts, opens doors for me, holds my hand, cuddles me, kisses me in public, he's gentle, he's there for me, he is selfless and he's a damn good shag. What more could a girl want?'

I said that he sounded 'perfect' and that he sounded just like me. She laughed her head off.

When people are devoted to each other, when they can meet each other's needs, emotionally, mentally, physically, sexually, financially, then it's a great place to be and even if Miss World or Mr World happened on the scene neither would get a look in. If the question of 'can I sleep with your wife for a million pounds?' came up as it did in Indecent Proposal (1993), Robert Redford, it would be laughed out of town.

When I left Chrissie I felt warmed and hopeful, because it seemed that her relationship was made of strong stuff and she was wise; she knew that the gloss would wear off eventually, between one or two years the psychologists say is the average (I know of longer), but she knew that they had enough in common, the same core values, the same song sheet, for things to work.

This happened to me. I was in lust. Physical lust. There was intensity, a real discovery of passion and sex, but once that faded, there was nothing left. I tried and tried and tried to find commonality but there was none and we had alternative views on love too, that is how to. Some people don't know how to love, people like to be loved differently and who knows how to make a relationship endure positively? There are no classes at school on it, Jeeze, there ought to be, there are no studies on selflessness, so no one knows what to do if there is a disagreement, if someone loses their temper, or if someone breaks the unwritten laws of trust, deceit, respect and fidelity. My ex and I had different visions. In my world people are a team and devoted to each other. Trust is never broken. Intimate knowledge isn't used as a breaker or as leverage. Remembering this spineless human behaviour makes me angry, even now. How the hell could she? Not my wife! But she did. A breach of trust; undermining me and us. You could call it a breach too far, boom fucking boom. I wanted a decluttered life without violence, with vocation. I didn't want idleness and forced happiness, so I walked away. No one else involved. But she didn't take the rejection lightly and still there are tantrums and bile. Good move on my part I'd say.

The issue of trust is so vital in a relationship that if one party abuses it it can cause total mayhem. I had a conversation with Ava last week and I made a mistake of lying to her. Just once. A white lie but a lie nonetheless and so I made it my priority to right the wrong and I made the bold statement that 'I would never lie to her again...ever.' She means that much to me.

It was a bold move but in terms of ingratiating myself into her heart I felt it necessary. Of course there are difficult questions to be fielded and there are ways of answering them without lying and without hurting the person asking, but being totally true really works. As I've said before, negative truth can be destructive so I try and keep that to myself, but positive truth can be the complete opposite.

'I love the way you look at me like that, that I'm going to be eaten for breakfast.'

'I love that top.'

'You have a great midriff . . . I could eat my dinner off that.'

'You have learnt so much in such a short time.'

'What a talent you are.'

'Your hair looks terrific; it feels great too, especially on my body.'

'You handled that situation perfectly.'

'Do you always cook food this good? I would marry the woman who cooked this.'

'You taste so nice when we kiss.'

To me these honest truths can only have a positive impact. Of course they are compliments but imagine the impact of the opposites?

'You're ugly, shop at Matalan, you're too fat, you're thick, talentless, need a haircut, have the social skills of a pea, you're a shit cook and you kiss like a camel.'

FIFTY-SIX

The new classes are always a great study in social skills, in social awareness. Everyone has to start somewhere and going to a dance class, especially alone, can be quite daunting, but if this process is followed it's a breeze. Here goes: have a shower, dress appropriately, have an open mind and mind your Ps and Qs. That's the first bit. The second? Be slightly bolder than usual (51/49), walk towards people when the teacher says 'find a partner', find out her/his name, smile and try your best without worrying; it is a peerless, non-judgemental society. And finally? If you are a bloke and mess up the female teacher will give you some personal tuition. Me, Dan and Billy used to go wrong on purpose when we first started. I know now that some of the women did this too, to get the personal tuition of the male teacher, obliged to educate, even when these girls weren't exactly rejects from a page three calendar. Poor lamb.

Not everyone can handle the 'find a partner' bit, the socially shy hanging back hoping that someone will make the move for them but it is highly entertaining to watch men dodging women they don't want to dance with and vice versa. At a class once I found a Chinese girl that I swear couldn't walk let alone dance and I vowed to never dance with her again. As luck would have it the following week the class was done in a circle and after a few steps the ladies were asked to move on to the person on their left. Sure as eggs are eggs I got lumbered with Hong Kong Phooey again. Dang!

This circular approach to dance teaching is common and it forces the issue of who dances with who, albeit for short periods of time, so guys get to dance with all the girls and vice versa. This gives you almost as much time to assess the girl as you would if you were speed dating and this way you also get to touch them legitimately albeit, again, in a dance hold. Girls benefit too, getting used to different leads, the strong and the weak, getting to know which men can dance and which can't, who's wearing Yves St Laurent and who's sporting eau de Toilet Duck or none at all.

At dance conventions this format is even better at breaking the ice. In the middle of one class a girl came around to me; she was wearing jeans on top of a leotard (the same bloke invented the trapeze) and the room was freezing, the air con set at sixteen degrees. Me though, I was warm, nay hot, and as I pulled her to my side she positively nestled into me.

'You are lovely and warm,' she said, 'I'm staying here for a bit.'

'Be my guest,' I replied hugging her.

Ah, the big convention...it rapidly approaches, its unique nature, the great attitudes, the party spirit and the girls, where people make life friends, where people let go of their inhibitions, where some people forget their marital status, where everyone's dancing improves just out of sheer repetition and occasion.

Me, Dan and Billy normally chalet together, sometimes Frankie joins in if he's in the country, and the arrival is like a military campaign: queue for keys, get spares, unpack, meticulous, wardrobe and draw space allocated, supplies put away in cupboards and the fridge, jobs agreed, Dan to cook, me to wash up, Billy to clean and do the bins. Dan sets up the music hiding Billy's classical shit, I crack the beers, wine, crisps and nuts, electric cards are stored for all to know so there's no blackout, and then we lock the door for a few hours to keep people out, do not disturb, to plan the weekend, to unleash some of the stagnant energy in our bodies. Jokes are ribald, opinions strong, our group peerless, we sing, we dance, we plot, high as kites, the power of expectation, we take the piss and slag off the world daring to be racist, sexist, ageist and ist anything. The unwinding and release is vital for the success of the weekend; it's a great set up process, it's really a bloke thing and do you know what, it's top fucking dollar.

What we have discovered, the more events that we go to, is that there will always be something that happens that makes the trip special and that really does heighten anticipation. It's not that we know there are certs, that we're bound to shag, because if you have that mentality you can guarantee that you'll end up on your own. But we know that the girls want company, that you'll always meet someone nice, someone you've never met before, and that the people that you do know are in a different zone and they are ready to party. The chances are too that you'll see some old faces — Ali and Sharon maybe — or girls from other events and there will be new people from your own city, ones you've never been introduced to before, seen from a distance and before you know it you have a new dance partner or a potential lover or even a bunk up for the night.

Unless you are chasing one specific girl the real skill is to just take each class and each event as it comes, to play what is in front of you, eyes up living, and then, when the time comes, to then make the right decision at the right time. I made a mistake at a convention once. Me and a girl were walking to a BBQ, hand in hand, and when we got to the barbie we ate, drank, danced, messed about and she ended up with her hands up the back of my shirt fondling my bare skin, pulling me close to her as we danced. The mistake was not to follow this through privately. No kiss, nothing, just a mutual understanding of affection. Maybe one day, if the timing is right, if we are both single and in the same city or at the same event. Maybe one day.

You can never second-guess these events; you don't know who'll come on to you or what will happen, best just to keep an open mind.

At one event Billy decided to take a Jacuzzi and a couple of girls joined him. As they relaxed in their bikinis, not Billy, obviously, and bubbles Dan and Frankie acted as waiters, tea towel over the left arm, and served wine for the ladies and beer for Billy. The ladies, delighted at the playfulness, then allowed a fifteen-minute neck and shoulder massage from Dan and Frankie. Totally off the cuff and it set a great tone for the weekend.

FIFTY-SEVEN

I wonder if you can remember life before the Internet, when computers were for geeks, the typewriter was the novelist's superior tool to the pen and the pad and when the only chance you got of seeing pornography was slipping a quick look at Mayfair or Penthouse off the top shelf at the local newsagent? On screen sex was all about suggestion and imagination. Dustin Hoffman in The Graduate was all about what went on behind closed doors with the light out. There were some scenes of nudity but most overt sex was covered up, regulated and restricted.

And then some clever bloke invented the video and films, real movies, became available to households that previously had to rely on three TV channels. Suddenly arguments ceased – 'Record It!' 'Watch it in the other room!' – and the big screen became so accessible that films became a prime form of home entertainment. And then another clever bloke decided to take advantage of this boom and introduced pornography to a willing nation. Every video shop had an 'under the counter' service for 'blueys' and the once restrained approach to sex disappeared. Every house had its stash of sex tapes, some kept by frustrated teenagers, some not hidden at all and some stashed by parents who couldn't wait for the kids to go to sleep or go away on a field trip leaving them at ease with their films and whatever happened next.

And then the Internet happened.

And now you can access anything you want at the click of a mouse. There are thousands of sites, subscription and free, for films, sexy chat and the chance to meet someone to fuck in your city. There is even one called ShagHappy.com. And in terms of sexual proclivity you can take your pick from whatever you want, any fetish, any kick, and I should add a rider here, as long as it is legal. Access to illegal material is easy too; the problem with that though is that you'll end up in prison and on the sex offenders' list for the rest of your life. So don't.

It's like using a mobile phone. Only when it is safe and legal to do so.

The ease of access is however a double-edged sword; great for adults over the age of consent but not so great when an eight-year-old can type sex into Google and see what happens. And you also have to be very wary of the gremlins that people try and infiltrate into your computer from their end; viruses are common, so too the attempts to steal identities and bank details.

But, for most adults, it is a great source of education, fun and frivolity. In the right hands, pornography is cool.

One of the lads sent me a video on email. In it a male monkey, balanced in a tree, is licking the genitalia of a female monkey, and then he gives her one from behind. After the first couple of thrusts another monkey, perhaps his son or brother, creeps up behind them, tweaks his dad's nads with his hand and then fucks off giggling, dad, not impressed, gives chase. Coitus interruptus in the primate world.

It was funny in a bizarre sort of way though I'm not really into watching other species of the planet copulating and when it comes to fetishes with animals, no thank you. But more and more in recent days I have noticed family pets on home movies. Let me paint a picture. Janet and John are going at it in a big way in the lounge or the bedroom and in walks Rover. You can see where this is going can't you and you're praying that that the dog doesn't go over and do what the monkey did . . .

There was a court case in Gloucester recently where a bloke was convicted of shagging his ex-girlfriend's family dog, a bull mastiff called Sasha. At least it was a girl. 'I was naked and slipped,' he said in court. 'I was just going to the bathroom.'

This was a man with three kids who escaped jail but who got a community order and his name on the sex offenders list as well as a four year restraining order keeping him away from his ex. The clinical proof came from an 'intimate' DNA sample.

In another clip I saw a girl is busy satisfying her bloke in the master bedroom. I say satisfying. She was licking his arse and whilst she is at it she enters a finger in search of the male g-spot . . . (as previously mentioned, if a girl likes anal sex why shouldn't a guy?) . . . all good visuals and then . . . along comes Rover. He wanders about a bit and then hops on the bed where he is presumably used to resting. Thankfully the nightmare scenario is averted as the bloke, momentarily diverted from his devoted searcher, leans over, picks the dog up and throws the little fucker off the bed. Hilarious. Thankfully.

FIFTY-EIGHT

Behind Dan's charm and smile he can be judgemental and frustrated when it comes to some dance classes. He says that he doesn't judge the girls anymore, he just dances with them, but he gets tetchy now when he sees people brandishing video phones to record the teacher going through the routine at the start of the class.

'Look at the fucking state of them,' he chided to Billy and me behind the back of his hand. 'Sad fuckers. There used to be a time when you did the routine and fucked off home to scribble it on a pad. Not any more. It's like a press conference at Old Trafford. And of course Tom (the teacher) is lapping it up like he's a fucking Hollywood superstar. Best get a chair. Wake me when they've stopped fucking about.'

Later, after his first pint though Dan's edge had gone, released with the dance endorphins. He told us about Loopy, one of the lads who lives up north who had taken the Internet route to pulling and the story is a lesson to men and to women. Loopy was a multi-shagger, that is having more than one bird on the go at the same time, girls out of town, girls in different towns, and happy as he was with his cache he always wanted more and he'd been targeting a tall single mum called Rachel for a couple of years. You know the stuff, a chat at a party, a hello in a pub, a nod walking down the street and after a patient and deliberate campaign (sometimes this takes years) she had agreed to go out on a date.

But Loopy, slick but naïve, left his mobile phone in the house whilst he nipped off to the shops, leaving his regular squeeze asleep on the sofa. In his absence the phone rang, it beeped messages waking her and true to form she scrolled through and read the text from Rachel.

Hell hath no fury like a woman scorned and his multi-pronged approach, going plural as Allan Leighton, Royal Mail and Asda, might put it, was exposed in a big way. Oh, to have more than one cock! On the phone there were other messages, photos, clear evidence. His squeeze rang Rachel.

Loopy, oblivious, to his outing and to the sting to come, went out with Rachel and after half an hour she asked him about his girlfriend. The date soon ended and Loopy went back to field World War Three. Sometimes it is not just the actions that are the problem more the duplicitous deceit. The harem was destroyed, silently he vowed to create another, but he and his girlfriend remained together.

I suppose the thing that cheered us all was the 'but for the grace of God go I' feeling and the thought of the look on Loopy's face when Rachel confronted him and then the row with his girlfriend. Hilarious.

Here's a statistic for you. Did you know that a recent study showed that in 708 of 849 human societies that polygyny was acceptable, that is men having more than one partner? Not ours though where the rules, even broken, are to have one sexual partner at a time, a few or lots over the course of a lifetime.

Another survey said that 75% of single men would have immediate sex with a total stranger. No women said that they would.

Now I know that a one-night stand would incorporate both sexes, and technically that could be deemed as immediate sex with a stranger but if that survey is to be believed then you can see the difference in the dynamics when it comes to pulling. Wired differently would be an understatement.

But once the barriers are removed and the stranger becomes familiar and friendly then things take a different turn. Loopy had preyed, I think that is a pretty accurate word, ladies beware of this approach, on the girls labelled with the following acronym: SINBAD Single Income No Boyfriend And Desperate. Of course he didn't know if he was going to be greeted by a mass murderer, a lentil loving tree hugger or a Bunny Boiler.

Or by someone slightly smarter than him.

FIFTY-NINE

In the press recently there have been two reports, one that made me laugh and one that was cringe worthy given that it centred on a man in the public eye.

The first was about a girl (37) in the south who, during the day worked for the Social and who, during the nights, administered beatings and torture for £100 an hour at her sex dungeon. Her bosses have found out and she's on garden leave.

The second accounted the story of the head of an international sporting body who went to a sex party hosted by five prozzies, dominatrices, two in Nazi uniforms, and there is a video clip showing him spread naked over a chair taking a beating to his bare arse. He denied it. Must have been his twin then?

The reason I mention it is not to condemn or to judge - why wouldn't the girl want to make £100 an hour? – but just to report that this sort of thing goes on far more regularly than 'normal' people would expect. The sporting head might not survive in terms of employment even though it's not illegal to want to have your arse smacked.

Personally, it's not my thing, but when you are dating and looking for that potential love partner you never know what you're going to come up against or what sexual proclivities either partner will have. But what is more, it is vital for the success of the relationship for people to know what these bed tastes are.

If you, as a woman, knew that your future partner/husband fantasised about getting dressed up in your clothes would you even order that prawn cocktail at that first dinner? If you knew that he craved to be dressed as a baby in an adult sized nappy, would you have replied to that text message? If you knew that he wanted to be beaten or have his cock squeezed in a vice would you have thought twice about the offer of a G&T?

The problem that all new couples face is that until you're there and in situ you might not find out until it's too late. That said it sometimes takes months or years for people to be brave enough to own up to their partner what they really like.

So what is the remedy?

I was talking to a girl once on the phone. It was tennish and we started talking about a date we had scheduled for the following Friday; she was coming over for dinner and she was going to stay the night for the first time. I'd been to hers and we'd kissed and groped and removed some clothes but there had been no full sex or orgasm from either side. I knew this girl was in bed and I knew that once we started talking about sex that she was playing with herself and at one stage she told me that she was licking her fingers. Sexy as fuck! She went into detail about what she was doing with her hands. This boded well for the Friday and I, unembarrassed, stated that I loved oral sex and that I loved a girl who wasn't scared of what happens during sex. So when I mentioned this to the girl on the phone and how it wasn't uncommon to come in a girl's mouth she thoughtfully said, 'I've never done that. Maybe we'll try it on Friday?'

My reaction, having sown the seed, was 'great, I can't wait for Friday'. But then I also deduced a few things about my potential lover; she wasn't very sexually experienced and she hadn't had many sex partners. Not a problem per se but it changed my approach to the date, a date that by chance didn't happen as planned when childcare got in the way. What a kick in the nads that was! A promise disappearing like blood from a rock hard cock.

The point, I guess, is that we had been bold enough to talk about it in a general, easygoing way, no judgements and no forcing of issues, as if we were discussing anything. Getting to this level of honesty and intimacy is amazingly difficult for most people who want sex that is anything other than 'normal'. There are some people I'm sure who think that sex is a fumble and a five-minute party. Others abhor the thought of oral sex. Some men think a one-minute shag after ten pints is heaven. Women don't. On the other hand how does a guy respond if the girl says, 'you can fuck my arse now'? Do you just get on with it? How do you refuse? Maybe the answer is to explore sexuality together?

Of course, if you are on a date, on holiday with someone, or if you live together both parties can pick up on what turns the other on. If he sees a bag of vibrators and porn DVDs on the kitchen table then he'd have an idea about her sex drive and stimulative approach. If she listens to his comments about sex he's seen on the telly or read about in the paper then she too can gauge his interest. Take the whipping story from earlier. 'I bet you'd love that,' she might say, testing, to which he might respond, 'not on yer ferkin nelly.' In that way ground rules are established but this is incredibly long-winded.

Imagine a guy discussing the normal threesome fantasy with a potential partner. For most guys it is a fantasy nothing more and they could live without it, they could die satisfied at it never having happened. But it's worth asking the question even if the answer is 'I'm definitely not into girls' or 'I'm definitely not bi-curious'. For girls who lick their own fingers during masturbation this almost seems a contradiction in terms.

Reports say that 90% of men have a secret fantasy that they never tell anyone because of the embarrassment. It might be wanting sex outdoors, or in public, or it might involve water sports (I just don't get that one), it might be a certain material, rubber for instance, or it might be he wants to be dominated, or even to be 'raped' in a role play situation. Whatever it is, unless you talk about it it will never happen and it may be a barrier to a fully fruitful relationship. As I said, sometimes this takes an age, to have the courage, but the protective layers can be peeled back one at time rather than a great revelation on the first date.

Let me give you another quick example. If you are dating and there is no opportunity for sex because there are kids or parents in the way what do you do? Do you have sex in a car? Not very comfortable and unfulfilling. Or on a bus? In a public toilet? In a wood? On top of a mountain? Or do you just hire a hotel room for the afternoon? If one party wants to do this, fuck in a wood, and the other doesn't, then you're bollocksed aren't you?

SIXTY

'I got arrested at the weekend,' I said as Ava came into the studio for a private lesson, just me and her, yeefuckinghaw.

'Oh!' she was shocked.

'It was because I was impersonating George Clooney.'

'And that got you arrested?'

'Yeah, I was dressed as a doctor, stethoscope, white jacket, the full works . . . they just didn't see the fun in it down at A & E.'

She giggled.

Dancing with this girl and teaching her is as torturous as it is pleasurable. She learns quickly, she likes the physical nature of the dance and there is a real chemistry between us. Anyone can see it. To be honest Stevie fucking Wonder could see it but it is so hard to hold back, so difficult to restrain myself from taking her right there and then, but I have always stopped myself.

It's funny that one; I wonder how many women would just go for it if a bloke kissed her behind closed doors? If it was just a part of the dance? Almost. It only happened once, with Ali at the convention, and the rebuke came quickly but these situations are extremely intense and personal and sometimes a kiss is just a natural evolution of what has already happened.

In the bar I carried on my comedy approach.

'Ava, pick a card...'

I had designed four packs, all with the same line on, not that she would know that. She picked her card.

'What does it say?'

'Will you sleep with me?'

'Thought you'd never ask.'

'No, cheeky, that's what it says.'

'You'd better pick a card from the "yes" and "no" pile.' She did. It came out "no". 'Take another card,' I suggested undeterred and she did. 'What does that one say?'

'If you had a week to live would I sleep with you?'

'Of course.'

'No cheeky, that's what it says.' This time she drew a "yes" card and she was embarrassed to show it but did after a little blush. Really quaint. Hidden desire or what?

'There's one last pile to pick from.' I offered and she took. 'What does this one say?'

She crumpled into a fit of laughter, holding her stomach, tears pouring from her eyes. The card? It said: Can we pretend?

'You are quite a funny guy aren't you?' she said eventually.

'Not everyone's this funny,' I said. 'It's taken me thirty years to get this good.'

'Oh,' she said, 'bit to do yet then.' This time it was my turn to burst out laughing.

When I spoke to her later, calmer, I said that if she ever fancied a coffee or a walk in the park then all she had to do was to call me. Of course, she was busy, she had to work, to be a domestic goddess, a mother and a partner, but amidst everything I knew that she wasn't happy, that her life lulled, it was fuelled with dullness, anonymity, a plateau so low, and somewhere in her head she was trying to work out if she deserved more, if the stagnation was the best that it could be.

I gave her my number, I didn't get hers, probably just as well, and I told her where I lived. In her mind I could see her working it out, from where she lived, or where she worked, how long was it, in miles, in minutes. I was sowing a seed; I sensed this would be a long game rather than a short one but I checked for rejection. All she had to do was to say 'no', but she never did. All the signs were positive, there were the smallest of signs in her body language that said she was comfortable with my presence, her gestures were encouraging, there were looks in our eyes, we both really wanted to devour each other.

SIXTY-ONE

I have never been a great one at containing jealousy. Not that I get all antsy for people to see, but inside me I hate it, I hate it when I see someone with someone I want to be with, holding her or touching her. If I'm with the girl I get a bit defensive, put an arm round in a protective 'she's mine' statement, something that not all girls appreciate. When I see someone hit on my girl, something that has happened in my lounge at home, I control the physical rage but not the feeling. If I was a tennis player I'd be Borg rather than McEnroe, calm instead of lambasting the line judge, but inside I would be boiling.

This is the same when I see Ava out and when I see her dancing Salsa with the klutz that is her partner or when someone else tries to shake their thang with her and I don't mean ballroom stuff. I fucking hate it so much that I have to look away. You know, as I've said that Salsa is sexy as fuck, sex with your clothes on, and me, as a funky exponent, use that to its fullest extent when I am dancing with Ava. With others I tone down, less hump, fewer hand trails, no thigh to thigh, but with Ava I go the other way and she loves it. The problem is is that she does dance with other blokes and they all have their own style and some like the bump and grind too. I hate watching her with other men. In one way it is quite sick and on the other it is just a dance.

But I know as well as anyone that that is bollocks. Of course it's not just a dance. There's a girl I dance with who is married and she is all for the bump and grind, the groin on thigh rub, and if I were her husband I would be incandescent. He does the decent thing and stays away and never watches her dance. What might scare him a little is not the guy getting his kick but what his wife does. There's the flashing off of her body, provocative smiles, wiggles, body rolls, arse shakes, arse rolls against the guy's thigh and some moves are simulation, the man's hands can get as close as he wants...and is allowed...to her tits, arse, midriff and her crotch. Look, not every guy dares to dance like this, you get to know which partner is up for what, but like I said, this husband does well to stay away.

I spoke to Curly about this, sex on legs she is, and she has had rows with her blokes in the past over this very subject, as has her blonde oppo, Carly. 'If he can't cope with it it's his lookout,' she said with no hint of remorse. 'I dance how I dance. I dance how the dance should be danced, to me it's my thrill and that's it. Get over it.'

She has a point but Jeeze it is so hard. If you don't want to see the result look away now. Carly rarely gets out now she's courting. I reckon that's one of his rules.

Sometimes this stretches to other girls and other dances but here the subject isn't necessarily pure jealousy maybe it's just having some fifty-year-old tosser wanting to dance with the same girl as you, one of your schooled few. There's one bloke, beard, bit of a trier, dresses out of the 70s and there I was chatting to this tall beauty and every time I started to chat with her – we have a natural rapport but she is married – in he steps to join what was essentially a private conversation. There she is, stuck in the middle, loving my patter and flattery and then some twat distracts her. My choice would be to tell him to fuck off but I keep schtum until it's time to dance and I claim my prize whilst he goes off with some other hapless fucker. I know it sounds wrong, but we're all on the savannah and not even I can relent from being an alpha male. Perhaps I should have roared and bit his head off?

Which brings me back to Ava.

At one gig I normally dance with her for half an hour, just her, four, five or six tracks, it's practice, it's schooling, it's me getting my kicks and her getting her rocks off before she has to go back to Alcatraz. Most people in the room know the dynamic...if me and Ava are dancing it's like an exclusion zone, do not disturb, maestro and protégé at work, but this one fucker walked up just as I was showing her a new step. I knew him. Neil.

'Hi, how you doing?'

'Cool.'

'Can I borrow this blonde beauty for a dance?'

'No.' I gave him the filthiest look I have ever given anyone. He was visibly rocked so I recoiled a little. 'Oh, go on then, as it's you. Just one though,' I smiled through gritted teeth. The cheeky cunt. Who said that he could spoil my night?

I saw him a few days later and I went straight up to him when he had finished, my smile more genuine.

'Neil, can I offer you some advice?'

'Don't dance with your bird?'

'I wasn't going to mention it, but now you have, good idea,' I laughed with him but he knew the rules now. 'No, what I was going to say was that when you dance Salsa it's a backwards and forwards motion not up and down.'

'Yeah, I've developed it on purpose not knowing it was wrong . . . thanks . . . message understood.'

I discovered that he was the ex boyfriend of a mutual acquaintance and she regaled me with the story a few days later. I really had put the frighteners on him. She pissed herself.

So there you go, a Jealous Guy, feeling insecure, shivering inside, she might not want me anymore . . . so the song goes. I'm sure girls get jealous too but their take is less animalistic more about disrespect. You have to have respect.

SIXTY-TWO

When I walked into the pally Dan was sitting on his own dressed all in black, a full pint on the table, another half-finished cradled in his giant mitt, the first drinks of the night. The big lug obviously had a thirst.

I went to get one from the bar, fighting my way through an early evening throng and when I returned there were five gorgeous chicks at Dan's table. How did he manage that one? Little Flower Girl, Sparkly, Kate, Becky, Vicky, all dressed to the nines for a mid-week dance. It was great that they'd made the effort in more ways than one. They looked terrific, that was cool, but only two of them danced, so they had sacrificed their usual cocktail bar for a Salsa pally, maybe checking out the talent; there would be plenty at this gig, and it was traditionally one of the booziest venues where things were known to happen.

'Come and join us,' said Dan. 'It's like a scene from a Bond movie . . . do you know the girls?'

'I'm always keen to meet true glamour,' I said sitting on a lone chair, Dan and the girls having commandeered a curved bench backing a wall, him at the epicentre. I wondered if any of these five were on his radar? I doubted it. Three were too young, one was leaving to see the world and the other was just a little wacky and Dan knew that. His targets would be on the dance floor.

'We were just talking about kissing techniques . . . what the girls prefer, you know, soft, hard, open, shut, tongues, teeth, banging noses . . . '

'Don't suppose there's any practice sessions going?' I chipped in.

'No!' they all said in unison. Tra la fucking la.

I remember my first French kiss, a busty blonde rough house of a bird from a neighbouring village when I was about thirteen. She had offered me open or shut and frankly I didn't have a clue what the fuck she was talking about so when she widened her lips I sort of felt short-changed because up till then I had been brought up on the Errol Flynn school of kissing. Closed mouth, intense, perfect for the Hollywood censors. I don't think the world shook for her either. If ever there was a sympathy snog, that was it.

'We were thinking of that Carly Simon song,' Dan said interrupting my reverie. 'Kissing With Confidence . . . you know the one…you may be a smart dresser . . . the spinach on the teeth song . . . unless you can trip it in the kissing stakes it doesn't matter if you dress flash, dance well or are a sharp conversationalist . . . there's no second date.'

Thank fuck for that, I thought. Snappy dresser? Mainly. Razor sharp, empathic talk, yeehaw. Dance? Do me a favour. But instinctively I went back to that kiss with Ava, the very first one, had it been a good one, had I done myself justice, did she enjoy it, did I let myself down?

There are a few things to take into account about the Ava kiss. I kissed her on the mouth, hard, with intent, but I was severely dehydrated and kissing with a dry mouth is not advised. I only held her shoulders. And there were thoughts going through my head. Does she really want to kiss me? Does she want me to open my mouth? Does she like French kissing? It was in public, even though it was late and the car park was dark. Was she conscious about being seen? The CCTV cameras? And what if she recoiled? What if she pulled back embarrassed? It's not just as simple as puckering up. The psychology is more powerful than anything.

Billy walked into the bar to distract my thoughts.

'Dan? You auditioning for a Bond movie?'

I vowed to make sure the next one was perfect, electric.

SIXTY-THREE

Kissing's a funny thing isn't it? I mean proper kissing, the full, I want to fuck your head off type of kissing. Why kissing? Why mouth to mouth? When did we learn that this was the thing to do as part of emotional expression? When did we learn that to open our mouths and to touch someone else's tongue with ours would drive our loins crazy? It's a bizarre business.

Okay, look, most people kiss differently, from the amount of pressure they apply to the width they open their mouths, what they do with their tongue, what works for you and what doesn't, and how often and where to kiss, behind closed doors or in public but what is sure is that if the kissers aren't compatible then they might as well stop before it all starts. Forget sexual proclivities and wanting to talk about how many times you want to fuck and in which position, kissing is the start to everything of what happens next.

Mouths have to be compatible. Sometimes it's hard to kiss someone with thin lips when yours are thick and vice versa. Some girls don't like to use all their tongue; others are delighted to try and lick the ice cream from your tonsils. What I can add is that, given what goes in our mouths, that getting the right taste is vital too. Brush your teeth. Floss. Avoid foods that give off a stench unless you both eat them. Take garlic for one. Fags for another. No thanks. Avoid foods that repeat on you, upper airwave and lower. Girls, go gentle on the lippy and the gloss. And get one that taste's nice. It's amazing what an intoxicating effect a great taste can have.

I'm not sure what happens inside a woman's body when she kisses with passion save for the body getting ready for the next step in the process but in a bloke it is easy to see and feel the impact. The question is, what does the bloke do about it? If he's lucky his hard on will be comfortable; if he's unlucky it will strain at an unfortunate angle in his pants and be torturous. What then? Does the bloke draw the bird against him so that his cock brushes hard against her body leaving her with little doubt the impact she has had on him? Is this best practice on a first date? If sober? Or does the bloke try and remain more distant until he gauges her level of interest? And lest it be remembered girls, an erection is a response to which you are a prime creator and beneficiary, so once it's there don't piss the poor bloke around and send him home for a quick wank. Not only is this too unfulfilling it really is unfair.

I was with a beauty once and one day just before Christmas we had talked for a while in her kitchen and as I was due to leave she pulled me to her and we kissed as if our lives depended on it. There was no mistletoe but there was electricity, a great taste and an immediate response. So, what to do? I backed off a little and then she went to attend a kid in the neighbouring room ('Hey, Junior, here's twenty quid, fuck off to the pictures.') I adjusted my pants just before she returned and we then immediately picked up where we had finished. My erection was still prominent, hard and full on, but I thought fuck it and I pulled her arse forwards so that our crotches met. To my delight she just wiggled, got comfy and she grinded her body against me.

'I guess you know by now,' I said, as we broke for air, my hands still holding her arse, pulling her onto me, 'that I really quite like you?' She pissed herself.

Personally, I love kissing, the intimacy and the closeness. Okay, it's no fun when you have the flu, impetigo or a cold sore, but generally it is one of life's great gifts. It's funny how some things work out. When I was twenty (yesterday) I was due to meet a girl after not seeing her for an age and I had impefuckingtigo, welts and boils and inflammation around the mouth. It was almost as bad as that first tingle of a cold sore and there's no Zovirax to sort it out. Well, smart fucker as I am, I went to the doc's and I got my cream. By sheer fortune – or fate – the impetigo fucked off and I was in for a tongue fest.

I also love what kissing means, not in a teenage 'I'd kiss anything for the experience or the notch on the belt' sort of way, but in the 'I think I could really like you sort of way' and the 'this is the first step to a full frontal fuck' sort of way. Most grown up girls don't just snog as a one-off, not unless it's a nightclub grope and who the fuck goes to nightclubs these days? Most girls snog because in this enlightened age they want affection and sex too. God bless 'em.

SIXTY-FOUR

I'd just danced four records on the trot and my back was turned to the main dance floor. It was time for a breather, a towel off and a drink when someone tapped me on the shoulder and asked me if I wanted to dance. Now this is a tough call. The blind acceptance. Do I? Don't I? If she sees my face when I turn around and react with a 'no' then that's her shot away and I'd have broken one of the golden rules of the Salsa pally. Refusal is not done. When asked 95% of offers are accepted and that is a conservatively low estimate even when you've just danced for fifteen minutes.

I did refuse a girl once, at a beginners' class, when I knew Jack and couldn't move for the life of me. This girl, taking the brave and the courageous steps, the first move, the 'will you', was mortified when I said 'no'. She'd made an effort this chick, done up, nice cut of trousers, pristine blouse, her first dance class, and then some cunt like me says no. What a twat! She walked away, chastised only by rejection.

Seized by a cataclysmic sense of guilt I quickly walked over to her, took both hands, looked her in the eyes and said that I was really sorry, that I would love to dance with her but that I couldn't do a step. She immediately melted, felt right with the world again and now, many years down the line we dance a lot together and are good pals. Before you even think about it, she's married. No.

So I turned around and there was Jenny Glasses, the Nordic beauty who I think thinks I'm a bit of a twat. That said, a good dancer, and a twat, and in demand.

'You never ask me to dance anymore,' she said as we skipped into the middle of the dance floor, the crowd clearing like Moses at the Red Sea – just a picture not an analogy so you can fuck off before you start.

'Sorry, Jenny, every time I look at you you're with some good looking guy . . . I thought that you were all loved up and

stuff so I was giving you a polite berth . . . nothing personal.'
She had been hanging around with a 'dude' with just a tuft of
facial hair under his bottom lip. What is it with some blokes?
Don't they realise that they look fucking stupid?

'No, I'm happily not loved up, thanks.' So we danced.

Dancing with tall girls can be a problem, as it can with
short ones, but the taller girls aren't always as light on their
feet and if their hands are tight and heavy too you might just
as well be Sumo wrestling. It's the same if a girl tries to
second-guess the lead, then it's the guy that has to adjust.
Jenny was a bit cumbersome but fine. I could do with an
hour with her to smooth her up.

During the dance her top kept dropping precariously
low; there was a real danger of her tit dropping out. Why do
birds do this? They know they're going to a dance, an aerobic
event, that there will be body contact and they turn up in
clothes that don't fit, that ride too high, that drop too low,
where there is the chance that body parts will be revealed.
Are birds really that thick? Well, I guess, to be nice, in their

defence, maybe they don't do a dress rehearsal before they go out to play. I do. How flexible is the shirt. Which are the comfy knickers, that sort of thing.

Back to Jenny Glasses and her loose fitting clothes.

'Shall I get you some Superglue? Double-sided Velcro? I knew a girl who had Velcro on her knickers . . .' it just came out. She just giggled. 'So how come you don't wear contact lenses?'

'It's like putting acid in my eyes . . . don't you like my glasses?'

'They hide you . . . I'm not sure that's a good policy.'

After that dance I reckon that Jenny Glasses is back on the definite maybe list.

SIXTY-FIVE

'I do it a lot on my own,' I said in all innocence.

'Do you really?' asked the cute Irish girl with red hair. I know, typical stereotype but there you have it, she was from Ireland and her hair was red.

'Well, sometimes it's good to have a partner,' I added.

'Glad to hear it,' she said and giggled.

Of course, I was talking about dance practice, nothing else. There are some dances that don't lend themselves to going solo but when a routine is structured like the classical ballroom dances you can practice it, turns, drops, tempo and sharpness, it only gets fucked up by adding a bird and music.

Later me, Dan and Billy were having a beer at a bar on The Strip, chewing the fat about the best way to pick up birds when one of the bar girls came over to clear the glasses and wipe the table down. We moved our drinks as she cleaned away.

'You do that beautifully,' Dan said, oozing charm.

'I'm very good at wiping tables,' she said, 'that's all that I am good at.' She smiled and walked away.

'Such low self-esteem,' I said, 'Dan, you'd better ask her out, you might have a chance.'

'Birds go dating just for the free dinner,' Billy said, 'so you really might have a chance Dan.'

The big fella looked at us nonplussed ignoring the jibes and took the centre stage.

'I was on a date once,' he said, 'and the bird asked me why I buttoned my shirt up so far and I told her that it was to hide those ugly little skin growths that come with middle age (skin tags). Couldn't you get a balaclava, she asked, cheeky fucker. There was another . . . I'll get the beers I said, you just make yourself at home. Does that mean I can fart, scratch my arse and pick my nose? Didn't last very long that one. Another time I was smoozing this chick when some twat barged me from behind and the beer spilt in my face and onto my clothes. You can lick the beer off my face I said to her. You lick the fucker off yourself she said. No chance of a knee trembler in the car park there then. Eh, lads, do you know what my best chat up line was? I'm writing a book about all the birds I've been to bed with. Do you want to be in it?'

'Small book is it?' I interjected.

When Dan gets like this it's best just to let him go and enjoy the ride. Between them, he and Billy compete for stage space and getting the laughs. They should do a double act but which one would be the straight man, I don't know.

I always try to read bars; who's there, why, are they happy, what's going on, what the motives are. Some bars offer a good chance to meet people of the same class and religion, the moneyed middle classes trying to come to terms with life, the rat race and the huge mortgage.

In one corner a bloke was chatting up a bird who hid her left hand at every opportunity. It would have been easier for her if she'd taken her wedding ring off.

At the bar a couple were watching as a barman mixed a cocktail and then with a fifteen inch pestle he mashed the contents of the mortar, twisting like he was holding a pepper mill.

'You see his technique love, that's how you should wank me off,' said the guy to his girlfriend.

'I would but your cock's not that big is it?'

Which reminds me of playing golf with my mate Speaky.

'You're holding that putter like you're holding a navvy's dick,' he used to say. Still miss him.

Which also reminds me of the girl having a lesson from the golf pro. She was hitting the ball all over the place, left, right, high and low.

'Look,' said the pro, 'grab the club like you would your old man's dick.' The girl did that and the ball flew two hundred yards down the middle of the fairway.

'Fantastic,' said the pro. 'Now take the club out of your mouth.'

Back in the pub a bloke walked to the bar and ordered a pint. As he got some money from his pocket he put his keys near his arse and then they dropped to the floor.

'Bollocks,' he said to the barman. 'Someone's nicked my back pocket.'

Another bloke walked over to a group of girls to say hello to one that he knew. He was introduced, shaking hands, smiling, cocking his head, coy and charming, all but one girl looking him in the eye. Talk about the ultimate protection.

SIXTY-SIX

Did you know that there are over four million closed circuit TV cameras in this country, erected for security, to spy on the populace, to see if you're parked on double yellows, if you urinate in public or to see if your car is illegal. I'm not sure that they can identify people wearing hoods, caps or burkas.

The reason that I mention the cameras is that there was one right outside the bar we were in and I wracked my brain to try and remember when I had authorised their erection. When had legislation been passed to allow these things? I don't remember it in any manifesto and now the fucking things are all over the place. You can get clocked three hundred times a day in most cities.

But not only have the councils all over the country got in on the act so too have private establishments.

My old college features them heavily, security guards mulling over tapes of young kids pissing up the walls, couples cavorting on the sports pitches, young men sneaking through bedroom windows in the halls of residence, the occasional theft of a bike.

Banks have them too. A mate of mine was on holiday once up North and he picked up this bird. After a load of beer they got fruity on the beach and on the way to meeting some mates they nipped into the bank to get some money from an ATM (automated teller machine not arse-to-mouth) – it was after ten o'clock at night – and she decided to suck him off in the warmth of the little anteroom next to the cash machines. This was all on CCTV too. The stars of the film are now fondly called the 'NatWest Two'.

The reason that I mention these cameras, apart from the soapbox rant relating to the invasion of privacy, was to mention that there is another place where there is a sign that clearly states that for the safety of the patrons you will be filmed. The Golf Club. In the car park. Where I had kissed Ava. And where I kissed her again.

There is something about this girl that I feel will be intrinsically imprinted in my heart for the rest of my life. So I had to see her again and lo and behold when I drove into the car park I checked to see that her car was there, it was, and then I had to hope that she was on her own. She wasn't; she had a girlfriend there. But her bloke was nowhere to be found.

So I went through the usual pretence of being interested in the class, saying hello to the faces that I knew and to those that I didn't and then after half an hour I was delighted to see her girlfriend pick up her bags and skilladdle for the night. And I hadn't even had to give her twenty quid.

The class finished, people free-styled, I danced with Ava, and then, as the clock ticked, she announced her departure. I offered to walk her to her car just in case she was mugged by a gang of field mice and she consented. So without touching we walked out into the night, the car park well lit, and well-camera-ed, both of us tense, sensing what would happen next. The sun had just set but the air was still warm, musty even, t-shirt weather.

As we approached her car we slowed, she beeped it open, placed her shoe bag on the seat and then she turned to me. I didn't take her hands but her shoulders and I pulled her towards me, our lips met, I opened my mouth, she too, and we kissed with abandon, passion and fire. I pulled her even tighter with my right hand as my left pushed the underside of her right breast. She audibly gulped mid-kiss. We broke for air.

'You taste nice,' I said, looking straight into her bright blue eyes.

'You too.'

We kissed again and this time my hands trailed to her buttocks and I pulled her firmly against my hardness. Again she gulped mid-kiss.

'I have to go,' she said.

'A kiss goodnight,' I offered and she didn't refuse, the passions rising, tongues searching, bodies close, hearts beating. I could have taken her there and then.

As she drove off I knew I had fallen for her, that the kiss was on tape, and that I had just broken the rule of snogging someone in a relationship. But, as love knows no bounds, I knew instantly that I wanted her. For her part, what did it mean? A slice of colour in a dull life? Some passion in a tired relationship? A sneaky taste of the forbidden fruit? Or . . . . or . . . did she feel the same for me?

SIXTY-SEVEN

There's a dating website called www.mysinglefriend.com, created by TV presenter Sarah Beeny and her pal Amanda Christie where your friends can recommend you to the dating populace. The way it works is that, with the person's say so, a friend will write a testimony, a tribute, a mini-profile and then the person will modestly thank them. 'Ooh, am I really that nice?' The thought is that if you are recommended the copy is more sincere and friendly, genuine, with more chance to attract sincere, friendly and genuine people. Whilst skimming the files I came across three girls that I know on the local circuit. Not one, but three!

The minimum cost to advertise your wares on this site is £18 a month as long as you tag along for three months, £54 in total (there are other packages), and at a glance that doesn't seem too bad a price to pay; most of the profiles, for men and women, look better than the average biffer you get on Dating Direct or Plenty of Fish. Maybe it's the format, or the colouring – the green background highlights the photos well – but the people do look nice and lo and behold there I found Morag, Catherine and Jenny Glasses, not all at the same time, their availability has differed, but there they were, one in a bikini, one in a nice frock and one with just a headshot.

Morag looks like Wendolene from the Wallis and Gromit films, should you ever need to picture her. The Travolta

Twins look like Mike and Sully from Monsters Inc, whilst we're there.

Morag's profile said she was terribly witty, independent, pretty sexy and a family type, ergo she wants kids. There was no mention of her penchant for chocolate, Archers or everything fluffy. It also doesn't say that she fucks like a jackhammer, but then again most sites don't encourage that sort of openness. Now there's an option . . .

Catherine is in her early thirties and is a really smart dancer. She has done what most people who can't dance don't do, she has put the miles in and it shows. Her turns are classy, her timing impeccable, her pretty face an advert for a shy, cautious girl, lacking in brazen confidence. She's great company – perhaps I should write her profile? – and I'm surprised she's single.

So too Jenny Glasses. But I know a little more about her than her profile shows. I know that she has been dating and that she is targeted by any bloke as tall as she is; she is gorgeous under those protective specs. But she is a little on the rebound, her heart has been broken and she knows that I'm into Ava, not physically, sadly, given her relationship.

So where does that leave us? What will be, will be, said one wise guru once and that is absolutely true. Something will click for me but with who? Will it be Morag? Catherine? Jenny? Ava? Or someone that I've not met yet? All three know about Ava.

SIXTY-EIGHT

I had lunch with Curly at her house. Just good friends, remember. Her semi was at the corner of a nice estate and it looked like it had only been built in the last five years or so. In the kitchen there was a laptop, a DVD showing Salsa styling and in the lounge was a piano, some serious novels, none of that chick-lit shit. So apart from being a sexy fucker, she's a serious kiddy too, independent, strong, defensive, protective, wary of men and all the foibles that they can bring to any party.

The night before Curly had been to a dance and she regaled me with her commentary of the evening, who was there, her eyes lighting up at certain names, and then there was that air of dismissiveness when she mentioned others. And I thought it was just Billy and Dan.

'He's lovely to dance with is Tony, with his snake hips, great eyes and a strong lead. But he does wear a baseball cap sometimes, back to front, and it makes him look a right twat.'

'And Pete was there . . . lovely dancer . . . but fat.'

'And Gary . . . needs to wash more . . . '

'And Steve wasn't (one of her exes) . . . I miss him, he's lovely to dance with but you wouldn't want to live with him.'

'And Neil wasn't (another ex) . . . manicfuckingdepressive . . . I tried to help him through his tough times but he's a nightmare.'

I hadn't really asked for this mini-tirade but it was fun nonetheless. I laughed and pointed at her.

'Bit judgemental today Sugar? Christ knows what you say about me.'

She looked me in the eye and smiled mischievously.

'Few extra pounds but if we were going out I'd fuck you thin.'

Yikes.

For some reason this reminded me of a story that Dan told me about his brother. The story came from Churchy, his brother's mate. They were in Cornwall and pulled two locals and after a few pints of cider they all went back to Churchy's place and within minutes they paired off, turned off the lights and they all got naked in the same room. Churchy tells the story from then on.

'There we were, my bird rolling her tongue all over my nads and it was fucking lovely and then I heard the other bird talking. "Why is it all hard at the end and soft in the middle?" she said and then she followed it with, "shall I tell you about my first blowjob?" To which the girl who was licking my nads stopped and looked over towards the sound. "Fucking hell

Gloria, don't tell him about the first one . . . tell him about the next fucker!"

Minutes passed and then Gloria yelped with glee, as if she'd just won the lottery. "Yee haw! Yippee! Janice, I've just gone and fucking done it . . . I've just done my first proper hand job.'"

Piss me self every time I hear that story.

SIXTY-NINE

Being a dance instructor has a lot of advantages, least of all the amount of attention you get from the girls in the class. Of course, you don't want to get off with the biffers, but the single girls seem to be attracted to the position rather than the man under the clothes and under the badge and that makes it easy to get dates.

To be honest it's pathetic really seeing these groupies falling over each other for their little bit of the high life, the time under the spot light, the precious moments when they are with the best dancer in the class. It's all about prestige, a little tick on the self-importance list. Let me put it another way. If the instructor wasn't an instructor, would the girl make a beeline for him? This is the dance version of the Tebbitt Test (who would an Indian born in England support at cricket, England or India. Most say India but were England to play against any of the other subcontinent teams they would all support England. Indians don't get on with Pakistanis, Sri Lankans or Bangladeshis.) I suppose this is the acid test and more often than not the answer is no; most teachers are really ordinary people, some would say dull, others would say self-absorbed. There is a colour issue, sometimes prohibitive even in this modern age, an age issue and who wants to be seen with that twat issue. But still the girls fawn around the 'charming', dreaming that one day that Mr Luscious will drop his harem for some desperate thirty-something or for some really desperate forty-something.

Let me bring in a total contradiction here and introduce you to Romeo, black, lean, six two and better looking and more photogenic than Eddie Murphy; Romeo really should be in the movies, stunning looking, great smile, white teeth, come to bed eyes, and no, I don't fancy the fucker, I'm just doing my duty as your correspondent to report accurately. The girls fawn all over Romeo and when I say that he was gay, they said they'd fuck him even if he was. He isn't.

There is a Tango teacher who has a reputation as a Lothario, tall, gangly, an unlikely hero, too much hair, but he can dance and the Tango really is a licence to print...and a licence to rip clothes off with your teeth. I should explain the term Lothario here. It's old-fashioned speak for player, an eighteenth century word for a bloke who is just looking for affairs, no relationship, no wedding, no living in sin, just a bloke that wants to fuck. Don't we all dear? He does only teach one dance though...compared to my seventeen. LMTO. Laughed my tits off.

There's another teacher local who used to have a pigtail and now doesn't. Somehow he's picked up with an illegal immigrant from Bulgaria. Stunner she is. He must be more interesting at home than he is out.

And then there's another couple – both blokes – who are so into their selves, so much so that the birds are peripheral and they try and outdo each other by teaching harder routines, routines that only pros or semi-pros can get. Pointless really. You have to teach to the level of the class. Do these two have such low self-esteem that they have to play the cunt for an hour each lesson?

And what is it about a bloke who is black or Latino that he thinks he can teach just because he is black or Latino? All bollocks really.

SEVENTY

Not everyone has courage when it comes to dating but when people drop all pretence and are up front it makes for captivating viewing. It's a primeval thing, carnal in its attraction.

Me, Robbie (5' 6") and Syd (6' 5") went to Dublin a few years ago to watch some rugby and to have a night on the Craic, Dublin, the home of the Craic, hen parties, stag dos, the hospitable Irish, their 'I'm going to live forever whatever I eat, drink or smoke', culture. At five o'clock we had our first pint, the two lads on lager, me on Smethwick's before hitting the Guinness later. In the bar we chatted to a couple of girls who said that they were going for a swim in the hotel pool before hitting the town.

'I bet you look good in a swimming cozzy,' Syd said.

'I bet you look better out of it,' I added.

'You're a saucy fucker aren't you?' said the girl as she giggled into her lager.

As soon as they had disappeared Syd spied a couple of beauties and without a blink he was over there chatting, both tall, one blonde and her hair crinkly, one brunette in a bob, both statuesque, nice tits.

'You just undressed me from top to bottom with your eyes,' said the blonde.

'I could use my hands if you like,' said Syd.

It turned out that both girls were policewomen from Yorkshire, the blonde a D.I. and the brunette her sergeant.

They disappeared – we bumped into them later briefly – and we moved on in search of more fodder. It didn't take long; soon we were tagging along with five girls on a birthday bash, three from Birmingham, one from Lichfield and the other from Leicester. Two were married, two had boyfriends and one had a partner. At 7:30pm they were very keen for us to know this, they were prim, quiet and pleased that we'd spoken to them sober. Two hours later we were singing along to the jukebox, Summer Nights from Grease, and I clicked with the girl from Lichfield, blonde, petite, not my usual thing, but there was great chemistry.

At midnight we all headed on to a club, and fuck me, we, the lads, paid for all the birds, all five of them. The next two hours are a blur but I can remember losing the girls and then finding them at about two, Syd pulling one who he found out had had a boob job, Robby was with a mousy looking girl and me and Lichfield...for some reason our eyes met across the crowded room but the river of people was insurmountable and we both went home alone. We both wanted each other but her friend, probably sober and her advisor, took her away, much to the thanks of her partner back home.

It does beg the question though...what were they playing at, these girls? All five of them, well four, up for it, once the beer and the occasion kicked in. You can't imagine being Lichfield's bloke back home thinking that his babe had gone on an innocent weekend only to find that she'd had a bunk up with a relative stranger. Maybe he was doing that whilst she was away?

SEVENTY-ONE

Ava and me are officially history.

Stop crying. I have. Just. What will be will be. Let me explain.

I'd managed to get into Harry's Bar, I say 'managed' because getting in and out of revolving doors sometimes is a fucking nuisance. So too waiting for a beer whilst some twat orders four daiquiris, three pina coladas, two slippery nipples and one black Russian. There should be a 'help yourself' beer tap like we used to have water fountains in the school playground, an honesty tap, three quid in the pot, pour your own beer, job done. It was a cocktail bar though.

Looking around I saw a girl and thought, 'she's tall,' that was until I realised she was standing on the stairs.

The Love Theme from The Godfather was playing on the sound system and whilst I waited for Ava I sang along, everything pitch perfect until that last fucker of a note that is too high for my baritone range. Andy Williams creamed it, I cremated it. That would explain the difference in our record sales I suppose.

On cue in walked the blonde bombshell that is Ava, her short hair bobbing soft and warm against her gentle skin, blue eyes sparkling like chips of ice, black cargo pants and matching t-shirt revealing her midriff. Makes me hard just thinking about her.

She came over and we luvvy kissed, once on each cheek, soulless, so I took her in my arms and held her close to me, hugging her for four or five seconds.

'Wow, you're lovely and hot,' she said.

'I'm always hot,' I replied and she giggled.

What followed was half an hour of sparring, small talk, a couple of drinks, her just halves, she was driving, me pints, I wasn't. And then came the crunch time, the softly delivered question about us, about our future. She looked at me in the eye and spoke with tenderness and affection, so much so that I just wanted to hold her, to kiss her, to feel her warmth, her heartbeat and the sizzle in her eyes. Her monologue was short and then I took my turn to talk.

'Do you know something Ava,' I smiled gently at her, our eyes not moving, 'that sounded like you actually quite like me.'

'Oh, I do like you, big guy, I do really like you.'

'It's okay . . . I understand.' I wanted her to tell me that she was leaving town, emigrating, out of sight, out of mind, but she wasn't, she just couldn't commit to anything over and above her family even though things weren't great back at the Manor. I carried on. 'I know and have known that this would never really work.'

'You have?'

'Yeah, you have too much at stake, you need peace in your life not turmoil and even though you need lots of TLC your home is more important than any fling or affair. You really are lovely, you are easy to like and who knows what would have happened had things been different . . . it'd be easy to fall in love with you and I use those words rarely and never lightly.'

She smiled and smiled.

And then I let her go.

So, history, even though that's not strictly accurate; in truth we never really got started. But we are done and it's hard to take.

It is a foolish world that stops people who really like each other from being together. Perhaps that's just part of God's test?

SEVENTY-TWO

I was talking with Dan recently and he told me about a porn DVD he'd watched where the male lead keeps on getting caught with his pants down, interrupted by the bird's bloke putting keys in the lock of the front door and the last scene of each clip is the male lead running from the house with his pants in one hand and with his shoes, shirt and socks in the other. Whilst we both knew that this was a stage-managed movie it seemed to capture the mood of the moment – Dan's frustration at finding a lover and a dance partner matching my own frustrations with Ava, work and the world in general. The last six years have been the least fulfilling of my life.

But the tale of sexual frustrations got me to thinking about my own back-catalogue of coitus interruptus. I was once having sex in a kitchen when in strolls her brother. Then I had a bird in my bedroom at home and my mother waltzed in like she owned the fucking place, which, in fact, she did. 'Any chance of fucking knocking?' I thought. 'Should've locked the fucking door,' was the second thing that came to mind. And there was that time when I'd locked the office door and this bird had straddled me after giving me some head and the cleaner tried to get in. Thankfully the door was solid, that is, no glass.

But all this pales into insignificance when you hear what happened to a mate of Dan's called Jimmy. Dan tells the story.

After a night on the pull Jimmy woke up wondering where he was. He didn't recognise the decor, the curtains, the shape of the windows or the smells of perfume and pot-pourri that filled the room. The quilt was warm and definitely not his. Then he replayed the events of the previous night. Great. Fantastic. Superb. He smiled, rolled over and was greeted by a welcoming Emma Wilson. 'Ah,' thought Jimmy, 'that's where I am.'

Half an hour later, during another replay of what happened when they got back to the flat, Jimmy's flow was interrupted by the sound of stones being thrown at the windows. At first he ignored them but when half a house brick shattered the glass and landed with a deadening clump on the floor by the bed he was compelled to stop what he was doing and ask a few quick questions.

'Who the fuck is that? What the fuck's going on? Are you going to call the police? Do you want me to? Have you got a gun?' Emma rolled over and banged the pillow in frustration and anger before answering.

'It's my ex, John. He got out of prison yesterday. I was hoping he wouldn't come round. We finished ages ago. You'd better get dressed and go. I'll have to deal with him.'

'What was he in for?'

'GBH.'

'Shit.' Another stone came through the window.

'I know you're in there!' Boomed a voice from below. 'You've got a bloke in there, haven't you? If you have I'll kill him!' The next sound that Jimmy and Emma heard was a frantic banging on the flat door and fearing for his safety and not wanting to see this crazed lunatic put his hand through the door and do his Jack Nicholson impersonation ('Here's

Johnny!') Jimmy decided to leave. The only way out was the window. It was a first floor flat. More shit.

Jimmy opened the window and stark naked he jumped onto the lawn below. He knew he'd be okay once he hit the ground. It was only twelve feet or so. But instead of lowering himself by his arms so that the fall was only six feet Jimmy jumped from a seated position, the twelve feet fall did the damage and Jimmy winced with pain when he hit the grass. The crack of bones was a bit off-putting too. When he tried to get to his feet his frail ankles buckled and his body ended prone on the turf. He couldn't walk. Both his ankles were broken. If Jimmy could have kicked himself he would have.

SEVENTY-THREE

In the flat Jimmy could hear screaming and shouting. John was issuing threats, throwing crockery and breaking glasses. Jimmy had to get help. He had to call the police before it was too late. Somehow he hauled his naked frame over the grass towards the rose bed and the wall that divided the buildings. If only he could get next door he could raise the alarm. The soil was cold under Jimmy's knees. The brick wall grazed Jimmy's arms as he pulled himself onto it. On the other side he dropped over arse first. Only to discover that next door had limestone chippings not grass. It wasn't Jimmy's day.

Blood poured from the gashes on Jimmy's knees as he crawled towards the door and more than once he thought he would pass out. His ankles were killing him, his hands were cut and to cap it all off it was a cold morning too. Not the weather for a naked commando crawl. Eventually Jimmy reached the door. At last. Relief. Soon it would all be over. The shouting seemed to have died down. Maybe John and Emma were having a quiet chat? More likely he had beaten her in to silence. He had to get help. Jimmy knocked on the door with all the strength he could muster. There were voices. He could hear footsteps. He saw human shadows through the opaque glass of the door. Great. Soon it would all be over. The door opened, Jimmy put his hands on to the hall carpet ready to pull himself into the warm. However, whoever answered the door was only looking at eye level and seeing no one slammed the door shut. Well, not quite. Jimmy yelled in pain as the door shut onto his hands. It was only then that the person that answered the door realised that in fact there was someone at the door. Crying in pain was a naked, male thirty-something. Truth be told he was sobbing like a baby. All he needed was a punch on the nose and Jimmy would have had a full house.

The homeowner covered the nude form with a blanket, rang the police, called for an ambulance and Jimmy was taken to the local infirmary where he was sedated, cleaned up and his broken bones were set in plaster of Paris. Wouldn't have the same ring to it if it had been invented in Middlesborough would it? Plaster of Middlesborough. Aided by Valium Jimmy slept for twenty-four hours.

When he woke up he was still a bit groggy. Once more he played over the events of Friday night and Saturday morning. Some story that. 'One day I'll write it down,' he thought. He rolled over and was greeted by the smiling Emma Wilson. Both her ankles were in plaster and the bruises around her eyes made her look like a panda. When Jimmy realised who it was he half smiled and asked her what had happened.

'I thought he was going to kill me so after rowing and avoiding anything that he threw at me I had to get out. He wouldn't let me get dressed and he'd locked the door and so when his back was turned for a split second I made a break for it and I jumped out of the window. However, rather than lowering myself so that the fall was only six feet I just jumped from a seated position. I thought I'd be okay on the grass but as soon as I landed I knew that my ankles were broken. The crack of bones was a bit off-putting too. The police found me in a naked, crying heap a few minutes later.'

'Shit.'

'What happened to your hands?'

They were married three months later.

True story that.

Anyway, here's a quick question for you. Who is the most important person on the shoot of a porn movie? The cameraman...and he, and it is invariably a he, has to have the ability to hold the camera steady with one hand.

SEVENTY-FOUR

One or two websites seem to be just jumping on the bandwagon in terms of dating, not that you can knock that, we all need more than one supermarket to shop in, and some people have aimed for specific niche markets in terms of clientele.

The posh birds target the broadsheet newspapers; The Telegraph's is great. The slightly less posh birds that read the red tops fix their aim at Match.com. There's one called Bumble, another called Zoosk and every commercial radio station has their own version. Same business model, same fees. As said, the biffers go on Plenty of Fish.

I'm sure there must be sites for one night stands, not that I can find it, swingers, doggers and goers, as they used to be called, great word that, she's a goer, bit like the East German athlete back in the day, Marlies Gohr, but there are also some aimed at single parents and there's a site called Loopy Love which claims to keep dating fun. Not quite sure it's the best unique selling point that I've ever seen but there you go.

One alternative to the Internet, and something that me, Dan and Billy didn't come up with originally as where to find women, is at a function, any posh do that you can get access to. It could be a Summer Ball, a localised film premier, the opening of a new building, it could be a race night, a charity gala or a Ladies' Night with the local Masons. As long as there is alcohol you're on to a winner.

Go back to the Dublin trip and how the girls behaved early on in the evening. Chilled, proper and spoken for. Five hours later, energised, pissed and free they were up for anything or anyone. It is the same at functions.

Picture the Christmas do held in one particular room at a hotel. And in the next lounge there's another firm, and in the next another and another and another. And all you get, as time moves on, is birds all frocked up, half-pissed and game as you get, inhibitions in their handbags with a 'I don't care what the fuck people think I'm going to snog that bloke over there,' attitude.

There are many things that us blokes have to take into account at these gigs, predominantly whether or not the girl is with someone in the same room. If a girl is there with her hubby or bloke then it's a real no-no and a danger zone to be avoided, but if it's a table full of girls then that's a different story. That's when the 'Dublin Factor' hits in.

- o I might be seeing someone but it's not really that serious.
- o I might be living with someone but he hasn't gone down on me ever.
- o I might be married but he smacks me about.

o I might be engaged so what's wrong with one last fling?

One great benefit of these dos, especially the posh ones, is that the birds get seriously frocked up, they make a major effort with their hair, their make-up, their frock, obviously, and it is a great sight. Is there anything better than a bare back underneath a soft gown? Or tanned legs? Cleavages aplenty. I suppose being a DJ and spinning discs at these gigs is almost as good as being a dance instructor?

Dan recalled to me that he was at a work's party once when Bryan, one of his co-directors, appeared carrying some champagne for Dan and the two girls he was chatting up, both from telesales, one mid-twenties, one late-thirties, both glammed up showing off plenty of cleavage, expectation in their eyes as alcohol and lust merged into intent.

'Did you know that there isn't much in life that Bryan doesn't do well,' Dan said conspiratorially. 'Maybe there is one thing though...what do you think Bry? Begins with W, ends in K, four letters...'

The girls giggled and sipped at the sparkly, thinking the obvious.

'What's so funny?' asked Bry, smiling, 'what's funny about the word "work"? Never thought it'd raise such a titter.' His choice of words deliberate and provocative.

'Ooh, sorry Bryan,' chorused the girls, 'we thought it meant something else...'

'Wink?' he offered.

'I bet you're a bit of a winker Bryan,' said the girls, oblivious to his position.

'I bet you are too,' he smiled.

'More champagne?' Dan offered.

SEVENTY-FOUR

Ever on the look out for that elusive love match me, Dan and Frankie did a small Salsa convention as a pre-cursor to the big event, the one with over a thousand people, with all those girls away for the weekend.

There is no harm in these small conventions; they are very personal, you get to meet the teachers, some of the locals, and there's more to it than just dancing, you're all together in one hotel, you eat together, drink together, chill together and these trips form indelible memories.

When we got there a class, like an informal welcome, had already started and whilst Frankie took all the kit to the room the three of us would be sharing Dan and me watched the instructor, studying his technique, his skills and his teaching style. Physically he wouldn't have looked out of place in Lilliput and he spent a lot of time grabbing his crotch in a Michael Jackson sort of way. We reported back to Frankie.

'Well?' Frankie said, as he put away his clothes and raised his suitcase onto the top of the wardrobe.

'Hard to believe,' I said, 'but the fucker's more arrogant than you.'

Frankie laughed.

'It'll be a tough night tonight . . . you two fuckers fighting for airtime,' Dan chipped in. 'I see the Squealer's here . . .'

Frankie's attention rose, you could see him thinking, 'ah, the Squealer . . . mmm . . . now there's a thought.'

The couple had a bit of history.

'You'd better get a pillow ready if you're going to bring her back to the room,' I added, 'and make sure we have earplugs available.'

There is a common fallacy about men and women, that women talk about their sexploits with their girlfriends and that blokes keep schtum and say nothing. It's not true. Whilst I'm sure that the girls go into graphics a little more, exercising the left side of the brain, more and more men are more direct about sex, especially when you are friends and more so when the liaison was just about the sex rather than affection. If it was the love of your life silence is the only respectful strategy.

'Did you go down on her?'

'Did she go down on you?'

'I was going down on her when.'

'I was just about to spray her tonsils.'

'She's definitely into anal sex now.'

'Swallowed the lot.'

You can see that most of these statements are action based, practical in many ways. There is little mention of the atmosphere, the wine, the music, the candles, how long the session lasted, what the undressing was like, who came first, how pleasurable the orgasm was, how much affection was shown in the process. That's where women come into it.

Well Frankie had told us about the Squealer's first orgasm at his pad, how she screamed loud, so loud that any passer or neighbour by would be in no doubt what was happening, so if there was going to be a repeat performance we deserved to know about it in advance so that we could plan our contingencies.

People are funny when they orgasm, it really depends on how comfortable they are with showing their innermost pleasure. I think I mentioned before that depending on the given era or your country of birth, showing real pleasure was either totally normal or not the done thing at all.

Some times you don't know if a girl has orgasmed or faked. You should do, really, given muscle and fluid response, but if she chooses not to verbalise it then maybe you don't know. I'd even heard of men faking orgasms as well. Surely the girl could tell too for exactly the same reasons?

I suppose the orgasm is similar to going for a shit in a public cubicle. Do you just let it all out, the wind, the explosion, so that everyone using the urinals can hear or do you try and control the release as if to say, 'I don't shit really.' I do know one thing that has never been addressed. Why do toilets always smell of toilet?

SEVENTY-FIVE

I warned the big lug that it would only end in tears and sure as sure can be it took Dan a month to get over the loss of what he thought was a new permanent squeeze. The dopey fucker only went and fell for an FUD – fucked up divorcee. Dopey fucker.

It all started innocuously enough but Dan pulled this stunner and they dated for a while and then she just disappeared off the radar totally, moved house, changed her email address, mobile number and job and he was left high and dry. One minute she was there, the next gone, it was like she'd died but she hadn't and that made it worse.

It nearly destroyed the poor lamb. In such a short time he'd got very comfy with the idea of a permanent squeeze and potentially someone to spend his life with, that was, after all what he had been looking for, but she wasn't up for any commitment, felt terrified, her emotional tank was empty and as a result she just fucked off leaving Dan like a lost sheep.

So the warning?

FUDs. They do not act like normal people, that is the men too, not just the birds, but given their species this makes women even crazier and the advice is simple. Unless they want just a shag every now and then, do not get involved.

Sure dance with them, be nice to them, and yes, if they want a good seeing to then give it a shot, but do not get emotionally involved. There are a myriad of reasons and most of it is to do with timing and phases.

Look at it logically. They have just come out or are still involved in a life-changing event. He has been Mr Bastard and fucked half of the female population of say, Salisbury, whilst wifey has been dutiful back at the ranch. So she has to cope with the rejection, the deceit, the lies, the moving house, the selling of the matrimonial home that emblem of security, the loss of status and money, and the tag of divorcee or singleton, her life a mess, her dreams shattered, her postcard picture life in ruins. So why on earth would she want to get serious with anyone after all that? I told Dan but he thought she was different.

Let's add some more context. She probably blames herself and feels guilty even if it is him who has problems with his cock and self-worth. She probably has some self-loathing to cope with, she won't like herself very much and her self-esteem will be lower than a snake's belly and before she gets back into the real world she has to go through phases and processes first before she can come out of the other side.

Her biggest motivator will be fear and she will not want to go through such crap again. She'll be in shock, maybe shake a lot, cry a lot, drink too much, decision making dodgy and probably lacking the courage to face the demons of her feelings, stabbing her like a knife. There'll be anger, pain, acrimony, a certain measure of grief, in fact bundles of the shit, and she has to rebuild everything. She will be the centre of her world, selfish, unable to give, fearful and emotionally empty. Only when she can bag all that will there be any chance for her to move on.

Dan got her very early on. Wrong place. Wrong time. Sad. Maybe when she realises that she can be better than she once was will there be any chance of a resurrection. Maybe she'll realise in time just what she could have with Dan and what she has lost? But only when the mists have settled.

SEVENTY-SEVEN

I mentioned before that men hurt too and they respond like women do. They drink too much, cry, shake, don't eat and try and work it out. Men apply logic but that is just not anything that any female can comprehend. Logic? Totally fucking irrelevant.

Me, Dan and Billy were sitting in the pub, Dan scratching his head and crying at the same time.

'We were so fucking good together. And I offer her everything that women want...'

'Normal women,' said Billy.

'Not FUDs,' I added.

And it was true Dan did offer an attractive package – funny, compassionate, writer, dancer, singer, sensitive, good looking, educated, few quid, great cook, great listener – in fact, if I was gay I'd date the fucker, but this CV is irrelevant for the FUD who doesn't know what day of the week it is let alone what she wants from a bloke. In fact she doesn't want a bloke. Of course she'll go for the wine, dine and sixty-nine but that's about it. And she'll probably fancy a bit of that with a long fucking queue before she even thinks about a new commitment but she will eventually. We spoke to Dan about this. Her trend management shows that she's always been in a relationship and that once the funny stuff is over and she finds herself again she'll be up for it. Question is though, will Dan still be available? Funny, life, isn't it? You search for 'that' person and through circumstance you're not together. Daft really.

Fuck me, was just picturing Ava then and getting hard as rock. I wonder how she is?

Anyway, back to the logic. If you read books about relationships, books written by men and women, counsellors and psychologists, PhDs, whoever, they all come with the same wish list for women – love, fidelity, kindness, commitment and intelligence. Of course, you can't overlook the hunter gatherer bit, the provider of resources too, but if one person can offer all that, as a package then you'd think that the woman would bite your hand off wouldn't you?

That's what Dan thought. But it only applies to normal women, not FUDs.

SEVENTY-EIGHT

The dance world, that eclectic mix, has a new species as part of its social network: the predator. I'm not talking about a player, a dance-tart, but about the bloke that goes to a dance class for skirt and he targets the vulnerable and the naïve. There's a certain amount of sleaze about the predator because he's different than Dan and me. We are looking for long-term partners. The predator is looking for somewhere to dip his wick as often as he can, a new girl each night, or each week.

Of course, one-night stands are rare in dancing but not unknown, and that can happen to the best of us, but the predator adds slime to the normal chase. Remember, this isn't a night club where everyone gets pissed and then ends up snogging and groping before a cab home with some bird or on your own. This is a dance class or pally. Most people are sober, there is the chance to chat a little but the predator uses the class to his own end. Predators are normally okay dancers and they appear at beginners' classes so that they can help out.

'Can't you do it love . . . let me show you . . . that's it . . . foot there.'

'Oh, you're brilliant aren't you?'

'Thanks, any chance of a fuck?'

I'm sure that there are some philanthropists who help out because they want to and are big-hearted, because they want the world to be able to dance, but predators are the prime example of the dance-hall pick up artist.

You see, what happens is this. As soon as the girls walk into a class they forget where they are. They think they are in a dance class not in a nightclub or cattle truck so they immediately drop their guard. They forget that men are motivated primarily to procreate and that this is an audition. Because they think they're going to learn how to dance. And they do. And that is where the predator steps in attacking the gullible, when defences are down, when they least expect it.

Let me take this further. Men's motivations are easy; we are simple people. Sex on tap, regular blowjobs, oral, bit of domesticity thrown in, bit of TLC and love and then a bit of solitude and we're hunky fucking dory. He comes back from the cave (watching Man U maybe) knowing that he's number one and that he's going to get his nads licked. Simple. Birds, different story altogether. But that is the predator's world and little do the predatees, the predated, know that that is what will happen as soon as they innocently pitch up wanting to learn to dance.

SEVENTY-NINE

It's funny isn't it? You see blokes getting a bit ansty when their bird dances with another bloke, the old alpha male thing. You can hear their thoughts. 'Jesus, he's touching her arse.' 'They're so fucking close.' 'Is he touching her up?'

'Just watch the bastard's hands.' 'Leave her alone you wanker.'

And yup, it's tough sometimes to watch (then don't!) whatever the dance. In a ballroom it's not so bad because it's not such a predatory school as clubs with Latin Fever. But in the Salsa pally you know that there are predators aplenty, single blokes thinking they'll get lucky and single blokes looking for a love partner and you never know, it could be with your bird . . . you'd hope not but I have seen it happen.

What also happens, and it's not often exposed publicly, is that some women go alpha female too. They might not know it or even acknowledge it but if you put a cam on a couple all night you'll see it from time to time.

Let me give you a for instance. There's my pals Rich and Gemma. They were dating, loved up, a proper romance in the making and of course they danced out a lot, well they used to, they don't talk much these days. They used to spend a lot of time together but you can't dance with the same person all night and because of the way Rich dances he's not short of a queue. Gemma is gorgeous so she is a target for anyone.

Here's something that maybe you didn't know. There's an unwritten etiquette when it comes to blokes, especially when they're out dancing. Single blokes clock who comes in with who and who is shagging who, be that girlfriend or wife and 99% of blokes act with respect. They don't dance the same with someone else's girl, they hold back a bit, rein themselves in and are courteous because the last thing they want is some big lug whacking 'em round the ears with the warning shot of 'watch it you cunt, that's enough.' Not many men hit on girls who they know are with someone; it would take a wanker to do that, and a brave one at that.

Anyway back to Rich and Gemma. They go to a dance and they say hellos around the pally, still with coats on, shoe bags in hand. Then they sit down and change shoes and Rich is faster than Gemma. And then someone comes over to say hello to Gemma, one of the girls up for five minutes of girly chat. Rich, ready, does the rounds and says a few more hellos.

He's talking to Rog who's talking to Jenny Glasses. He shakes his hand and kisses her on both cheeks and being friendly he leaves his arm around her as they chat for a minute. He is empathic, listens and smiles. Jenny tells him that she has lost his number (that he gave her before he was seeing Gemma) and she asks for his business card. As is, he doesn't have one but he says that he'll email it.

Whilst all this is happening Gemma is sitting in the corner watching. She hears nothing but sees the scene unfold, the touching, the eyes, the obvious attraction that Jenny has for him and inside she is fuming. Her face gives nothing away, a smile and a sparkle, but she knows that someone is hitting on her bloke.

Suffice to say that Rich was looked after in a spectacular way for the rest of the night.

EIGHTY

There's an unwritten rule in the dance world that isn't worth the paper it isn't written on. Teachers never date pupils. Well to be honest that's bollocks isn't it? And also, what a waste of opportunity! I mean what a great attraction, being able to teach someone a life skill. And how many teachers do you think met their current squeeze on the dance floor? Or in a dance class? Tom & Lola, Ian & Lucy, Phil & JLo, Helen & Troy, Rob & Pam, Daz & Delilah . . . the list goes on. Of course, there is a downside, if it doesn't work, if it goes tits up, what happens next?

If you date on the scene things will go one of two ways if it goes tits up. Either you will both be mature enough to know that it was just a trial, an audition and it didn't work out and you get on with life. As long as there's honesty and openness about what is happening normally that's not a problem. Plan B is that you never talk to each other again, avoid each other in classes, blank each other at functions or one of you leaves the building when you meet by accident.

I saw a couple hook up, two young things, her at uni, him just out and I wondered for them. In six months it'll have gone tits up and then what? Do they organise their calendars so that one dances on Mondays and Wednesdays and the other on Tuesdays and Thursdays? Do they agree to go to different functions or risk the chance that they will bump into each other? I suppose it depends on the level of attraction. If there is strong emotion in the air then it can be tricky.

But what about the moral issue? Is there a teacher/pupil line that should not be crossed? Or do you just follow your heart? Or your loins? Is it a sin to bow to temptation? I'm not religious but you get the drift.

EIGHTY-ONE

One Friday night before Christmas, after the Seaside Convention – more later – I pulled. It was one of those nights when I had nothing planned, no-one lined up, no intention of trying with the opposite sex and I was just happy to have a few drinks with my mate Spud, chat to whoever wanted to chat and just chill out. The DJ played some 70s disco stuff, a bit of Abba, a slice of Ricky Martin and a fair smattering of rock'n'roll. The atmosphere was just right. It was a good night.

Even when Spud fell over the first time things were just dandy. Spud did this from time to time. It was as if someone had chopped off one his ears and, staggering like a baby giraffe, Spud inevitably ended up on his arse. The surprising thing was that this sometimes happened when Spud was stone cold sober, sometimes when he was half full and never when he was up to his limit. It was almost as if the alcohol had a reverse impact.

The first time that Spud fell over I just let him fall before bending down to help him to his feet. On the second occasion I was sitting on a bar stool talking to him. I saw it coming and I tried to prevent it but trying to catch a dead weight of sixteen stones is virtually impossible and all I managed was to be pulled down on top of him. One down, two down, like we were both being suctioned towards the carpet, like the last two pins in a bowling alley. Spud banged his head on the floor. I held on to my bottle of beer for dear life like a circus performer and didn't spill a drop. However, there was a group of five girls that once stood where Spud had fallen and the closest of the group took the full brunt of Spud's fall.

The victim was tall, had shoulder length light-brown hair that was brushed away from a gorgeous face whose eyes looked like they'd been dipped in a glass of Crème de Menthe. She wore leopard skin leggings and a satin-white blouse that wrapped her voluptuous body like Clingfilm. 'Wouldn't mind having some of that in my sandwiches,' I thought.

There were traces of white wine on the blouse so I asked for a fresh bar towel and then began to dry the damp bits on the blouse as if I was tending a wound, dabbing gently so I wouldn't sting. As my hand moved from her shoulder downwards the girl gently pushed it away with one hand and took the bar towel with the other.

'I'll do that if you don't mind.' She smiled when she said it. Was this courtesy or was it a signal?

'Shame,' I said, 'I was just getting to the good bit . . . I'm sorry about my friend . . . he suffers from an incurable disease and he only found out today . . . it should kill him by the age of 90 . . . can I get you a drink? Didn't you have one? Oh, yeah . . . there it is.'

'I'll have a large glass of Chardonnay please.'

'Sure.'

EIGHTY-TWO

Now what happened next was unusual. Normally the girl accepts the drink, says thanks and then turns around and continues talking to her mates. But that didn't happen. The girl sipped her wine and began chatting to me, just little old me. Spud got the picture and fucked off for a dance. Her opening gambit was intriguing.

'I suppose you're married then?'

'Happily and successfully unmarried, thanks.'

We then shared stories about music, favourite records, the first one that we bought, the best ever album, the funniest song, why records were called records still when they were CDs, why people still called CDs albums, why the 'Hit Parade' had more than one song in it . . . (surely it should be plural?) . . . because the Stock, Aitken and Waterman recording studios was called the 'Hits Factory' and one day the 'S' fell off and no-one was really sure which end of the word it had come from. And when the DJ played Don McLean singing 'American Pie' we sang it together. And the duet continued into Jeff Beck's 'Hi Ho Silver Lining', Meat Loaf's 'Paradise by the Dashboard Light' and 'I Don't Like Mondays' by the Boomtown Rats.

And when the DJ slowed it all down a bit with Chris de Burgh's classic from 1986 'Lady in Red' I took my new friend by the hand and lead her to the dance floor where in less than a nanosecond we were snogging for England, groin to groin, wanton lust, public, late, but who cares? When we finally broke for air the room was emptying, the other girls and Spud were nowhere to be seen so we left together.

'This might seem a daft question,' I said, as we ambled arm in arm towards the taxi rank, 'but what do I call you?'

'Anne. Anne Hathaway.'

'You messing?'

'No.'

'What, the actress?'

'No.'

'Not Shakespeare's wife?'

'No.'

'Thank goodness...you'd be about 450 years old.'

'So . . . are we going to share a cab?'

EIGHTY-THREE

Anne Hathaway was an interesting package, her first words telling me so much in so few. She had been out with a few guys since her split and every one of them turned out to be married, chancers preying on a beautiful, single and vulnerable girl.

Her split hadn't been planned and she hadn't suspected anything. She had been a dutiful partner, always there, living together, not married yet, and she fulfilled all the roles of a wife, and more, and they had a good sex-life, so it begs the questions why do men cheat? Or women for that matter? I threw the subject at Billy and Dan and we formed a list that isn't really rocket science.

- o Alcohol/drugs
- o Ego, to prove that you can still pull
- o Cowardice, too scared to leave a shit relationship but who still fancies a bunk up
- o Lust
- o An ex

- Won't get caught

- To hurt

- Opportunity

- Not getting on with current squeeze

- Not getting it at home

- Revenge after a row

- Too easily forgiven

- Boredom

- Sexless relationship

- To achieve a sexual high

- An open relationship

- No strings, no responsibility

- An agreed arrangement

- Selfishness

- Disrespect

- Because we're cunts. I say we but I was faithful for 17 years.

We also thought of ways of nipping this in the bud, what to do when you get so horny that you just have to kiss, or more, and the results weren't quite as comprehensive.

- o Walk away
- o Read the sermon on the mount
- o Submerge your bollocks in a bowl of cold water
- o Think of the most recent family death
- o Pray

EIGHTY-FOUR

If you teach dancing, as I do these days, you are exposed to a number of different women and generally I only do private lessons with girls that I want to. The girls have to be talented, pretty and nice people but my intentions are purely honourable, there is no ulterior motive other than to teach the world to dance.

I've just re-read that. What a load of bollocks! There was me thinking that as I pass 62,000 words that the whole point has been to search for a life long lover, so surely my intentions are honourable in one sense but not in another? I am not looking for the opportunist shag, that's for sure, though would take one or two if offered. Hey, I'm just a bloke. But why shouldn't a girl I teach fall madly in love with me and become the next Mrs Travolta for I am, like Dan and Billy, the third Travolta Twin? Teaching gives you credibility and status and it makes you attractive, the bringer of a life skill, whilst the knees still work that is.

But even when you're teaching, as a philanthropist every now and again, these scenarios do throw up real difficulties that you have to conquer. Let me paint you a picture. A pupil buys in to the entire process and the two of you are gobbled up by the music, the performance and what the dance means. It isn't just about moving the feet and the body in the right direction; it's about the artistry, living the music and the story it is telling.

And when this happens the entire process changes. Bodies move differently, holds get more personal, tactility more sensitive, heartbeats quicken, ardours heighten, sensuality more sensuous. That is when things become critical, the tipping point. That is when hands stray, kisses to the side of the head, the cheeks, even the mouth. And it can happen in any dance that is close contact, which is most of them.

I know a lively chick called Emily who I danced Salsa once with in a car park. A few months later I chatted with her in the local and after a few drinks she pulled me to one side. 'Can I ask you a personal question?'

'Of course, fire away Em.'

'Do you ever get a hard on when you're dancing?'

I did ponder this for a while because normally it's a simple answer, a simple 'no'. But every now and then there are mitigating circumstances. You couldn't quite apply the 80/20 rule. Maybe the 98/2 rule?

EIGHTY-FIVE

You'd think that certain dances would generate more horn wouldn't you? Bachata, Salsa and Lambada, the latter I've never done, are all up front, full on and sexy. The Tango is steamy, the Waltz exotic, the Rumba erotic. So which one delivers the most horn?

I danced a Tango with a girl and she just wanted to kiss me in spite of her betrothal to someone else and the fact that she was half my age.   Another did the Tango too and she got so hot that she had to change her blouse in front of me. I didn't look away. The same girl responded even more after a Waltz. But none of these produced a hard on. I guess the thought of the bowl of cold water worked.

But there are certain songs that get girls going more than anything and the only two words I need to utter are 'Dirty' and 'Dancing'. If there's a girl on the planet who hasn't seen the movie then I don't know her. Is there a woman alive who hasn't dreamed of being in Jennifer Grey's shoes being seduced by the male lead which is a bit off given that he was a chain smoker? Which should really inspire every bloke to watch the relevant scenes and to try and replicate some of the moves. There is little in the seduction scene of technical demand. Anyone can do it. Just have courage boys.

It's handy too to have the piece of music ready, 'Cry To Me' by Solomon Burke and The Blind Boys of Alabama. In proper speak it's a Rumba. In Dirty speak it's anything you fucking want. Girl straddles gent's right thigh. He holds her back and flops her backwards forcing her groin directly against him. And he does it again. There might be a circle thrown in, a few fast thrusts. She walks around him, kisses his back, he takes her top off (she was wearing it) and then he kisses her cleavage and neck. Presumably, after all that, he fucks her.

Well, this was one of the few times that I got a hard on whilst dancing. I put the tune on and she bought into it. There was no undressing or kissing, or fucking for that matter, but hard is an understatement.

Dirty Dancing has a lot to answer for and a lot for dancers and teachers to be grateful for. The scene that does it for me is the Water Melon Shack where all the young rebel against the formality of the ballroom. Couples, professional dancers, pretending to be actors, pretending to be party animals, dry hump their way through 'Do You Love Me' by The Contours. There is a smattering of dance steps, not many, but there is abandon, a smidgen of oral sex simulation, hands on tits, breath on cleavage, a thrust from behind. I know the film has some proper routines but this'll do for me.

EIGHTY-SIX

Most blokes like porn. Some don't. Some women like porn. Most don't. Dan told me about a girl he was with once who copied what the girl did on the film they were watching. Drove him wild. So I asked him the obvious question. Have you ever filmed yourself?

Now there's a chat up line in the making. 'Alright love, fancy starring in a porn movie with me?' Or 'I want to film you sucking my cock . . . fancy it.'

Layla told me about her brother who had made a film of him and his girlfriend of the day shagging for England. They had placed the camcorder on a tripod and tried as best they could to stay within shot and the film captured everything. The other option would have been to have someone else doing the filming but that isn't everyone's cup of tea, either being filmed or doing the filming. Surely you'd get so horny that you'd want to join in and that can be problematic too . . . I guess . . .

So Layla's brother made a film, a mix of the tripod and some hand held shots. When he came no one would know that it was him, not unless they knew his cock intimately, but the girl's face, smeared, and her mouth, full of cum, was there for all to see should the tape get into the wrong hands. That's how long ago it was, when tapes were tapes, before digital took over the world.

Inevitably Layla's brother and the girl broke up so another obvious question, who got custody of the tape? As she was the guilty party in the split, he kept it and as he was in the army he sent it out to The Gulf for the rest of the battalion to see. She wasn't impressed but the troops were. There were a lot of requests for her number; guys like a game bird. These days the film would have just been uploaded onto the Internet, maybe onto YouPorn. Other sex sites are available.

Dan said that he hadn't filmed himself but he thought that it was a pretty good idea and one that he would broach with his next squeeze. The beauty of modern technology is that the images are stored digitally, you can take stills as well as moving pictures and everything can be stored on your PC, a memory stick or your mobile phone, so when you're all alone in that hotel room you have the ultimate in porn, watching some bird licking your own nads.

Of course, should the material get into the wrong hands . . . it's not exactly the sort of thing that you'd want your parents to see. Or your offspring. Makes me shudder just to think about it. What makes me shudder more? The likelihood that one day there will be such material featuring your parents. Or your offspring . . .

EIGHTY-SEVEN

At the next Salsa gig Terri and Lola were on the door. I was alone, Anne Hathaway was back at her cottage; it hadn't worked. Nice, but short and sweet, she wasn't ready for anything more than a fling, her mind dominated by the damage and pain caused by her split. In twelve months, who knows? I've still got her number, no, not written on the back of my hand.

Terri looked resplendent, beautiful, blossoming. Lola fluttered her eyelids, her face pretty, innocent, hiding the real her, her legs stunning beneath a tan coloured dress. Dan was paying.

'Ladies,' he said, 'what a greeting. Which one of you has the lucky ticket to dance with me tonight?' No mention of making a porn film then. 'If I'd known I would have been greeted by such beauty I would have dressed up.' He walked off to change his shoes.

'He's right,' I added, paid and followed him.

The room filled over the next half hour: Curly, Lulu, Billy, Jenny Glasses, Norris the News, Pastel Pete, Thumper, Bobbin' Robin, no sign of The Spaniard, Tamsin without Morag, no Ava, Arlene, Lizzie, Princess Grace, some new faces, some old ones, some old people, all levels, there for the breeze of the dance.

Lulu came over to me, Dan and Billy, kisses on each cheek.

'Looby Loo, I was just talking to Dan about my brother,' I said. 'He lets his dog lick his feet. As a sex guru where does this sit in terms of fetish and fantasy?'

'Pretty disgusting really,' she said. 'Just imagine where that dog has licked before?'

The world stopped as tumbleweed flew past our faces; we all considered the tableau of a dog licking its own arse or the nads of another dog before licking human feet. Bestiality is definitely not best. I tried to lighten the mood.

'I bought a little rabbit for my niece for her birthday.'

'I've got a rabbit,' said Lulu.

'This was a cuddly toy.'

'Mine's not, mine's a big fuck off vibrator called The Rampant Red. There are five other types – The Purple de Lux, The Three Way, The Pink Elite, the Platinum and The Blue Thruster.' I marvelled at her product knowledge.

'You've got them all?'

Lulu smiled.

'Thought you were walking funny,' I said.

'What are you talking about?' asked Billy joining us when she'd mentioned the word Red.

EIGHTY-EIGHT

When you study motivation, whys and why nots, most people, above carnal lust, are motivated by fear or love, away from something or towards something. Both are great propellants. Love begets love. Fear inspires survival.

Remember the beautiful girl I mentioned, another selfish FUD? I asked her why she came round to see me. The flesh is weak was her answer. She felt horny and she liked me enough to want to lick my nads. God bless her. I wasn't prepared for the fall-out though, being used, auditioned, but I learnt a lot from the experience.

Let me take it further. Go back to the girls in Dublin? Pure lust, fuelled by a not insignificant volume of alcohol, and fear geared them towards recreational sex with a complete stranger. They didn't want to miss out. They wanted to see if the grass was greener. They craved some skin, some sexual satisfaction that they probably weren't getting at home.

Some girls will try and seize the moment. I was chatting to one girl. 'I know I shouldn't,' she said, 'but I could do with a beer and some fun and sometimes your heart has to rule your head . . . go with your instinct . . . your feelings . . .

not logic.' I suppose you could apply this to the Dubliners too.

Some women are pragmatic rather than spontaneous, fear meaning that they want to keep the stability of the status quo rather than encouraging dramatic changes. Upheaval is an unwelcome bed friend and as a result some women tolerate shit relationships and live unfulfilled.

With all this in mind is there any wonder that finding a potential lover is such a quagmire. Factor in other things. Just split up. Rebound. Too old. Too young. You're in the wrong phase. She's in the wrong phase. She won't leave him even though the relationship is dead. Even though he is fucking anything that moves. Even if she wants kids and he doesn't.

I have two very special friends who are facing the latter dilemma. Their body clocks are ticking, 37 and 41, they both want kids and both their partners don't. So what do you do?

Let me tell you about one of them. We had an honest conversation at a Salsa class. We stood by the bar as others took part. It was almost as if I was her girlfriend.

'It is no fun being me at the moment . . . everyone I know is having babies . . . except me . . . '

'So what does he think?'

'He thinks everything's hunky dory.'

'Have you told him?'

'We've talked about it.'

'But does he know how much you want kids?'

'He already has two . . . he says he doesn't want any more.'

'So you have a decision to make.'

'Yes . . . do we split up? And then I take three months of total heart ache, cry, don't eat, try and recover and then I have to find someone else...and what if I don't, I will have lost a great bloke, and for what . . . and anywhere, where do you find smart, professional, solvent, nice, good looking men?'

'You could try here?'

'But look at them! Not exactly the greatest selection of the food chain. And they are all so short. And wimpy.' This girl is tall.

'That would just leave me then.'

She laughed but I knew that she was thinking about it seriously.

EIGHTY-NINE

You girls are forgetful things.

There's a drawer in my bedroom that is a little like a trophy cabinet. It's not but you get my drift. In it are earrings, the odd necklace, a leather belt and a toothbrush, all the spoils of sex. Maybe the girls have such a good time that they forget what they came in with? Maybe they are in such a rush to get out that they can't be bothered to search? Lmto. Laughed me tits off.

You can understand the jewellery, an earring that comes out, or a necklace that is taken off because it is not meant to be slept in. But a leather belt? I wonder if she still wonders where it is? The toothbrush? I'm trying to entice her back for another go and maybe she'll use it again.

What there isn't in the drawer is any underwear. The reason I mention it is because there have been reports in the papers that the Mayor of a small town in Lancashire has recently been arrested for breaking and entering. Okay, so the local mayor is a bit of a hood. But it's not that. The reason that he broke in was to steal knickers. And not only that, parade around the bedroom wearing them. The papers said that he performed a sex act too. That'll mean that he had a wank then. Sorry, a bit of self-love. He was caught because a girl put in a secret camera. 'Fucking hell, it's the mayor! Oh, no, he's jerking off!'

You can understand a woman's horror when this happens can't you? First off there's the cost. Nice knickers are not cheap. I have a girlfriend who'll make you a pair out of leather for ninety quid. But more than the money it's the violation of your home and privacy. It's creepy, pervy and sends a tremor, a fetish too far.

Apparently it is quite common. The Japanese call it shotagi dorobu. Knickers are stolen from bedrooms, during hotel raids, nothing else just the knickers, from washing lines and even from people's baskets at the launderette. So you just have to ask why?

Apparently not everyone is good at intimacy and the knicker stealers see it as trophy hunting in one sense and compensation in another. If you are shy with women, if you have a poor self-image, if you fear rejection then having the knickers, the gateway to intimacy, is almost sex by proxy. In a world where a relationship is primarily a simple negotiation for sex on terms that both parties are happy with this irons out a lot of issues for those people who haven't got the courage, confidence or skills to cope. Perhaps I should teach it at night school?

NINETY

They say that the way to a man's heart is through his stomach. I think the aim is a little high but if it is a truism for men then it is equally the case for girls. Food is important in the dating stakes whether you are taking someone out, planning on seducing them back at the ranch or providing little treats, little signs of affection like a small bar of chocolate or an individual piece of candy. And then there's sploshing. More later. Sploshing? What the hell is that? I know, just educational.

Guys, listen up. Girls love to be pampered and cared for in every field. They might pretend that they're all independent and sassy and needless but we all know that is bollocks. They love flowers, jewellery or a pack of their favourite wine gums. I lied about the last one. Replace it with chocolate, Lindors, if you like. We all want to be liked and loved and have people do things for us; it makes us feel valuable.

And as part of this process - for dating is just that, it could be a short game or a long game, but it is a process – buying them dinner is as good an opportunity you get for developing the relationship and for anything further to happen, whether that is a step towards marriage, a bunk up or someone to scratch from your list of potential love partners.

So what does having dinner mean? It means that she has chosen to spend an evening with you, that she has accepted the proposition, the chance for you to sell yourself, and for her to reciprocate, for her to get a free feed and for you both to enjoy the moment. There is also the seed that is sown in her mind that she has to reciprocate in some way or to say thanks and this is almost the mildest form of prostitution there is. You buy dinner, you get a snog. Or a blowjob on the landing outside the flat. Of course, that is no guarantee and the bloke should never presume but the girl does feel compelled sometimes to even the favour stakes. 'Fuck me, that steak was nice, better shag him then.'

Let me take this theory a little further before we get on to sploshing – talk about a tease! Eating, and don't forget the mildly numbing qualities of a little alcohol too, eating has a profound impact on the brain. Check out the somatosensory cortex. The human cognitive capacity transforms and elaborates pleasure. Food is a stimulant. Hormones go crazy as the woman's appetite disappears. She stops worrying about where her next meal will come from and she can then concentrate on other things, like pleasure, it's almost as if a new door is opened, or her legs. And if she's had some food deemed as a natural aphrodisiac then you'd better hope your bollocks can cope. We're talking oysters, avocado, water melon or chocolate, all containing phenylethylamine (PEA) - a substance found in the cocoa solids in chocolate - they release the same feelgood chemicals as having sex. Some cheese has ten times more PEA than chocolate. That said I'm not big on oysters personally. Aphrodisiac? Normally a naked or half-naked body is enough for me.

NINETY-ONE

Entertaining a girl, that is cooking dinner for her rather than doing an hour of stand up or singing the songs from her favourite musical, is a sure fire way of winning affection. First off, if she agrees, then she's happy to be behind closed doors with you, a sign of trust and maybe things to come. Girls know this too; they're not stupid unless you're talking about the black girl Desiree Washington that Mike Tyson supposedly raped. (Why on earth did she go back to his suite? Was she so naïve or was he really an animal? Really tough to call when it's one person's word against another.)

Girls know the rules. They know that it's the spider's web scenario. (That said, a girl I know was propositioned by TV's Nick Knowles; five star dinner at the local Hotel du Vin. She thought it was an innocent offer until I explained his plan. Perhaps she was just joshing me but she seemed genuinely surprised. She tells me she didn't shag him. Yeah, right.) Anyway, back to the real rules. Of course, it's best to play it stage by stage and not to greet her naked with your cock in your hand but cooking is a great sign of intimacy and investment in your own emotions and if you get it right then it really is hard for the girl to refuse.

There is this myth that to seduce you have to have candles, soft lights and gentle music. It is no myth. If you create the mood it signifies that you have made the effort and girls like that and what's more it does make the whole process more memorable, warmer and perfect for seduction. Appeal to all the senses, not just one. Of course, if it's lunch you might not be able to sort the lighting but keeping the house warm is a good starting point. She's not going to strip in the cold now, is she? It really does help if you can cook though and do cheffie things rather than serving food ladled or dollopped onto a plate. Presentation sells.

So make sure you think about the date. Plan it. What special touches can you apply? Clean up. Hoover. Dust. Plump the cushions. Clear down radiators. Apply clean sheets. Shift the washing basket. Clean the bog. Don't have photos of the ex all over the bedside cabinet. Close cupboards and drawers. Shift the lads' mags. Give the place an airing. You might think these things are obvious but you'd be amazed at how many girls turn up and are quickly turned off by the state of the place.

The mind set is important during a date. What do you want to happen? What does she want? Has she come for the food? The company? The sex? Or all three? Of course, if you have an adult conversation first, like, 'are you staying?' that makes things easier but even without that don't be obsessed with the result, just let the process work for you. Remember Dublin.

Normally the alcohol intake is enough to gauge her interest in staying over. Of course, she might ask for the spare room, she may be your best girl friend, but even then, make sure you have enough drink in the house, a variety, maybe the ingredients for cocktails that you can make together? Put wine glasses in the fridge. Chilled Chardonnay from a chilled glass is so classy.

And after all that maybe you'll want to give her a little treat. A copy of a new CD. Or maybe a small bottle of massage oil? I did that once and after dinner we massaged each other. Totally sensuous. She was a funny one though, insisted on condoms even though she had a coil fitted. I don't know whether she was concerned about catching something from me or protecting me from her. I like to believe the latter. Lmto.

NINETY-TWO

As much as the film 'Dirty Dancing' gets the girls' juices flowing so too does 'Nine and a Half Weeks' starring Kim Basinger and Mickey Rourke a film I profess to never having seen, which, given Kim's beauty and on screen sensuousness is a surprise but this film is when the world was introduced to sploshing. Hey, maybe it happened before 1986 but I'm running with this one.

There's a scene in the film when she's in her white fluffy gown and her white fluffy socks and they are in the kitchen, him in just his jeans and thong. I guessed about the thong. He gets her to sit down and close her eyes and then he feeds her an eclectic mix. It starts with olives, another guess, cherries in juice, strawberries, a glass of wine, some cough mixture (true!), jelly, a chilli (that she spits out), she glugs at milk and then he sprays her with sparkling spring water, all a precursor to fucking each other's heads off. Oh yeah, they finish off with honey.

Technically sploshing fits into the fetish realm of wet and messy (WAM) where people get aroused when someone is covered, generously, with substances, normally fluids like whipped cream, custard, shaving foam, chocolate sauce, oil, paint, slime or gunge but it can be baked beans or spaghetti hoops though depriving the third world of such processed crap would be a sin.

Sploshing can happen when someone is clothed not just naked and I suppose the best description is bukkake with fluids not spunk. So when Mickey Rourke hits the sparkling water and drenches her, therein is the splosh.

I watched one of these videos in the name of research. A good-looking girl wearing jeans, v-shaped t-shirt highlighting an ample, inviting bosom and nice shoes was gunged by her pal, another girl. It was gently applied, bit-by-bit, cold and warm, as she sat on a chair. The gunge, different colours, started on her head and dripped over her body but somehow missed her cleavage, a mighty fine cleavage at that. The girl applying the gunge seemed to notice this too and made it her quest to make sure that her tits were part of the show. And do you know what, it was mildly arousing, her body covered in gunge, her profile there to see. Not my first choice and I don't know anyone who would want to sit through it but mildly arousing nonetheless. I suppose Tracey Emin would call it art?

The attraction of the Mickey and Kim scene, apart from trying to enter her in the wet dressing gown category at Butlin's, is that she is totally compliant, runs with it, even with the cough mixture, there is trust, fun, that willingness to experiment and the joy of watching a woman have something put in her mouth and we're not talking a banana or a Cadbury's flake. Watching a beautiful woman eat is erotic. And when the cherry juice dribbles down her chin it is almost a replica of things to come though with the cherry juice I'd be more inclined to lick it off. Don't you just hate that porn when the guy snogs the bird after he's come in her mouth? Not for me. Nor felching. I'll let you look that one up.

The simple message is that food and sex go. Don't tell me you've never used a banana on your girlfriend . . . or on yourself, ladies. And where would we be without a fresh tube of squirty cream to lick off her body and her yours. Honey, dripped onto naked skin is very popular. Chocolate spread works. A good pal of mine said that he used to stick his cock into the peanut butter jar but I think he was only teasing. That said I always avoid the toast when I stay over at his.

NINETY-THREE

I read (past tense) lots of books about relationships. Lots about girls. About life. About self-improvement.

Anything to give me an edge, an inkling. Something that would open a door or two. You have to keep developing or you just stagnate.

And with the development there came change, a wisdom, an understanding, a more global view of people and life.

Sounds a bit pious doesn't it? But bear with me. Please.

I discovered from a genuine sage that there are five languages of love, no, not French, French, French, French and French. I did a psychometric questionnaire on my own love language and discovered that it is easier to retain a partner that you want to retain by using the language that your partner prefers, not your own. (Do unto her as she wants to be done to – not what you want.)

Many people get their kicks out of being told that someone loves them. There is some reassurance in soliloquies that contain, 'I love you with all my heart', 'God, I love you', 'I love you so much', 'You really do mean the world to me'.

But not everyone digs that. To some people you might as well be speaking Mandarin.

Others think that love is offering and giving 'Quality Time' to their partner, you know, that undivided attention that says, 'I give you my all; I can't give you any more than that'. This isn't necessarily an activity but more a proximity, where the time and its quality, the abundance of eye contact, the lack of distraction, speak volumes about your feelings. Truth be told, the most valuable thing that you have in life is time. What else is there to give? Save, your life?

Did you know that there is an international rule that says that hugs have to be six seconds or more long for them to be worth anything? I may have mentioned this already but when I see people meet at an airport and the hug lasts a blink I cringe. Give them a proper hug! For physical touch is another way of showing love, a connection, a movement in union, no fear. This is why dancing is so intimate. There is as much contact as either party wants and allows and there is complete trust. Barriers melt, bodies soften, desires arise, and away from this intimacy, it hurts.

Each time I see the film 'Evan Almighty' I cry. It's normally the bit when God explains life to Evan, or should I say Morgan Freeman to Steve Carrell. It's when the term 'random acts of kindness' is turned on its head and God creates the TLA that is ARK, acts of random kindness. Being kind is a great sign of love. Being nice, thoughtful, considerate, all great Christian characteristics, in a non-religious sort of way, matter. Being selfless doesn't mean that you think less of yourself, it just means that you think of yourself less.

So being servile, offering service is a sign of love. So too offering services, help cutting a hedge, de-frosting a car, scrubbing a patio. Something to ease the burden. Anything to take away responsibility.

The fifth language of love is the giving of gifts, however big or small. One chocolate. Or a hamper. A gift that says I have put thought, love and effort into this process. My spirit tells me that giving is good and therefore I give. This is why birthdays and Christmas can be so special. It is not about the day or the religious celebration, it is about the thought that goes into the giving.

So once you get the girl best find out what her love language is.

Don't at your peril.

Not sure how each auditionee would react to a psychometric test being placed on the barstool on the first date though.

NINETY-FOUR

Me, Billy, Dan and Frankie went to a dance that was themed. The promoters do this sometimes. Vicars and tarts. Caribbean. Gangsters and Molls. Cubano, whatever the fuck that is. Black and White.

So we'd dressed up in black and white clothes and so had most of the room except for the odd waif and stray who'd turned up in jeans and a t-shirt and looked like a cunt. Couldn't be arsed to make the effort.

I could see Eve and Adam, her in a number that faded from black to white to grey. She looked terrific, the hem length perfect so she could still dance (you wouldn't believe the number of dopey birds who turn up to a dance in clothes that they can't dance in.) The kicker came when you looked at Eve from the side; the dress was slit every few inches revealing tempting flesh.

'She looks like a fucking sausage roll,' said Dan, himself adorned with black Italian trousers and a white Italian shirt.

'She looks fucking gorgeous,' I qualified. 'Shame she's with that twat.' Not popular, Adam.

Tamsin appeared with Morag, hadn't seen them in an age.

'So you do have legs then,' quipped Dan at the sight of Tamsin in a frock.

'Nice pins,' I said to Tammy.

'You look lovely,' said Billy. Frankie just stared at her chest, prevalent.

'Nice party frock Morag,' I added.

'You look lovely,' said Billy. Frankie was still looking at Tammy's tits.

'Good to see you have some white jewellery to suit,' said Dan.

'Yes, the earrings are pearls,' she closed.

'Shame you couldn't find your necklace made of pearls,' said Dan. Tammy started laughing. The others didn't get it. 'Didn't I give you one of those for your birthday a few years ago?'

Indeed he had.

NINETY-FIVE

The idea of a pearl necklace, that is, coming all over the bird's neck or tits appeals sometimes and occasionally it happens anyway, by accident, depending on the power of the spurt. In fact I used to own a greyhound and I called it 'My

Tits' so that when it was running down the final straight everyone who backed it would be shouting, 'come on My Tits, come on My Tits.'

Almost like when someone asks you what you do for a living. 'I used to breed race horses . . . now I've got a girlfriend.'

The only thing that doesn't appeal, as previously mentioned, is when it's the bloke that finishes himself off. All that prep, foreplay and fucking and he ends up wanking himself off. Just fucking pointless really. I mean, if he's had ten pints and can't come that's different, all hands to the pumps and all that, but surely the beauty of sex is what someone does to you? Sex is about mutual pleasure, stimulation, giving orgasms and the only time you should do it yourself is when there is no one there to do it for you. It should be a rule papered on the bathroom wall. 'It is the job of the bird to make the bloke come . . . where and how to be agreed'.

You could take it down when you had visitors.

The thing that isn't taken into account on occasions like this is what the bird wants. Maybe she wants to do it? Maybe it is part of her mantra:

'I am giving him pleasure,

I want to give him pleasure,

I need to give him pleasure.'

It might just make or break her self-esteem. Maybe it's a notch on the belt for her too. She might even have a monthly target to hit? Or a yearly target? Or one for her life? You can imagine the conversation can't you?

'I'm going to shag forty blokes before I get married and then remain faithful forever (seems a lot, most girls don't get to double figures.) And that's in five years. I've done my targets: two hundred orgasms a year, same with hand jobs, three hundred suck offs, fifty facials, one hundred in my arse and the rest inside me.'

Equates to about three times a week if you're wondering about the maths ☺.

'And what about that Derek bloke, the one that likes wanking off all over you?'

'I can't be doing with him anymore . . . he fucks up my ratios . . . I want to do the wanking . . . what is it with some guys?'

I rest my case.

NINETY-SIX

The Black and White gig was in full swing and the overwhelming feeling in the room was one of relief, relief that the week had passed, that the weekend had arrived and that for a few hours everyone could throw away the shackles and let go.

I decided to use the evening to put some markers down and to see if anyone would match the tough criteria that I had set in terms of someone making the grade as a potential love partner. Nice. Tough one that. All right, as said I don't like overtly huge women, I am attracted by traditional beauty, by brains, by a heart, by someone who has the courage to love and by girls who are rampant in bed. But nice is the starter.

It's funny, you walk into a room full of girls, they know you're good, they might be a bit frightened of asking you to dance, most girls are shy when it comes to asking a guy to dance – they think it's sexual, in Salsa it can be but generally it isn't - and you can pick and choose who you dance with. But of all the girls in any one given room there might be one that you think looks all right. One. Two if you're lucky. The other thing that affects results is that if you've been on the scene long enough the girls that know you have already made their mind up and you have been categorised, just as they have by you. That means they have judged and if they haven't made their move, some do, most don't, then they're not likely to. And if they do or you do it is a shock to everyone's system.

Over by the bar was a girl called Sam. Used to live in The States, five eight, size fourteen, heaving top shelf, pretty face, sandy coloured hair, layered, cropped at shoulder level, always prettier when she smiled. Then again most birds are.

We met one January when she came to a gig where I performed. I do that if asked. We danced, she was impressed that I topped the bill, and within seconds we had clicked. The dancing was fun and sultry and by the end it was difficult not to kiss her. The look on her face said, 'do it big guy,' but I backed off. The next morning I sent a text to her mate (I didn't have Sam's number) and asked her to get her to text me. Nothing happened. Don't even know if she got the message. I said hello.

'Hello stranger . . . haven't seen you for an age. You ok?'

'Good thanks . . . you're looking well.' Sam was a one-time FUD now 90% recovered, probably just entering phase five of her recovery, more later.

'So are you . . . gorgeous.' I kissed both her cheeks and cuddled her. She didn't back off. As she settled in my arm Dan and Lulu walked back to their chairs, away from the dance floor and they hugged and kissed each other as a way of thank you for the dance. It was on the mouth. Some girls like this. Some don't. Lulu does. No tongues.

'Oy, you two, that's enough,' I said, joking. 'You can get a room if you want Dan . . . they rent out for periods of fifteen minutes.'

He mouthed 'fuck off' through his smile.

NINETY-SEVEN

At gigs like the Black and White Dan, Billy and me tend not to talk to each other much. We dance in different parts of the room and don't normally go for the same girls. It's like Team Travolta is split into three. But in between dances we stood with a short girl that Billy had schooled, Rose.

'Rose is emigrating,' said Billy, sad to be losing a talented dance partner.

'That'll hurt your arms,' said Dan. 'All that flying.'

'You can't,' I said, 'the shares in Matalan and Primark will plummet.'

'You can't,' said Dan, 'where will I get me drugs?'

'And Thresher's will go bust the day you two fuckers stop drinking,' she countered.

We all pissed ourselves. When a girl swears unexpectedly...

'Where are you going?' Dan asked.

'New Zealand.'

And she's still there.

At the bar a group of girls were doing tequila slammers, you know the drill, lick your hand, put on the salt, lick the salt, neck the drink, bite the lime. A bird did this to me once off body parts – my chest, the swell of hers, gratuitous licks thrown in, bizarre given her boyfriend was five yards away (alcohol obviously.) It was unusual to see at a

Salsa gig, alcohol and proper dancing are not normal bedmates.

Leading the group was Rozzy The Prozzy (Likely Lads, way back) who was starting to look like she'd been at it a while, she wasn't looking well.

'She's into alternate medicines,' said Dan.

'She might need the fuckers the way she's going,' I said.

'And she's into Pilates,' said Billy.

'And Tai Chi.'

'And Reiki.'

'And incense burning.'

'Recycling.'

'The environment.'

'And she's definitely going green,' I said as she staggered towards to the exit. 'She's going to puke her guts up.'

After the tequila floorshow all our attention quickly moved to a new girl who had just entered the room.

'Who the fuck is that?' asked Dan, his tongue reaching the floor.

The girl was five eight, willowy, sultry, auburn hair caressing her shoulders. She walked in a slinky, curvy way, her arse swaying, hitting imaginary cymbals, her stomach bear, muscled, a white bikini top showing off an ample, welcoming bosom. You wouldn't mind some of that for breakfast. Dan wolf-whistled as she passed. She smiled and walked on by. I think Dan's in love.

NINETY-EIGHT

Dan tells me that the only person he is in love with is the inventor of the Internet, pornography and the left-handed mouse. (Have you ever tried writing pornography? It takes you twice as long because you're only typing with one hand.)

When Dan said this, funny as it is, there was some genuine sadness in his delivery.

'I'd love to fall in love again big guy,' he explained to me, 'but I can't. The experience with the FUD nearly destroyed me; I gave it everything and all that she did was abuse my trust and betray me. After all I'd done for her! It's the incredulity really. I couldn't believe it. After I'd given her so much. Ever felt used?' He stopped to wipe away the birth of a tiny tear in the corner of his eye. He looked away and tried not to think about her, about the good times, about the photos he'd yet to burn. Then he looked at me again, filed his thoughts and continued. 'It's knocked my self-esteem, my faith and I've put some barriers up now to protect my heart. I feel a bit helpless and not worthy of much at the moment.'

I listened hoping no one would disturb his soliloquy. He needed this.

'I pulled a bird the other day, a few shags, no emotional attachment at all . . . I might as well have fucked a hooker . . . it was soulless, empty, quickly forgotten. Can't for a minute think that is was any good for her either. You know what . . . I threw in some one liners, had her giggling in her knickers, she had a fucking boyfriend and still she came back to mine . . . and do you know what? I didn't give a toss; it was just a shag. She wanted it. I wanted it. The bloke? I thought about it for a fucking nanosecond. Am I really that bankrupt of morals? There's an obvious fucking answer to that: yes.

You know what, I was in that rugby pub once and got chatting to a bird from the south coast, up for the weekend and I spent an hour stroking her legs, her body whenever I wanted and snogged her in the middle of the bar. Sexy fucker she was. I told her. She said she was organising her bloke's 40th birthday. What the fuck was that all about?'

He stopped to drink then carried on.

'And there was that night in that club, another fucking 40th birthday and there's this chav and a little hottie, him, knuckles on the floor, IQ of a gnat and I made a play for her whilst he was in the pisser. We made eye contact. It was all that was needed but the goon was soon back and I moved on and pulled a right fuckin' loon, high as a kite, not totin' a machine gun. It would be really nice one day to fuck someone that I actually like.'

Dan was where a lot of people find themselves, wary, wanting to be loved, lonely, but scared and facing a terrifying balancing act that he, like many others, failed to achieve.

NINETY-NINE

I am blessed to know some people with wisdom beyond the ordinary. I got this note from a girlfriend.

'I don't think FUDs do it deliberately. Emotionally you don't know where you are! You just try and get through. Having someone around who cares, helps. You want to believe that this person could be for you. But really it is all too soon.

Hormones and lust get in the way of logic, maybe? But at the end of the day, we are all responsible for the choices we make. I know how hard it can be to come to terms with wanting and loving someone who is not there for you. But real love is being able to let go. Negativity is not good for the soul AND WILL NOT CHANGE ANYTHING. So people need to stay positive and strong. What will be will be. FUDs are just looking for a form of escapism from reality. They need time. When a woman feels under pressure that is when she backs off. Given freedom, time and understanding, no pressure is very seductive. Let time heal their wounds, and who knows what the future may hold.'

I kept the note and thought better of sending it to Dan for the moment.

ONE HUNDRED

Lulu shook her hips and bounced her arse off an imaginary wall. The Black and White gig was all but over but everyone still watched her remarkable gyrations. Shaking your booty was never like this. She danced like Betty Boo on speed and we were all glad of it. She left the floor and took a drink before introducing us to Ellie, a pal from Birmingham.

'Wow, you're beautiful,' said Billy. 'You should be in the movies.'

'You might have seen her in a porn film,' said Lulu. They both giggled.

'Welcome anyway,' I said.

'Stunning,' added Dan.

'She's naturally gorgeous,' offered Lulu, 'hasn't washed her hair for a week.'

'It looks lovely nonetheless.' Me again.

'Her and her bloke were shagging last week,' Lulu, unstoppable, 'he came all over her face and hair . . . that's why she hasn't washed it . . . she loves the smell . . . every now and then she takes a bit in her mouth to remind her of what she's missing.'

'Remind me not to kiss you on the head,' I said. 'Dance?'

I'm not sure if Lulu did this for fun, to shock or because she thinks it's just normal language. Some men do it, they talk dead pan about oral sex or fetishes, and they do this in mixed company, and you wonder if it's to make them look big, liberal or just a cunt. There was a time when a group was discussing deep-throating, something that you would assume, if you did the maths, was almost impossible. The distance from a bird's lips to her throat is about four inches so if the cock is longer and it all goes in how does she do it? Try it . . . with a banana . . . and see how you get on. I suppose it's an acquired skill.

Did you hear about the porn film with the male amputee? Talk about getting your leg over.

Anyway, Ellie and me danced and she wasn't half bad, a natural sway and she didn't mind close contact. Her eyes were like dark milk chocolates.

'That was great,' I said, 'thank you, an absolute pleasure.' Me.

'Why? Did she make you hard?' Lulu.

'You can both walk me to the car when the night's over,' I said.

'Where's you car parked?' Ellie.

'In the garage at home.'

'Saucy fucker!' Lulu.

ONE HUNDRED AND ONE

Lunch with Layla was always a fun event and this time she introduced me to her pal Sarah, forty something, hippy chick, mad, mild, mixed up, musical, mentally marooned, messed up, middle class.

When guys are together they don't normally get too graphic. Birds do and as I was the guest these two just ignored me and talked about whatever they wanted.

'Do you know,' said Layla, 'there's a course at a college in America where you can learn how to give blow jobs? They talk about preparation, technique, positioning, the gag reflex, the sensitive areas, what to do with your hands, your tongue, how to stop him coming, how to give him the most pleasure.'

The hippy joined in. 'They even tell you about not forgetting his balls . . . lick . . . suck . . . guys love it . . . that's why they want two girls, one to suck his cock off and the other to lick his balls as he comes.'

'Sounds pleasurable to me,' I hinted.

They both looked at me as if to say 'no fucken hope'.

The last bit cheered me though. You see girls, that's what it's about, giving pleasure.

Funny this, let me delve further. Birds get all antsy when a guy puts his hand up her blouse to have a fondle. Why? 'Get off.' 'What do you think you're doing?' Well, all the guy is doing is giving pleasure.

There is a common misinterpretation that a guy is getting to bases, numbers one, two or three, or more, that they tally it all, take it home and wear it with a badge of honour. 'Yeah, baby, got my hand in her knickers. More points.' That's the last thing on his mind. All he is doing is giving pleasure. He gets more pleasure from getting his cock rubbed and sucked, believe me and that is what he is thinking about. When is she going to make her move? The tit fondle is for the physical benefit of the girl and the emotional benefit of the bloke, adding to his self-esteem that someone will be intimate with him. Why birds object is just bizarre. Maybe they don't want to seem cheap? Or easy? Or accept the fact that it is just nice and that this kind and generous bloke is going out of his way to make her happy?

Anyway, back to Layla and Sarah and they regaled me with a story on how Sarah had pulled a guy just for a bet. The bet, with Layla, was whether or not he had a big cock. I kid you not. Big is about comparison and perspective but anyway the bet was for one full penny. He is now known locally as 'The Penny Bet'.

So how do they find out? Rather than stalk him in the gents or ask for a signed photo the only way was to dance with him and rub their thighs or crotch against him. I suppose they could have ripped his clothes off and done the deep throat test – probably did later – or they could have asked him but given that most cocks change in size depending on the weather, the situation and what you do to it what would have been the answer?

'How big's yer cock?'

'Big enough to choke on darlin'.'

Gents are far too polite to reciprocate, to look at the bird and ask her how big or small her fanny is.

ONE HUNDRED AND TWO

It has to be said that unless you are desperate, and many are, that love and relationships are a minefield. The desperate accept anything.

But if you are choosy, even though the loneliness is killing you, finding someone singing from the same song sheet is difficult at its easiest.

Take the word 'Love' as an example, Love with a capital L. What does it mean to you? What does it mean to your friends? Your siblings? Your colleagues at work? To a girl in a dance hall? To you it may mean passion, to another it may mean infatuation. A girl I dated once used to drive a red Lada when they were freshest from the Eastern Bloc. Love was looking out for every red Lada and hoping it was her.

Others may think that Love is the physical ecstasy. Some may favour companionship, that bond, the sharing of goals, (I typed that as gaols by accident, and that fits too. Lmto) the commitment to each other, to care for someone else. Others may just be altruistic, meeting the needs of others by sacrificing their own.

As said it is a minefield.

Add this to the mix. If there are three levels of a relationship and you fit into Band One and your girl Band Three where does that leave you?

Let me elucidate some more. Band One is where you are dependent on each other, Band Two is that of equality and Band Three is about contribution, who brings what to the party. If that doesn't drift down to Band Two I'd say that was for the high jump.

ONE HUNDRED AND THREE

I want to talk to you about Direct Marketing and how it influences dating and pulling. Now, you might be scratching your head now thinking what is this twat on about but run with me, eh?

When you pull on a one-night stand there is an instantaneous result. It's like being in the supermarket, sort of, when you eye up that packet of biscuits, except with dating the biscuits have got to want to be eaten as well. One-night stands are a real magical mystery tour. You don't know what will happen, whether the sex will be any good, whether she will leave or stay, whether you will ever meet again.

'See you again.'

'Do it again sometime.'

'You haven't even got my number . . .'

And then there's the friends turned to lovers scenario when courage takes over and people decide to risk the friendship by gambling on love, or just sex. If it works, it's cool. If one person doesn't fancy it much the friendship struggles for a while and will probably be rebuilt.

But then there's the long game, the strategy for winning the girl, a game that might take months and years rather than minutes. Let me give you a scenario and then compare it to Direct Marketing. And then I'll give you another example when my pal Spud actually used a communication strategy – he is a Marketing graduate - and see what you think.

There's a girl in my sights. I have known her for about four years and she likes me and I like her. She's quiet, intelligent, beautiful, really beautiful – I have seen a black and white still photo of her and it just enhances her looks – and over time she has had a few boyfriends, an ex FUD ready to commit her heart again. I dance with her but as she has always had a boyfriend she's always been off limits.

And then, eighteen months ago she tells me she is nursing a broken heart after a recent split, no fun, no fun at all. As a chosen counsellor I gave her my card and said that if she wanted to talk she knew where I was. Non-invasive, friendly.

So we saw each other out and she never called.

Over the next few months though I emailed her once or twice and she responded, answering my queries, listening to my support, accepting the ethereal hug over the Internet.

Then she said they were back together, I said I was pleased but I still sent her the occasional note. And when I asked her out for a beer she came, just for an hour, to talk about life, I could see that things weren't all right.

And then she went to work Down Under for a couple of months. I wished her well but at 12:15am GMT one December I sent her a text. It was her birthday and she would have received the text at 10:15am local time. She was in a café having breakfast and the message delighted her. Will we get it on? Who knows but you get the gist of the process don't you?

So there you have a bit of Direct Marketing and a typical long game.

ONE HUNDRED AND TWO

On then to Spud.

Spud's been married a while and he has a theory that he applies to his life. He devised two communication strategies as part of his life path, the first, some Direct Marketing, to get the girl and the second, some more Direct Marketing, to keep the girl.

New business and existing business, if you like.

Let's check out the first.

Spud met this blonde (now Mrs Spud) and they clicked but she played a bit hard to get and although they had a beer every now and then it was all a bit platonic and he wondered if they would ever up the ante and move from this staid existence into a whirlwind of frenetic sex, emotional bonding and end up as life partners. He knew there was a way but how to convince the girl? That was the big question.

He had her phone number and rather than bombard her every day to the point of stalking her he sent her a text every Monday morning at nine o'clock. It could have been about anything, saying how he hoped how great her weekend had been, wishing her a good week, asking what she'd been up to, or condolences when her favourite actor or singer died, all non-invasive, just nice. She grew to expect his text.

After five or six weeks he felt brave enough to change the form of contact and after some minor investigations he found out where she lived and as well as the text he then sent her a little card every week, posted on a Monday so she would get it on Wednesday, sent second class purposely to stagger the communications, two brand placements a week.

In the card that he sent over eight weeks these were the messages:

1. It would be great to fall in love with a princess.
2. Making you laugh is just the greatest thrill.
3. I'm always here to listen to you, I'm always here for you.
4. All I want from a girl is faithfulness and her heart.
5. Acts of Random Kindness are inspirational.
6. I'm going to New York in the spring and it won't be on my own.

7. My restaurant has just been awarded its first Michelin star.

8. After five years of trying I now know that I can dance. Fred seeks Ginger.

Throughout this period of almost four months, when they met, Spud never mentioned the cards at all, neither did she, and then she called to arrange a meet in the pub and he surprised her with a little packet of tangy Haribos (sweets), beautifully wrapped in gold paper. She surprised him by reaching over and kissing him on the mouth and the deal was done.

Of course love isn't always sweet and had Mrs Spud not been up for it whatever he did would have been in vain – simple lesson on unrequited love – 'get the fuck out of there and get over it, it really isn't worth it' – but the softness, gentleness and romance of his strategy was beautiful. In fact tears are streaming down my face as we speak. (Soppy twat.)

ONE HUNDRED AND FOUR

We all know that the chase is fun, thrilling, a roller coaster, ups and downs, fears and phases, and is there any better feeling than the undressing on the first date? God, makes you hard just thinking about it. But the mistake that most men make is that once they applied Direct Marketing to get the girl they stop applying it to keep the girl and this is just naïve if not a bit fucking stupid. You spend all that time and effort, maybe some cash but not least of all your emotional investment and then you just stop, as if getting past the winning post was all that mattered. I should add that it's not just blokes who fuck up here; women are typically bone idle when it comes to doing things to keep the bloke happy, and I don't just mean putting his meat and potato pie on the table at six o'clock every night.

Let me put this into context. If you want the relationship to survive then you have to treat that union as the most important thing in your life and act accordingly.

Remember birthdays. Anniversaries. Her/his favourite song. Film. Restaurant. Surprise her/him with a special treat even if it's just a packet of sweets. Write a love note. Do what she wants you to do. Talk in her language of love as previously described. Even hard faced bitches that think they're immune to affection like it when someone tells them that they love them. Send flowers. Just do anything but for fuck's sake, prioritise. And girls this applies to you too. No fucker's ever bought me flowers. I got some lucky heather from a Gippo once. I don't think that counts.

My pal Big Davey got divorced in another life, so long ago. He told me that on his sixth wedding anniversary he walked in the house after work bearing six bunches of flowers, one for each year. A really nice touch. His ex thought it all suspicious – she had done nothing to celebrate. And because he'd bought three new shirts recently she knew that he was having an affair, guilt written all over him. Obvious. The silly fuck up got it all wrong. He was just carrying out his marketing strategy. Little wonder that this marriage was just waiting to disintegrate, which it did in a fairly calamitous way.

I suppose the point is that he made the effort and she didn't. We can all do little things for each other. Call it point scoring, call it banking favours, but it works. If you read 'Men are from Mars' by John Gray chapter ten deals with this beautifully. I won't re-write the twenty-eight pages but suffice to say that even though it's not simply quid pro quo it ain't far away. Women associate the same value on a packet of sweets as they would a night out or a weekend in Paris but if people empathise and act selflessly then the chances are things'll go well. But think about it, do it and see what happens. Write the fucker up on a spreadsheet if you like because as much as spontaneity is a terrific boost behind every successful relationship there is a great Direct Marketing plan. Just ask Spud.

ONE HUNDRED AND FIVE

The search for a love partner was getting frustrating. How many fucking auditions would I have to go through to find someone worthy? And as the frustration mounted it also made me question whether I was looking for the right thing.

We are programmed from birth to believe that when we grow up we will get married, have kids and we'll all live happy ever after. As I've already mentioned, the average marriage lasts eleven years so that's not the case. So with this in mind maybe I should be looking for someone else?

Why do people want a partner anyway? Why do they want a relationship with someone else when normally the relationship in its most peril is the relationship we have with ourselves?

In the bigger scheme of things it is the mechanism that we have been naturally given to ensure the survival of the species, given that we're great at making people but not great at peaceful co-existence once we've done that. Bit of a double-edged sword this one. Human beings are really the most mindless killers and destroyers on the planet.

Anyway. We meet, we shag, we have kids, the human race survives. Bosh! Job Done! But what else happens? If marriage isn't for life anymore, what is? And what sort of existence should we have? Friends with people? Fuck who we like? Live alone? Take each day for what it is rather than looking at the long-term picture? Get married but have a mistress? As long as she can have a lover? Just have a list of fuck buddies? Another list of girls to dance with? Another list who you want to drink with?

It all seems a little unfulfilling.

So the search continued, me, Billy, Dan and Barbara Finn hitting a club to check out the talent and to see if the clientele could dance. 'Let's see if there's any competition,' said Barbara, a bit of a mover herself.

'There's never much,' Dan said objectively.

Dan and Barbara danced and took the piss out of the rest of the floor, mimicking the fake John Travoltas and then they just danced, grace, class, outshining all-comers. They didn't do it on purpose, it was just a bit of fun.

Billy danced with a random girl, her happy to be asked, him gentle, dancing at her level, making her feel comfortable, grateful, whisked away on the surf.

I took over from Dan with Barbara, we was bringing the funness back to the dance. We stopped every now and then for a swig for as documented Barbara likes her pop.

Once the track had finished we all congregated at our table and as we sipped and glugged this bloke came over, straight from the dock of the Magistrates' Court, stocky, blinged up, big collar, small jacket, sleeves up, glass of Asti Spumante in his hand. He grabbed Dan by the hand, shook it, tried to arm-wrestle, lost and said, 'great dancing.'

'Thanks . . . we are dancers.'

'Oh . . . '

Nonplussed he fucked off back to Bambi, his girl who had been giving me the eye all night, not that I mentioned it to Fred Flintstone. She was tall, pretty, size ten, blonde, curly hair, dashing blue eyes, a waistcoat and shorts set, leopard skin patterns, ample amounts of thigh, edible, a snippet of buttock, edible. She seemed too bright for him. If there is a God she will be in a dance class close to me very soon.

ONE HUNDRED AND SIX

Layla was back, not having quite managed her mission: to fuck her way through the male population of Turkey. The good news though, for her, was that this was a fleeting visit and she would be able to reconvene with the Marmaris Massive within days.

She can be ribald can Layla and sometimes that makes others feel awkward, men and women alike, especially good God-fearing Presbyterian folk. She was with Dan and me in an Irish club and somehow the subject of confidence came up, confidence of people in the social world and on the pulling scene.

'Some blokes are scared,' I said, 'they don't want the rejection or to queer a patch, you know, they suddenly profess to undying love and the bird looks at him like he's got three heads.'

'True that,' added Dan. 'It would be so much easier if the bird just walked up to you and kissed you. That would stop all the fucking about.'

'Spoken like a true romantic,' said Layla.

'Well, you know what I mean?' Dan came back at her. 'How do you know if she fancies you? I was at a gig with two birds once. I was chasing one who wasn't having any of it. She was pissy because she could see that the other one was all over me. I couldn't see it at all. Why didn't somebody just tell me?'

'You're supposed to be able to spot the signs you dozy cunt.'

As soon as Layla said it the bar stopped and the world stood still.

'All right,' she added, 'let's make it fucking easy then. Let's introduce a coloured t-shirt system at the next gig we do.' She stopped to think a minute. 'Right, got it, here's what we'll do...Jesus fuck, the things I do for you blokes! Talk about a total lack of social recognition skills.'

'Present company excluded,' I added. 'I know when a bird fancies me. She just has to be breathing.'

Layla ignored me and ploughed on.

'Right, here's the t-shirt code...' and she announced it for all to hear.

'Black - unavailable. Yellow - married and up for a one night stand. Red - goer. Blue - I don't shag on a first date. Pink - gay – obviously. Green - I don't give head. Purple - I give really good head.' There's a thought. Is there such a thing as bad head?

The bar had stopped. There were some knowing looks, some nods of acknowledgement, some tuts and the sound of a body hitting a sofa as Mother Theresa fainted.

A colour code would help but it might stop the fun a little.

ONE HUNDRED AND SEVEN

Where a colour code is desperately needed is in the world of the FUD to help us all recognise true signs and to prevent people of both sexes being fucked about. Remember Dan and that FUD? Not healthy. So, how?

Well, FUDs go through a five-stage process of recovery after a split and only when they are in stage four or five are they going to be thinking straight enough to make proper, rational decisions about relationships, maybe only in phase five, to be honest. There is so much shit going on in the first three stages that, to be fair to the rest of the population, FUDs should be sent to Devil's Island or simply sectioned to protect the real world. Here's the detail.

Phase one should be a black t-shirt.

The FUD has just had the life changing news that he or she wants out, that there has been extra marital fucking and that there is no way back. This is the highest impact phase where paralysis, disbelief and denial combine to produce tears, fears, shock and agony. 'This is not happening to me!' is a popular mantra, one that once phase five kicks in FUDs look back on and realise is totally futile.

Black equals gloom and emptiness.

Phase two should be a red t-shirt.

Here the FUD realises that the partner isn't fucking about any more and a bit of reality hits home. Anger! Anger at the world, anger at the adulterous cunt they were living with or married to, anger at the selfish cunt who has decided to fuck their partner and ruin their perfect life. Anger generates hate and there are still tears, fears, shock and agony.

Red shirt spells anger and danger.

Phase three should be a blue t-shirt.

This phase is where the FUD enters a period of depression and anxiety because there is the beginning of reality. They have been rejected, they are confused as to why, they suddenly become very scared, lonely, defensive, protective. Remember that bird? 'I will never be beholden to another man, ever!' Her goal was survival, as I said, she'd take the wine, dine and sixty-nine, but she would do what she wanted, when she wanted and fuck the consequences.

Selfishness abounds as the brain goes into 'today I'm going to make fucking stupid decisions' mode.

Blue is a cold colour, icy, impenetrable.

ONE HUNDRED AND EIGHT

During these three phases FUDs are needy. Their personal circumstances have been turned on their heads and even if they have the support of their family, minus cheating spouse, obviously, the reactions are almost universal. They look for outlets and invariably turn to drink. They try and keep occupied. They work harder. They might take up a new hobby. Like dancing. Or they might go off on a singles' holiday or to a spiritual retreat where they can find themselves. Or a fuckin' hippy commune in California.

Funny that, finding yourself. Really it is the search for some sort of understanding, to try and make some sense of someone else's behaviour and your reaction. FUDs are martyrs, victims and focus on the negative, maybe not wanting to cause more damage and not knowing how, because their emotional tanks are empty and the only thing that will really work, even more so than trying to find yourself, is time, and that period varies from each individual.

Phil was married for 35 years and she fucked off with a younger bloke. It took him the best part of four years.

Taff was married for 18 years and she decided that she didn't want to be married anymore even though they had four kids. After two years he still doesn't date.

The Mambo King was like Phil but it took three years.

Christy was like Taff but with two kids. He's now in love with a girl from the Far East and has thrown the Prozac away. It took him six months.

Dr Kerry is two years down the line and you wouldn't touch her with a barge pole.

As I said it takes time because anything that happens in this period is a distinct threat to their unhappiness.

They won't allow happiness.

What's the secret of great comedy?

Timing.

What's the secret of dating an FUD?

Timing.

Because there is always a eureka moment when it suddenly hits the FUD and this is where phase four comes into play.

Phase four should be a green t-shirt.

This is where there is a glimmer of acceptance that the dream has gone but that because happiness just is, it shouldn't depend on external factors or another person, that the shit past can be boxed, filed away and forgotten and consigned to history.   Imagine locking up all your shit thoughts and shit memories and putting them on a DVD.   And then get that DVD and lock it up at the back of the filing cabinet never to be seen again.   It happened but it's gone. Move on, get positive, find some courage to believe in love and good things again.

Green is the colour of nature, gentleness, acceptance.

ONE HUNDRED AND NINE

And this leaves the last phase.

Phase five should be a yellow t-shirt.

Because phase five is where the defences come down and FUDs are nearly ready to step back into the real world. Yes, they may be wary, cynical even, but they won't be naïve and the wisdom gained through experience will be invaluable. This is the phase of readiness, of optimism, of hope.

Think about the colour yellow. What does it mean to you? Bananas? Custard? Butter. Brazil (football shirt)? Lager? Beaches? Gold? The leader of the Tour de France? The sun? So far, apart from, say, the custard, this is all good. Yellow is a colour associated with strength, intelligence, joy, happiness and brightness because sunlight is a life force and stimulates the nervous system, balancing energy, refreshing and a celebration of life.

Now once an FUD can get to this stage, this is when sober, correct and brave decisions are made to re-engage with the word emotion in a positive way; this is where people are ready to fall in love again or to even think about committing to one person.

So with all that going on you can see why it's imperative that the government introduces a t-shirt system. Maybe we should just go the whole hog and get people branded? Or corralled together when they go out on a night so the rest of us can live in peace? Best make their t-shirts striped or quartered though so that it doesn't fuck up Layla's colour scheme.

ONE HUNDRED AND TEN

Manners maketh man.

I was talking to Billy about the male population, their lack of intelligence, their lack of class, their caveman like qualities, and yet they still get the girl.

'Ah, that's because the girl doesn't know any better,' said Billy. 'And once they've got a bloke they tolerate a lot more than they normally would because they're not single anymore, they feel lucky to get a bloke, they're not on the shelf or lonely, they're getting a bit of cock and there's maybe someone to share the bills with. And more than that they tolerate Mr fucking Average because then they can go on a fucking campaign because think they can improve him beyond all recognition . . . it's not a case of change as most men think, it's about making someone better. . . even if they find he's a bit of a twat.'

'That's right,' I agreed not wanting to interrupt such an elegant and well-delivered monologue. 'There was my pal Porky at a wedding in 1989. He was with this stunning blonde and weeks later they'd split after they'd chatted at a bar about how he should drink less, dress smarter, shave more often and use mouthwash. (Toothpaste would have been a start!) To be fair to her she had a point, in fact she was right on all counts, but he thought she wanted to change him. All of those things pointed to one thing. Improvement.'

'But what women don't get,' added Billy, 'is that unless the bloke is of my vintage when we used to treat women with respect . . .'

'Or a 21st century man like meself . . . '

'He ain't going to buy all that bollocks. And that leads to frustration on her part. And then, if he stops doing the nice things he did to woo her in the first place, then as soon as something better comes along, she has her eyes opened and the thought process kicks in…grass greener…and she's off.'

'Nearly happened to me that.'

'Really?'

'Yeah, you remember that glamorous Indian bird . . . I taught her . . . we went out a few times but she was married so I backed off, but I treated her well, looked after her and all she could say was, "if I found someone better" . . . than her husband.'

'She was beautiful, I remember her . . . didn't fancy the ceremonial sword up the arse then?'

'I was just selfless, true to me, gentle and kind.'

'True that,' said Billy. 'How many blokes open doors any more? Or compliment a girl about her looks? Or walk road side of the pavement? I was talking to that bird Chrissie last week and she'd been out on a date with the baboon. He held the door for her, she said thanks, and he said, "Best make the best of it, won't happen again".'

'The stupid cunt.'

'Suffice to say that they don't date any more.'

'She's well shot.'

'Blokes just don't get it. Birds want class, quality and attention,' said Billy. 'I know I'm a bit old school but you can imagine the chav mentality can't you? Won't even walk her to the car on a night. What's all that about? And what do they do when they've just shagged some poor unfortunate after fifteen pints of Guinness? Growl, roll over, fart, pull the duvet from her, fall asleep and snore like a jet engine. Not exactly attractive.'

Quite.

What happens is that once a bird cottons onto the fact that you have manners, smile at them, look into their eyes, are genuinely nice and selfless, and that you aren't scared of saying warm, positive things, legitimate compliments, then you have far more chance of success than the Neanderthal.

ONE HUNDRED AND ELEVEN

'What's it like working here?'

This young kid in an England football replica shirt, white, circa Euro '96 was standing next to Dan at the Latin Pally.

'I'm not staff, mate . . . '

'Oh, I thought you were the bouncer . . . '

Dan was wearing black trousers and a black t-shirt, his normal kit, and he's a big lug, so the kid could be forgiven.

'If I was you wouldn't be allowed in.' The kid backed off and Dan laughed out loud. 'Only joking mate. This place doesn't need bouncers. This lot don't drink. It's only ale that causes problems. Hey,' Dan shouted to Billy, Curly, Barbara and me, 'do I look like a bouncer?'

'Black and black . . . a bit,' said Barbara.

'Black and black. Yes.' Added Curly.

'Knuckle duster on your right hand gives it away,' said Billy.

I didn't have to say anything.

JFI knuckle dusters are illegal . . .

We were watching, checking out the style, the talent, Barbara and Curly the same, Barbara window-shopping, Curly on the pull, something that meant that Dan and me had already been passed over in the selection process. Not a problem for us, we can take rejection, he lied.

A blonde approached me and said, 'Hi.'

Everyone stopped. Me too. Who the fuck was this? Five four, size eight, beautiful face, midriff on offer, sky blue eyes. I had to think on my feet and there it was, sprung from the memory bank like magic.

'This,' I presented her to the group, 'is Margarita from Sofia, beautiful, blonde and Bulgarian.' I kissed her on both cheeks. 'We met a few weeks ago over cocktails in that . . . cocktail bar . . . you were with your . . . French girlfriend . . .

and if I remember rightly you said you were married to . . . an English policeman.'

'No, we met at a dance last week and my name is . . . '

'If that's your story that's fine,' I butted in, 'if you don't want me to inform the authorities that you're an illegal immigrant that's okay with me.'

Margarita didn't know what to make of it. The others neither. Until a minute later a girl called Jackie came over and spoke to the blonde.

'What are you drinking Kasha?'

'Who the fuck's Margarita then?' asked Dan pointedly.

Fucked if I know. I'm sure she was the same chick. Obviously not.

As Margarita/Kasha sashayed away Dan opened his wallet to get some money for a beer and by accident a condom fell onto the floor. I think that's Karma; teach him to have a go at me.

'What's that for?' asked Billy picking it up and handing it back to him, 'a posh wank?'

'Better check the use by date,' I offered smiling, revelling in Dan's discomfort. He blushed.

'Better check the purchase date,' said Barbara, 'I bet you've had it for years.'

We all looked at her and began pissing ourselves.

'What?' she asked. 'What? What? What?'

ONE HUNDRED AND TWELVE

When Dan returned, less red in the face, the girls had gone for a dance.

'There's only one thing for it,' he said, 'it's going to have to be the convention. The weekender. The seaside. 'Cause to be fair, looking at this lot, I'm not going to find the next Mrs Travolta in here, am I?'

He had a point. All the regulars were in this pally. There was plenty of a new crop too but we'd thin sliced the lot. Miss Bulgaria, whatever her name is, would probably go and pull one of the teachers, a lot were too young, I mean teenagers not birds in their twenties, some too old, over fifty, some too fat, size sixteen and out, some just didn't make it out of the blocks. It was mildly depressing.

But at the convention . . . well . . . different ball game. Five hundred chicks, maybe seven hundred, maybe more, and with the added abilities, to dance and to teach, where else would you getter a bigger gene pool, a bigger captive audience? Apart from hitting on every chick in a supermarket or shopping mall where will there be such opportunity? And to be fair, their guards will be down, birds on tour mentality and all that.

Dan finished his drink, he sometimes drinks like a piranha, went for another and came back with a smiling Belle, someone we hadn't seen in a while.

'Wow, Belle,' I said, 'you look lovely. Super outfit.'

'Thank you kind sir.' She smiled some more.

'This is my last night on the pop,' said Dan as he etched towards the bottom of another glass. 'Time to clear the system a little. Costs a fortune too. Especially in here. I'll take a month off and then have a little wine when we get to the convention. You going Belle?'

'No, working away.' We both sighed, disappointed. 'Let me get you a drink,' she continued looking at Dan's empty glass. 'I'm only on coke . . . it doesn't take much to get me drunk and then when I am I get all soppy, I go around and tell everyone that I love them.'

'Would you like a bottle of champagne?' Dan asked.

Billy came back over to us, his coat on, ready for the off, a beautiful girl on each arm, looking like a Mafia Don.

'I need to bid you good night gentlemen, the time is nigh. Madam, what a stunning example of the female species you are. A true vision.'

'Belle, this is my twin,' said Dan. 'William.' They shook hands. 'I know, identical. Uncanny, isn't it?'

Belle played along in spite of clocking the differences in height, weight, age, hair colour, eye shade and skin pigment.

'Daniel, marry this lady, set up a home and let her have your children.'

And then he walked off.

'No,' she said, 'before you ask.'

Dan looked hurt. I pissed me self.

'Don't think you'd be that lucky Sugar.'

Dan has a sharp brain to match his tongue.

ONE HUNDRED AND THIRTEEN

I've got a pal who tells me that he fucked three different girls on the same day. First up the receptionist at work just after nine. Then his girlfriend at lunchtime. Ending with his wife before going to sleep.

It reminds me of that gag.

'Doctor, I've got a problem. I have sex first thing in the morning with the wife, then I come home for elevenses and we have sex again, and then we have sex at lunchtime, and then in the afternoon, and then when I come in from work and then before we go to sleep.'

'Well, you certainly have a healthy sexual appetite, what seems to be the problem?'

'It hurts when I wank.'

Funny, I know.

Anyway, back to my pal. Morally corrupt you could argue, I agree, but what about the girls, where do they fit into the equation? Why would the receptionist shag him? Especially if she knew he was married? Or the girlfriend? Morally corrupt you could argue, I agree.

But it also raises the issues of appetite, enthusiasm and stamina.

Let me throw this curved ball at you. Sex is boring.

There you go. I think this needs some clarification.

If you have sex with the same partner forever you start with the usual power of lust, shag relentlessly and then the urges slow down, the chemistry changes and the volume dries up. Sex in the early stages of a relationship is magic. But monotony can soon take over.

Some men, and women, like to preserve the frequency of sex so that when it happens it is more special, you look forward to it more and you can create the right atmosphere to make it an event. This can sometimes diminish the need to shag someone else.

So too the type of sex. My pal didn't elucidate much but sometimes a 'quickie' works for both parties. Sometimes the bird just wants to be fucked. Sometimes she wants everything and the night becomes a fuck fest. Balancing both is a good shout.

So why did my pal shag three different birds? Because he could. He's not a sex addict, he just likes it. Three different venues, different mouths, different tastes, different bodies, different proclivities.

These days he has changed and he is delighted that his current and only squeeze wakes up and the first thing that she thinks about is giving him head. Now there's a happy match. I dare say most blokes would go for that?

ONE HUNDRED AND FOURTEEN

Whilst we're on the subject it is well known that Michael Douglas, the son of Spartacus, has had treatment in a clinic for sexual (and alcohol) addiction back in the early nineties. So it does beg the questions, who is a sex addict and what is sexual addiction?

You could be forgiven for thinking that this is just a psychiatrist's way of making a few quid because just because someone likes fucking a lot doesn't always make them addicted. Can't people just say 'no'?

The medics will point you towards behaviour and control.

What if you plan to look at porn on the Internet for an hour and then find that you have stayed on much longer that you wanted? Apparently this is a sign. Me, I'd call that research.

Dating escort girls for fun means you're an addict. No it doesn't, it just means you want some serious adult company.

Engaging in some behaviour in spite of the obvious harmful consequences. This is just blokes wanting a shag. Some think of the consequences. Most are just loin led.

If you take the moral high ground and throw out all your porn only to become a collector again a week later means you're an addict. No it doesn't, it just means you need something to stimulate you when you're wanking or watching the telly with the missus or the mistress.

What if your behaviour causes you to feel really bad about yourself and it disturbs your marriage and family life? Well, guilt created from conditioning is normal. Fucking another bird rather than your wife will cause problems if she finds out. This is nothing to do with addiction.

These habits cost a few bob. There is always the shadow of STDs too but this happens as a natural consequence of fucking about.

If you go back to the bloke caught stealing knickers the same mental issues raise their head here. Chronic low self worth, depression, anxiety or stress at home or work, anger, core loneliness, boredom, problems and bad feelings in the marriage or partnership, shame and guilt. Addiction? My arse.

Let's put this into perspective. Blokes are fired by lust. It is the core to the human race and just because we want to procreate doesn't mean we are addicted. Anger, stress, loneliness are just normal facets of life. People cope with whatever strategy they think fit. Fucking is one of those.

The medics would explain that sex is used, often unknowingly, to anaesthetise shame, low self worth etc and they would be right, it is a pattern of behaviour that closely parallels the medical diagnostic criteria for substance dependence.

Except sex is driven by the survival of the human race.

ONE HUNDRED AND FIFTEEN

Whilst we're talking about the son of Spartacus have you ever wondered what happens in the movies when they do bedroom scenes? Are they real? Do they actually get it on? I am sorry to be the bearer of bad news. I don't know.

I know, a right pisser.

Take a look at certain movies.

I have fond memories of Ken Russell's 'Women In Love' (1969), a movie full of love, obviously, tragedy, not so obvious, a naked wrestling seen between Oliver Reed and Alan Bates on a concrete floor (they shared a bottle of vodka beforehand to ease the pain Reed says in his autobiography) and where Ollie Reed sucks on Glenda Jackson's (Oscar winner and Labour MP) nipple. That actually happens. I think Bates has an alfresco shag too if I remember right. Not sure how many takes it took, maybe ten or twenty. Lmto.

In 1973 a film was made of the TV series 'Man at the Top' and it starred Kenneth Haigh as Joe Lampton and Nanette Newman as Lady Annette Ackerman. There is a scene where Joe enters a shower with two naked girls. Good shout. And there is also one where he suckles Nanette's left tit. I think she dropped the butter bowl. And he shags a bird in a wood. She's wearing jodhpurs and boots, dead sexy. It's like shagging a bird when she still has her heels on, sexilicious or what. Anyway, back to the girl in the hunt. You hear zips, moans and leaves being crushed and you see her toes curl. But I guess they acted.

At this stage let's bring in the Japs again with the 1976 cult movie 'Ai No Corrida' directed by Nagisa Oshima. This film was set in pre-war Japan where a man starts an affair with his servant, an affair that becomes intense and torrid, so much so that when he dies she cuts his cock off and carries it around in her handbag as a souvenir. Can't remember if she killed him or he died of natural causes. During this movie she gives him head for all to see. I think the Jap censors were more bothered by showing pubic hair rather than the erection or the blowjob. They're funny out East.

Check out 'Caligula' (1979) from that cheeky monkey Italian director Tinto Brass. There is plenty of simulation but plenty of real action too. But was it real? Maybe we'll never know. Bit scary as a film too but that's the civilised Romans for you.

Over a decade later Hollywood whacked us with 'Basic Instinct' (1992). Here we have serious sex vixen Sharon Stone, the unlikely 'Ice Pick Killer', with the aforementioned star son of Spartacus, this time a copper, clearly naked. They kiss. He sucks her tits. It looks like he goes down on her. And she reciprocates. And then they shag. But do they? And if they do what do Mrs Douglas and Mr Stone think about that? Or do they use a body double?

The son of Spartacus was also involved in 'Disclosure' (1994) (nowhere nearly as good as the book) where Demi Moore is supposed to have licked his nads. But did she? And did he really put his fingers inside her? Seems like an area the lads and me didn't consider. Become an actor and go for the female lead?

I don't know. Because if I was him and that happened on set, how on earth do you stop? You get hard, she gets turned on and then the director butts in with 'CUT'. So he gets up, stiffy aplenty, walks over to his trailer and watches the lunchtime news. Or does he grab the gorgeous Ms Moore and shag her head off?

Funny one this. I was with a great girl once whose fervent belief was that it was unfair, almost unethical, to get a guy hard and to walk away. God bless her. This is the dilemma when you do a bit of dry humping too. She straddles you, you kiss, fondle, feel her pushing against you. And then you've got to go and do the school run . . . Lmto. Ruined many pairs of my pants that one. God bless her too.

There have been a couple of movies in the last few years that have sneaked into the mainstream but which are just undisguised porn.

'Baise-Moi' ('Fuck Me'), was released in 2000 and the theme is two girls, marginalised from society (raped seeking revenge), who go on an orgy of sex and violence. It stars two French porn stars, the late great Karen Lancaume (Bach) and Raffaela Anderson, because mainstream actresses read the script and wouldn't do the full, real, sex scenes. There is a rape (acted), a pick up with oral sex, four in a room, a couple of great seduction scenes where the girls lead and there's also a minor clip of a brothel that is best described as open plan. It is French made and filthy. I loved it. Except for the violence. The French broadcast it at teatime.

In 2004 the film '9 Songs' was depicted as romance and music, an unknown actor and actress playing a newly dating couple, going to gigs and fucking in between. This film showed oral sex and ejaculation and did pretty well even though the premise was pretty thin and the sex tame and mildly passionless. It wouldn't have got much funding in this country and I can't see it featuring much on BBC1 either.

ONE HUNDRED AND SIXTEEN

So, this was it.

Me, Dan and Billy had loaded the car and I drove, taking the motorway towards our weekend convention. We were all excited, like little kids ready for a treat, each with our own set agenda.

Billy was going to have a few beers, fuck about, tell some stories, crack some gags, keep the chalet clean, entertain his harem and show off his techniques and physique. He'd packed his pinstripes, his gym kit and classical CDs, the latter of which wouldn't see daylight until he opened his bag again the following Monday when he got home. A Salsa convention is no place for any of that shit. Billy brought the red wine, peanuts and CD player.

Dan had packed fifteen t-shirts, numerous flannels and four hand towels. He also brought the omelette pan, cheese grater, peeler and machete. As head cook for the weekend he was in control of the kitchen.

My bag was full of wine, bottle openers and proper CDs. I was to be resident DJ, social secretary and events co-ordinator. That meant getting the right birds back to the chalet for lunch and dinner, not running out of alcohol and making sure that everyone was prepped for a fun time. Truth be told we all did this but I had to have some sort of badge didn't I?

On arrival, we queued, got keyed up, sorted the cards for the electric metre and unpacked. It was meticulous, military precision, fast. Then we locked the door, poured the wine and turned on the music. This was boys' time, the chance to share thoughts, dreams, opinions, plans and occasionally slag off one or two of the talentless birds or male numpties.

Of course, we had come to the convention to learn more about dancing, to try out different routines, test new dance styles, to examine new techniques. And we were here to party. But the prime aim, for Dan and me at least, was birds. Would there be someone worthy within the pack? We're talking a life-partner, a love partner, not just a quick bunk up, though we'd take it . . .

They're funny these weekends. Everyone has their own plan. Some girls just like to tart about, kiss here, grope there. They love the dressing up, me too, and most come along to learn. But I know at least one couple that came away and used it as the base for a fuck fest and were hardly seen out at all. And I know another couple, who weren't a couple, who used the chalet as the centre of their torrid affair. I say torrid, I'm guessing because there's no video available but you'll have to give them the benefit of the doubt. We'd never know. She wouldn't say, 'He was fucking great, better than the old man,' now would she? They tried to keep it a secret but you might as well have put a star in the sky above the fucking chalet. Everyone knew.

ONE HUNDRED AND SEVENTEEN

The scene in our chalet was an eclectic mix of boisterousness and serenity as music dominated, pop songs, current and oldies, and then some Latino stuff.

Billy lay on one section of the made up double sofa bed next to me in a very Eric and Ernie sort of way. He cradled his beer can, his fingers dipped into the nut bowl as he chilled, staring at the ceiling, occasionally harmonising with the tenor section of the music played.

I lay next to him cuddling my wine glass, my fingers caressing the remote control of the TV, my eyes flicking through the weekend's itinerary (a word I love seeing spelt wrong, makes me laugh each time), occasionally harmonising with the baritone section of the music played.

Dan was on his feet, checking the oven, shorts on, bear torso, one hand on a stirring spoon, the other cosseting a cocktail that he'd made at home and brought in a large pop bottle. Every now and then he would sing a chord, throw a shape, shimmy to the bedroom and back, bumping and grinding in mid air as the music filled his soul. The big man was up for it. He had the baton.

Every now and then we'd check the time and texts, in between refills, a snack or a story. The girls were already out. They wanted a dance. Well they could wait. We weren't ready. Clothes were ironed and aired, dance show bags were prepped, but mentally we were cruising around Cuba, that tempo, that rhythm, aided a smidge by the beer, starting to course through our veins. It was going to be a fun night, of that there was no doubt, it was like the first tingling of a cold sore. You knew it was coming. So did we.

Each of us showered, shaved and tarted up, three handsome fuckers, smart, full of nous, charm and talent. The dancing royalty was ready to hit the dance hall knowing that with such a life skill, knowing how to hold and to touch, and how to glide, we knew we would be in demand on the dance floor.

Off it and horizontal, who knows?

ONE HUNDRED AND EIGHTEEN

We walked to the main hall passed chalets, some alive, some dead, music pitched against the moon and stars, latecomers still unpacking. It was after half ten and there was anticipation in the air, as well as a modicum of caution and nerves, just a modicum, given that the room would be packed, the bar would be bustling and the dance floor, sprung, would soon be groaning.

We entered the hall side by side, Billy in the middle, Dan and me like book ends next to him, Bodyguards R Us. We slowed, smelling the mood, sensing the vibrancy, faces smiled, heads nodded, an occasional wave as we walked to our right, close to the bar and we stopped like landlords at the top of the steps, surveying the scene, lions checking out their kingdom. The dance floor was twenty yards in front of us, the stage another twenty, the floor some fifty yards long, the lighting out there sultry and suggestive. In front, tables and chairs, mainly full, glasses scattered, bags, coats, expectant visages filled the vista like a busy Michelangelo.

'Right lads, tell me who you can see,' said Billy, never a great visionary without his specs.

'Well,' I said, 'there is news. Over there is Ali,' pointing to the right at a Somerset-Italian beauty in a stunning knee-length frock. 'To the left, there, dressed as a punk rocker, bit Toyah if you get the drift, is Sharon. Down by the front there's Gail and Johnny. Keith and Olga next table. Morag and Tamsin. Fuck me, that's Anne Hathaway...'

'The actress?' asked Dan.

'Shakespeare's wife?' asked Billy.

'No, you daft cunt, she'd be over 450 years old . . .' Me. 'She's a gentle ex of mine,' I carried on. 'Ellie's over there,' I gestured, 'and some bad news for you Dan, Sissy is over there . . .'

Quick as a flash Billy grabbed my arm and raised a finger and put it to his mouth. He didn't have to say anything, he just looked at me and I knew. He wasn't such a blind fucker after all for over there with Sissy was the FUD that broke Dan's heart. Best steer clear of those two for the weekend. At the opposite end of the hall Dan suddenly appeared next to Ali and they were walking to the floor, jealous eyes marking his every step. The lad was off.

There was a tap on my shoulder and I turned around. Billy too.

'Hello,' he said, beaming, 'lovely to see you here.' He reached to kiss her on both cheeks. She bent forward.

'Hi,' I said, holding her hips and also pecking both cheeks, taking in the smell, the feel and the aura. 'Who are you here with?'

'I'm sharing with Annie.'

'Oh, thought you might have brought...'

'We split up,' she gently said.

There was a coruscating stir in my loins, a bolt of thunder went through my heart and strobe lights flashed in my own psychedelic world.

Ava.

Ava-ilable.

Fuck.

THE END

POST SCRIPT

Where are they now, in no particular order.

Cliff Richard:
Hadn't been around for a while but has resurfaced, thankfully, now living in The Village, plying his trade in the world of Latin & Ballroom.

Big Nev:
Last seen oop North looking after his ailing mum and his black brogues.

Bobbin' Robin:
Hanging on in there. It is ten years since his fling with The Italian but he's still here and there, an old hand still looking for adventure.

Karen Saturday:
Living in denial.

Curly:
After a surprising liaison with Beckham she finally found love with Big Dave, a man with a huge heart and compassion, something that her life had been lacking.

Baz:
Only talks to you when he wants something. A room in a care home beckons. Sooner the better.

The Italian:
In a better place now, after the divorce, our fling and a few auditions. She has a new man in her life and she has become a groupie with one of the local Salsa troops showing that everyone needs a home somewhere.

Arlene:

Another hanging in there. Seven years ago she said she hadn't had sex for seven years. Very Biblical. Not a lot of affection there. How does she survive?

Lisa:
Following a successful bout in the advertising business she is busy in The Smoke looking for TV work.

Jenny Glasses:
She ran off to the wilds of Shropshire and moved in with a giant. Desperate for a child she has compromised her life and will never become a mum. I cry for her.

Princess Grace:
Having upset her once, drunk, obviously, her and her beau are now my good friends. Who'd have believed it?

Eliza:
A big mama who got married and now has three young mouths to feed.

Hartcliffe Harry:
Resident Salsa DJ at many venues and he now has a girlfriend showing that desperate girls will do desperate things. Apart from that, he's okay is Harry.

Bandana Joe:
His long-term gal upped and left, off to The States. Undiminished he courted the buxom Kate. They were happily married but now aren't. Joe just needs people to understand him, big tits and a shag.

Robert Charlemagne & Pam
Still bossing it nationwide, Pam has fully recovered from breaking her leg in a fall but they have moved in different directions.

Belle Vue:
She was the resident Latin teacher at the local pally, a dress size higher as age catches up with her. Fell out with the host and was last seen boarding a slow boat, a boat that I missed, dang!

Morag:
The last time I saw her she was pushing a baby buggy with hubby. A wedding that I wasn't invited to. That hurt but I'm really pleased for her. Did I say that she'd been engaged three times?

Tamsin:
Proud mum of one, her husband one of the genuine nice guys.

Annie Tango:
Saw her with her partner in the local. Decided not to mention our evening and morning of filth.

ZF:
Her fiancée died on her then she took up with some Neanderthal with a speech impediment. They had a son and he left. She's still looking good.

Mickie the Lick:
Having gone through her mid-life crisis and half the population of Ceylon she is now back with hubby.

Kitten:
In Borneo.

Frankie:
The tightest, greediest bloke on the circuit. He is single again. She kicked him out when he wouldn't contribute to the cost of repairing the washing machine.

 June 2019

470

Ali:
Double edged sword. One that got away, a genuine gem, but as she is Mafia, is that a bad thing?

Terri:
She had a child and hubby left. Desperate for love and affection she took to a wrong 'un and eventually she sussed that that wouldn't work either. She' was still a maybe until she found God and a welcome widow.

The Runner & Moira:
Amazingly still together after a creaky start. Moira's lovely, he's ditched the machismo false front and is looking after her. I like that.

Connie:
Married and was expecting; now has two Bam Bams. Scarily, she's starting to look like her mum.

Lulu:
A vegetarian whose bedroom is like a sex dungeon. Her man in ten years her senior but he is 'the one'.

Layla:
Happy in Turkey. She won a legal battle, kept her house, she enjoys the warmth and there's only another fourteen million Turks left to keep her happy.

Lola:
After IVF Lola had twins. Makes you look at her partner differently, in a cubicle with a porn mag and his trollies round his ankles, tugging for Queen and country. JFI Barack Obama did the same . . . I wonder what he got off on?

Loopy:
Belligerent, narrow minded and he always knows more than the medical profession. His house is up for sale as he and his

latest squeeze look to move in together. Seems like he's setting her up as his live in nurse.

Barbara Finn:
Ethereal and still pals with Dennis, she has set up a website and a community group in search of God. Good for her.

Dan:
Dating a girl twenty years his junior but he knows that there may be trouble ahead with that. Will he ever let anyone else in? Is age such a barrier?

Billy:
Still teaching dancing and beguiling the ladies, working off his bucket list – diving in a shark cage, trips to the Middle East, Harley on Route 66 and getting wanked off in a bar in The Philippines.

Ava:
Guess you'll have to wait for that one.

Printed in Poland
by Amazon Fulfillment
Poland Sp. z o.o., Wrocław